Praise for *The Polite Act of Drowning*

"*The Polite Act of Drowning* is a beautiful and captivating novel, lyrical and sensuous, a precise and faithful evocation of the tumult and trauma of family life, and of emergence into adulthood, and the confrontation of truths about ourselves and the people we love"
Donal Ryan, author of *The Queen of Dirt Island*

"*The Polite Act of Drowning* is a beautiful and powerful novel about how the past never leaves us, and how secrets can destroy a family. Hurtubise writes so evocatively, I was completely immersed in the world of Kettle Lake, its colourful characters and the heartbreak of a community"
Elaine Feeney, author of *How to Build a Boat*

"Reading Charleen Hurtubise's sumptuous novel, I feel like I am suspended in her beautiful prose, deep in the waters of Kettle Lake, unable to come up for air. This is a novel of secrets, places and people who are lost even to themselves. An exceptional debut about an unforgettable summer in the lives of Joanne and her family, with writing that comes alive, lyrical and sharp, tender and heart wrenching, you cannot put it down. I adored it"
Olivia Fitzsimons, author of *The Quiet Whispers Never Stop*

"A luminous and gripping portrait of a teenage girl coming of age in a small lakeshore community. Filled with colourful, complicated characters and brimming with heartbreak, love, and redemption, it is an exquisite debut from a powerful storyteller"
Michelle Gallen, author of *Factory Girls*

The Polite Act
of Drowning

Charleen Hurtubise has lived in Dublin, Ireland for over twenty-five years, having moved from Michigan. She is a teacher and artist as well as a writer, and her short fiction, essays and poetry have appeared in various publications. She holds an MFA Creative Writing from University College Dublin (UCD).

The Polite Act of Drowning

Charleen Hurtubise

First published in 2023 by Eriu
an imprint of Bonnier Books UK
4th Floor, Victoria House
Bloomsbury Square
London, WC1B 4DA
Owned by Bonnier Books, Sveavägen 56, Stockholm, Sweden

A CIP catalogue record for this book is
available from the British Library.

Hardback ISBN: 978-1-80418-221-5
Trade Paperback ISBN: 978-1-80418-245-1

Also available as an ebook and an audiobook

1 3 5 7 9 10 8 6 4 2

Typeset by IDSUK (Data Connection) Ltd
Printed and bound in Great Britain by Clays Ltd, Elcograf S.p.A.

Eriu is an imprint of Bonnier Books UK
www.bonnierbooks.co.uk

for Dearbhaile, Donnchadh and Ruaidhrí
mo pháistí, a chuisle mo chroí

and Conor
for holding us up

1

Michigan, 1985

THE BEACH IS FULL of teens from the city. Two girls make their way down the hill toward the lake; the clean white edges of their bare feet trample the dune grass. Up and down the beach the sun is beginning to leave a lacquer over uncovered flesh – spreading up legs and over hips, following the curve of breasts above bathing-suit cups. It is the Saturday of Memorial Day weekend; the beach at Kettle Lake State Park has only just opened for the season and these girls are as bronzed and burnished as most of us will be by the end of summer. Still, the edges of their feet remain white. When they reach the hot sand, they glide through the crowd and claim a portion of beach with two reflective blankets that flash in the sun. I watch them from the shade of the only tree near the beachfront.

Aunt Rita slaps bologna between two slices of bread and stacks them on a paper plate. She calls to her sons, Gabe and Albert, and to my brother, Sammy. Her boys leap out of the trench they have dug further up the beach. They snatch their lunch from the plate and jump back into the hole. Aunt Rita walks to the trench and hands Sammy a sandwich.

My sister, Hare, sits beside me. Our towels straddle the line between shade and sun, sand and stubble. Hare is seventeen, exactly three-hundred-and-sixty-two days older than me, not even a full year between us but her breasts have been full and round for two summers now. She folds her arms over them as though she carries a secret under her shirt.

My swimsuit sags on my chest. Goldenrod yellow – that's what Mom calls this colour. 'You're athletic, Joanne,' she always tells me. 'You're tall, like my own father.'

I can't help feeling that my lack of development is related to something I have done – or failed to do.

Out front, the two girls splay on their blankets. The scent of their cigarette smoke and coconut oil drifts toward us. They pass the bottle between them, rubbing the oil down their thighs and into their tight calves. I strain to hear their conversation, catching only one of their names; everything else is a dull mumble. Cathy is the girl in the black string bikini. I watch her shin bones glint in the sun until I feel the weight of Hare's stare. A flush passes through me. I look away from the girls, out across the waters.

The town of Kettle Lake springs out of a fold along the curved edge of this bay; it belongs to the Great Lake, a lake so vast it feels like the sea. They are an unsettled force, these waters, an ever-changing vista. Today, sunshine fractures the surface into dazzling clusters of light, and the water comes alive. A boundless plain of mercury rolling like wind through wheat.

The wind shifts. Two boys stroll past. One is tall with gangly arms, the other stout with a broad chest and shoulders, which give him the appearance of a one-gallon gasoline can. They stop and stand in the girls' sun. Cathy flicks her cigarette out past them and inclines her head. They move on swiftly down the beach.

We didn't even want to drive up to the big lake today, especially not with Aunt Rita.

Heat and the scratch of sandpaper underneath my window woke me earlier than usual this morning, beads of sweat already pooling on my upper lip. I pulled on my shorts and crept outside, sliding the screen door soundlessly along its track.

I sat down on the step to watch my mother work. Soft trills of a robin in the lilac bush carried across the yard. Turpentine, strong and sweet, spread from her rag onto the breeze, opening the pores in my nose. She tipped the can again, filling the cloth, rubbing it across the surface of a dresser drawer I had helped pull from a dumpster in the city. The paint blistered and curled on contact; she scraped it off in a long run like dirty snow under a plough. When she spotted me sitting idle, she sent me inside for the first load of laundry: sheets, towels, shorts, Dad's blue mechanic shirts. I knew what lay ahead for the day – a constant cycle of hanging up and taking down in the hot air.

When Aunt Rita pulled up in the red bus, it felt like a better offer.

On the beach, my brother, Sammy, waits with my cousins for permission to swim. Aunt Rita pulls on her straw hat and leaves the shade of the tree. The boys run toward the water.

'Albert! Gabe!' she calls after them. 'Don't touch that water until I'm down!'

3

I walk slowly behind with Hare; we distance ourselves from Aunt Rita, tiptoeing over the hot sand.

Cathy has moved down the beach. She throws a Frisbee. Her friend, standing in the sunlight, catches the disk with a long, elegant arm and returns it. With each throw, her halter top rises slightly, exposing the softness of her belly, the way it extends and then settles gently back into the curve of her hips.

The lifeguard notices, too. He climbs down and leans against his tower, his back to the water. The girls pretend not to notice, but their posture is no longer loose.

An isolated squall has formed to the far north of the bay, shafts of rain empty from a towering cloud, its top flat as an anvil. From here, the formation appears benign as a turtle slipping off land, crawling over the bay.

The waves break hard on the shore and return like a churning river under the surface; the group of teens out at the buoys cling tighter to the orange and white cylinders bobbing above the water. Girls step up on the ballasted bottoms and scramble onto the boys' backs, playing chicken – a dangerous game in the deep water. Their shrieks bring Aunt Rita closer to where the cousins are splashing in the shallow water. She paces the shore in front of them.

Cathy misses her catch. The Frisbee skids across the sand and lands near the lifeguard. He picks up the disc. He passes Cathy, walks toward her friend. She cocks her hip, raising her hand against the glare of the sun. He leans back on his heels. I like to watch her do this, and she likes it, too: how, with the tilt of her hips, she can rule the orbit of his feet in the sand. He rocks like a pendulum on the beach; the waves break hard on the shore, the water rolling in behind them and out again, unwatched. Cathy doesn't hide her annoyance. She walks to the edge of the water, drags her fingertips along the surface. She steps out until the water covers her thighs. She glides onto her front, swimming toward the buoys – maybe to join the group of teens, maybe to let the betrayal dissipate, dissolve.

When we reach the edge, Hare runs straight in, flouncing into the water.

I step onto the cool sand where the water meets my toes.

Mom says I'm a bag of bones. I shiver on the beach, my entire body a rash of goose bumps. The water meets my ankles, my knees – they disappear, merging with the cold. I brace myself for the shock of going under. Any warmth left in my skin seems to be the only thing holding me together.

I hold my breath and plunge under, swimming out. The sting of the cold dissolves, and with it, I dissolve, too. I turn on my back and float, palms open to the sky.

When I look up, Aunt Rita is waving her arms from the shore, flesh waggling at her sleeveless cuffs. She cups her hands to her mouth and calls. She calls to the boys, calls to Hare and me, calls to the beach.

'Don't swim out! Don't swim near the buoys! Swim along the shore . . .'

We never swim near the buoys that mark the end of the swim line. Clusters of milfoil weed grow there. It's invasive; the green bristles trail up through the deep on long thin lines of umbilical cord.

We are different out here, too, Hare and I. The water churns at our shoulders. There is a pull, the gentle tug of an undertow.

'Handful from the bottom,' Hare shouts.

We hold our breath and sink like stones, then grab a fistful of muck. We count the seconds. I open my eyes and see my sister's face – translucent through the yellowish green of the water; an unearthly white found only on things that live in the deep, like the bellies of dead fish we find along the shore. I rise first, she a moment behind, triumphant. She swipes the grey silt on my cheeks. I slather her hair.

Sinking to the bottom again, we fight against our own buoyancy, tormenting Aunt Rita with every second we are under. When we emerge, she is staring at us from the shore. She is counting, too: the boys first, Hare and me last. Like a typewriter returning its carriage, she searches and begins again. We are all here. We are all safe. None of us is lost. Not yet.

*

On the beach, Hare changes under a towel. She throws her eyes over my suit, which is beginning to feel like humid breath on my skin – an aura of damp, like the perpetual state of annoyance that rings my sister. She drops the towel at my feet and walks uphill toward the parking lot. I don't know what I have done this time. I never seem to know.

The sun paves a silvery street running out toward the buoys. I shade my brow with my hand. The other teens drift back toward the shore in groups of twos and threes.

A lone figure remains out beyond the line. Her arms extend outwards, chin tilted toward the sky, the water holding her weight. I feel sleepy watching her, slipping in then out, floating like an otter on its back – drifting and falling with the swell, moving away from the shore.

'Grab those towels, honey,' Aunt Rita calls.

Albert and Gabe carry the cooler between them, Sammy trailing behind, back up toward the bus. I gather the towel that Hare threw at my feet, pack it into the bag and wrap the handles around my wrist, lugging it uphill.

Hare has already climbed in across the back seat, rolling down the window. She crosses her arms and scoots away as I slide in beside her.

2

At home, Aunt Rita sits in the shade, waiting for Mom to return. She drinks the sun tea I bring her down to the ice. Melted water pools in the bottom of the glass, and she tips this, too, to her lips, allowing the dribbles to seep onto her tongue.

Two fields away, out on the main road, the rising of a siren speeds past and fades as quickly. Another follows in its wake.

'I hope that's not your mother,' Aunt Rita says, in a way that always makes Mom crazy; she calls this Aunt Rita's doomsday voice.

Two more emergency vehicles pass in the distance, sirens blaring.

'Idiots,' Aunt Rita says. 'They're not happy unless they're killing someone.' She swirls her glass of ice at me. 'I have to get back to the shop. Roy can't stay all day.' It's as though I'm being accused of my mother's absence.

Rita's Bait & Tackle is a busy place. She started the business from a lawn chair, selling minnows to fisherman from a bucket at the edge of the Wildlife Refuge. It grew into a specialist trade, selling everything from lures and reels to rods, tackle boxes, decoys, fishing licences, hunting licences, ammunition.

Once her business started taking off, Mom helped Aunt Rita repaint the brown creosote shiplap cladding on her shed to a mossy green. Aunt Rita was happy with that, but Mom kept going. She salvaged window boxes out of a dumpster, painted them what she called a cerulean blue. She planted bright orange geraniums and trained peach-coloured roses to grow up the sides. A salvaged wooden fish leapt and curled over the door, bearing the shop's name across its belly. Mom even stencilled lettering on the side of the lean-to: MINNOWS, LIVE BAIT & MORE greeted fishermen arriving from the city, and on the leaving side: COME AGAIN REEL SOON. Mom had all sorts of ideas that Aunt Rita found foolish, but she let her try them anyway.

'I don't care what you do, as long as they keep stopping in and buying things,' she told her.

Dad said Aunt Rita was raking in the cash while our mom rummaged through dumpsters for her benefit. Dad called Mom's sister skinflint, but he still helped her build the outbuildings she needed, expanding into waders, hunting gear, guns and knives – all things duck, deer and fish. And since she is there anyway, the state gives her the contract to manage the gates and rental boats for the marina at the Wildlife Refuge.

She is a busy woman. And yet, here she is, waiting.

I take her glass inside to refill it. She continues to talk at me from the yard, her voice coming through the screen windows.

'Ask Hare if she knows where your mother went.'

'To drown herself in the lake,' Hare mumbles from where she is lying on the couch. Hare doesn't even pretend to let Aunt Rita hold the authority she thinks she has over the three of us. I bring Aunt Rita a fresh glass of sun tea.

She points to the empty clothes line. 'There's a waste of a hot day.'

I don't mind hanging the towels – they are small and give a satisfying crack when snapped in the air. But the elasticated corners on the fitted sheets twist in the breeze and refuse to peg with any degree of symmetry. I am wrestling with the last one when Edna McCarthy, Mom's oldest friend, drives into the yard.

My throat squeezes. I believe, for a moment, that something has happened to Mom; Mrs McCarthy always seems to know the sordid things first. Her husband has a radio scanner, which is illegal. It is always on in the background at their house, intercepting two-way radio calls between police or firefighters responding to an emergency . . . even though Mr McCarthy isn't a police officer or a firefighter. He works in a sugar-beet factory on the night shift, and Mrs McCarthy takes in an ever-changing roster of foster children. Her truck is full of children now; they burst out of the cab and merge with Sammy and my cousins, becoming a gang running wild through the yard. Mrs McCarthy sends out her cane, probing for level ground to support her weight.

'Rita, good, you're here. Thought I'd better come out and tell Rosemary first.'

'Rosemary's not home. Tell her what? What happened?' Aunt Rita's voice is stricken.

Mrs McCarthy speaks to the yard, sombre and resigned, as though she is addressing a crowd. 'There's been a drowning.'

'Oh dear, no.' Aunt Rita gasps. She brings her hand to her mouth.

Hare comes out to the deck.

'Who?' we both ask at once.

'Tell us, quickly,' Aunt Rita adds, bracing herself for the news.

'Some poor young gal from the city.'

Hare rolls her eyes and returns inside.

Aunt Rita holds her throat, as though something caught has been released. 'Nobody we know?'

'No, no. It wasn't a townie. It seems the girl got caught in an undertow. Her poor mother. Half the town is out searching for the body.'

'They haven't found her?' A strain returns to Aunt Rita's voice.

'That's why I thought I'd better let Rosemary and Danny know. Last thing she needs right now is another body washing up here on the shore. I won't stay – I just wanted to let them know.'

'Well, you're here now. We'd better wait for Rosemary to come home.'

'Did she go off in the truck?'

'No. The girls say Danny drove to work.'

'Well, where the hell is she?'

'In the lake,' Hare mumbles from inside. 'I suggest you follow . . .'

I know where Mom has gone, though this is not inform-ation I am willing to share with Aunt Rita or Hare, or anyone.

*

11

The Great Lake and the beaches along its shoreline are the dominant features of our town, though its name, Kettle Lake, is taken from the less celebrated, smaller kettle lakes that dot the landscape throughout this region. There is a cabin in the woods behind our house that sits above one of these kettle lakes. A glacier dragged itself across the land thousands of years ago and then receded, leaving behind big chunks of ice to melt and fill this depression with water. The spring-fed lake is much as it has been for thousands of years, surrounded by pines in one spot, dry oaks in another. The marsh goes back so deep through the cattails that you would hardly know it was there. It is disconnected from the shoreline of the Great Lake, where we swam today.

Keep walking through the marsh, however, and you'll find yourself surrounded once again by the waters of the Great Lake, along a peninsula we call Mulberry Point. Like Kettle Lake State Park, Mulberry Point is only one small stretch of land along this expansive shoreline, which runs the entire length of the state. The shoreline seems to belong to everyone and no one.

But this small kettle lake behind our house belongs to us – or so I like to believe.

Mom has a claim on these woods – or more likely, the woods have a claim on her. On rainy days, when we were small, she dressed Hare and me in matching yellow jackets and rain pants. We shoved our feet deep down into rubber boots; she took our hands in hers, and I imagine they felt like tiny warm hearts beating in her palms. We left the house like this, together, walking up the driveway and into the woods.

The woods were alive and pulsing with green under a grey sky. It felt like an extension of our own parcel of land, an extension of *us*. Before we reached Mulberry Point, when we came nearer the kettle lake and the cabin on the hill came into view, we pulled away and raced for the tree we called the crooked horse. Hare always arrived first and hoisted herself up onto the flattened trunk, where the tree bent at an odd right angle before it rose straight again. I'd follow close behind, struggling to shimmy up the trunk, lying on my stomach and pulling myself up behind her. I'd throw my arms around her waist, while she held the rising part of the trunk where it turned abruptly once again. I thought the tree looked more like a giraffe than a horse, the way its neck disappeared into the sky – or, in the snow, a deer bounding off into the woods – but the trunk was nice and flat, and Hare insisted we were sitting upon a saddle. We'd gallop off like this together, kicking our heels to spur the misshapen tree on its journey.

A few years later, when he was teaching us to swim, Dad pointed out that the bend in the tree was not an anomaly of nature; Anishinaabe hands had purposely bent this sapling, bent its stem to force a growth, shaped it to mark a trail, possibly to point the way home. Mom's own father showed Dad this very tree when he was a boy. I never thought to ask how Mom's father had known such a thing, mostly because it amazed me that she and Aunt Rita had a father at all – one who apparently had given me his height, one whom Dad had met. We never heard about her side of the family; very little was mentioned of her past, if there was any memory at all. But here, in its shape, the tree remembered.

At first, however, all we knew of the woods was how long it took for a stiff gallop at a furious pace. Mom would pass us by, smiling to herself, carrying on into the woods, skirting the kettle lake, out onto the peninsula with the fruit trees and old dilapidated bay house bearing its name: Mulberry Point.

Once, when we couldn't find her, I thought Mom was gone for good, faded along with the mist hanging over the bay – but then I saw her, standing on the long hook of land, looking out at the water, unaware of the waves washing up the shore, soaking her shoes and the bottom of her jeans.

I reached her first. She took my hand, and in a strange, hushed voice, reminded me of the Great Lake freighters we once watched from this hook. I didn't want to tell her that I couldn't remember, that her memory wasn't mine; I couldn't bear the thought of her letting go of my hand. Hare caught up with us, anyway, and broke the moment. We splashed in the foamy wash of the shore until Mom bent down to speak to us, as though she were only just discovering our existence, as if we had suddenly shown up out of the gloom.

She was a stranger, our mother, standing out there on the Point, someone we very much wanted to know. But she never stayed that way for long.

By the time we walked back up toward the house with our arms full of cattails and goldenrods, you could see the stranger had gone, like a visitor departing suddenly, taking all the joy from the house.

*

The only reason that these woods are still here, that this peninsula isn't now developed into subdivisions – fields full of two-storey houses with perpetual sprinkler systems and entrance signs declaring names such as Yorkshire Shadows or Finlander Farms – is because the university bought up much of the farmland and marshlands around the coast-line surrounding Kettle Lake, all the way from the hook out across the Wildlife Refuge to the edge of Aunt Rita's driveway.

A professor from the university has taken up seasonal residence here, in the cabin behind our house. On winter weekends, smoke trails up through the trees. In the summer, he brings a trunk loaded with boxes of books and stays for weeks on end. Mom says Dad is indignant about the way the professor sits on the screened porch and reads much of the day.

'I'm not *indignant*,' he says. 'I'm pissed off!'

Mom stopped bringing us to the woods years ago, but she returns, all the time, on her own.

I wonder how pissed off Dad would be if he knew that Mom visits the professor, drinks wine with him – how they sit together, talking, on the cabin's screened-in porch, which Dad, too, feels should belong to us.

His family once owned all these woods, the bay house and the cabin, many years ago, before it was sold to the university. The Kennedys are firmly rooted in Kettle Lake, with their centennial bunting and landmark sign out front of their family's farmhouse, certifying that one continuous family had farmed this land for over a hundred years. Their mother, my grandmother, likes to remind everyone that it is nearly a sesquicentennial farm – one hundred and *fifty* years since Daniel Kennedy arrived from Ireland and established this town. She claims that the road running through the farmlands, connecting one town to the next, is named for him.

'Bullshit,' Aunt Rita always tells Mom when she repeats this fact. 'That road was named after the president when he was shot. You remember that as well as I do.' Mom only shrugs her shoulders.

I know that what Aunt Rita says is right. I also know that the Kennedys' claim to be first farmers of the area is wrong. Even before I found the land markers on the heritage maps at the library, even before discovering the Kennedys' road had actually been called Ojibwe Trail, I understood that Native people had thrived on this land, these fields, this farm, and that they had been removed, displaced, expelled. Our crooked horse tree reminded me of this.

The Kennedys' claim on the land now only extends to a few fields near their old farmhouse. Our own home is divided from their farm by a fence that marks the two properties; it is converted from a fieldstone barn. Dad had planned to raze the structure and build a ranch-style house, but Mom convinced him to restore it. Dad and his cousins secured the barn's structure and built a new roof, a fire-place and chimney from the stones they hauled from the shoreline. They partitioned the walls upstairs where the hay was once tossed up onto the loft; they built a new kitchen. Mom learned how to salvage floorboards and cupboards from books she found in the library.

Our house is a triumph. I feel it off Hare, when she points out the original rafters to her friends, lets them marvel at the old tracks along which a barn door once moved, now a set of sliding doors out onto the deck. It's on the face of Dad's sister, Maureen, the way she sours whenever acquaintances ask about Mom, interested in hearing which exciting project she's up to now.

Dad can no longer drive out the field to the main road on his way to work in the city. Instead, we use the coast road, an old farm lane used only by us – and by the professor when he comes to stay.

It is early in the season to expect the professor, which is why I was surprised to see his car parked this morning, at the edge of the woods. And why I am not surprised Mom has disappeared, once again, into the woods.

*

'Come up and have some coffee.' Aunt Rita takes Mrs McCarthy by the elbow, helping her up the stairs.

Mrs McCarthy pulls away. 'I won't stay. I'll get these kids home and send Karl out to help with the search.'

'We were there earlier.' Aunt Rita lowers her voice. 'Those kids were going wild out at the buoys.'

'No one does anything about antisocial behaviour these days.'

'I'll go home and call Marylou.'

'*Marylou will know what to do*,' Hare mocks from inside.

I cover my mouth.

Marylou is Aunt Rita's special friend. That's what Dad calls her, rolling his eyes as he says it. I don't know what *special friend* means. I have met her only on occasion, but Aunt Rita defers to her at least once in every conversation.

'I bet the parade will be cancelled.'

'Yep. Even if they find a body before Monday, it wouldn't be right. Fetch the produce from the cab, darling,' Mrs McCarthy tells me. She turns back to Aunt Rita. 'That useless child would sooner suffocate than lift a finger to help.'

This remark feels unfair, but when I reach inside the cab for the bushel basket of earth-crusted potatoes, I realise that she does not mean me, but another girl, slouched on the back bench behind the driver's seat. Her cheeks are ruddy, like a doll's, from the heat of the truck. I can see she is my age, with one leg bent up on the seat, the other draping over the top of the passenger side. Her bare legs are stuck down inside a pair of cowboy boots that appear three sizes too big; her freckled thighs swell out of cut-off shorts.

She doesn't smile when she sees me staring at her, but her blue eyes lock on mine and brighten.

'There,' Mrs McCarthy calls to me. 'I brought you a friend, Joanne.' She turns to Aunt Rita and tells her this will please my mother.

'Joanne has always been her lonely child,' Aunt Rita says.

'You girls are about the same age,' Mrs McCarthy tells us. 'Lucinda's sixteen.'

'That's right,' Aunt Rita confirms. 'Same age.'

Lucinda glares at Mrs McCarthy through the side window. Her hair falls into her eyes, and she doesn't swish it out; she looks back at me through this strawberry blonde curtain. I already feel myself slumping in apology. Her eyes give a slow, lazy roll toward the sky, as though we share the same defiance and scorn for these women. I quickly conceal the smile erupting on my face.

Science is a subject I like – especially chemistry, the elements: the workings under the surface, an explanation for what is hidden from the eye. Take sodium: unstable and deadly, one electron to give. Chlorine: equally erratic, one electron to find. Their outer rings ache with the search, longing to fill the emptiness.

Separate: Deadly.

Together: NaCl.

Table salt.

Just like this, the girl and I are tied by the bond of some unknown element. Even after Mrs McCarthy gathers the other children, even as they pull onto the lane running along the coast, Lucinda's two fingers pressed against the back window, making a peace sign, even as the dust settles back to the road, I am smiling, so broadly it hurts my face.

For the first time in my life, I think I have a friend.

*

Soon after, Aunt Rita takes her boys and Sammy and heads back down the driveway, returning to the Bait & Tackle to finish the things that are not yet done.

Later, the phone rings in the kitchen. Neither Hare or I move to answer it. We know it is our aunt. She will have returned to her shop and changed out of her beachwear.

If I look out across the field, toward the Wildlife Refuge, I can almost see her standing at the counter, wearing her plaid gabardine pants and a pair of wading boots pulled up to her knees, a scarf tied like Rosie the Riveter covering her greying hair, wondering if she should get back in the bus and come over again, to check on Mom, to check we are all not dead.

'Please,' Hare hollers at me when it rings for the third time. 'Put her out of her misery.'

Aunt Rita doesn't wait for me to say hello.

'Marylou called into the shop. They still haven't found that poor girl's body. We are worried for your mother. Marylou thinks the parade will be cancelled for certain.'

I lie and tell her Mom is home but indisposed.

'Cut the crap,' Aunt Rita says, and hangs up.

When Mom finally does come home, her eyes are wide with knowledge.

'What happened?' she asks. There is something else in her face. It isn't annoyance at Aunt Rita and Mrs McCarthy hassling her, which I predicted; it is fear. She grabs my hand and holds it.

This frightens me. Mom doesn't usually overact.

'Headline news.' Hare comes into the kitchen. 'A girl drowned.' She opens the oven and stares at the empty racks. She looks under the lid of a cold pot perched on the stove top.

'How? Where?'

'We don't really know,' I tell Mom.

'Why don't you ask Marylou,' Hare suggests.

'Why? Was she there? Does she know?'

20

'Marylou knows *everything*.'

Mom turns back to me.

I shrug.

'I know as much as you,' I tell her, pulling my hand away. 'A girl drowned. She's from the city, everyone says. I don't know her name. I don't know how. I didn't see anything.'

Mom moves in closer. 'I don't want you girls anywhere near that water, you hear me?'

'Don't be stupid. We're surrounded by water,' Hare says.

Astonishment spreads across Mom's face at the hardness of Hare's words.

Hare doesn't catch the warning, or she doesn't care. 'What's for dinner?'

'Make it yourself.' Mom walks out of the kitchen. I hear her feet on the stairs, then on the floorboards above my head.

*

The next time Aunt Rita calls, I answer on the first ring.

'She's home,' I tell her.

'What did she say?'

'Nothing.'

'You told her about the girl? And she said nothing?'

'Yeah.'

'And?'

'Nothing.'

'Where was she?'

21

'Who?' She could mean Mom; she could mean the drowned girl.

'Your mother!'

'Nowhere,' I lie.

'Nothing, nowhere,' she spits. 'You're as secretive as her.'

I hear her rummaging around and know she is reaching for a cigarette. She lights it, then exhales.

'Your father stopped by on his way home. I've told him I'm hanging on to Sammy for a few days. He understands. You girls call me if there are any changes. He's bringing dinner home.'

Dad is coming through the door as she says this. Hare vacates the couch as soon as she sees him lugging a bucket. She runs upstairs and slams her door.

Aunt Rita gives instructions. 'Fry them up with a little oil in the bottom of the pan.'

The bucket swirls with the strong smell of fish. I associate this smell, like plaid, with my aunt – not the smoky scent permeating the house after frying fish, nor the pungent, putrid mess of a carp washed up on the shore, but fresh molecules of wind bonded with lake and damp and all things alive swirling at the coast-line where sand touches water, where water meets air.

Dad takes a beer from the fridge; he ruffles my hair, wedges the bottle top under the counter, pops the cap off with his palm. It spins and comes to rest on the floor-boards. In the living room, the radio is switched on; he tunes the dial. I wonder if he knows where Mom has been. I wonder if it bothers him. He flicks between stations, changing from Hare's favourite to his own. He lifts the volume on the receiver. It's a Creedence Clearwater Revival song, about a calm before the storm that's been coming for some time.

I have to put the phone down; the cord won't stretch to the door where the bucket sits. I slide it over with the edge of my foot. Catfish reel around the lake water, despairing of their circular captivity.

Dad always laughs at the way the old-timers still drop some of their catch at Aunt Rita's door. He says her business is successful because bachelor fishermen are casting out for a much greater find than perch.

When I lift the receiver again, Aunt Rita is still giving instructions.

'If you got sauerkraut, make some catfish Reubens. You'll have enough for tomorrow's lunch. Tell your mother to call me. I want to make sure she's OK. Everyone's worried about her.'

I nod and hang up. I turn on the cold water, filling the sink. We all know how to stun, how to bleed a fish, how to prepare one for dinner. I rummage through the drawer for the angler's priest, lift a catfish from the bucket. It flaps under my grasp and slips back into the bucket, swimming in circles, around and around in a furious bid for life. I dive my hand into the water again and this time firmly grasp one behind its eyes, slipping my finger down to hold its fin. It pulses – a muscle in my palm – then it lies still, awaiting its fate. I hold it to the draining board and deliver two blows to the back of the head. Life immediately leaves the catfish. I slice the gills, blood spurting onto the draining board. I hold it under the water, coaxing the remaining blood from its body, stroking my thumbs down its sides. A cloud of inky red fills the sink.

The breeze off the lake disperses the smell of fish. The cull taking place becomes mechanical. I wonder about Lucinda, out at the McCarthys' farm. Sometimes Hare and I are sent to help with the harvest. Last time, one of Mrs McCarthy's foster sons tackled me for no reason, and I came off the ground with a mouth full of blood and dirt. He didn't stay long with the McCarthy family. But it is too early in the season to ride out and offer myself in the orchard. I will make a cobbler, say Mom sent me to deliver it.

With the catfish, cleaned and gutted, piled on the draining board, I wipe the blood from my hands, feel the thud of my heart travelling through a vein in my neck. And there is Mom – walking past the kitchen window, leaving again. The sky is turning copper over the woods; the peepers call from the lake as the sun sinks behind the trees. I sense the terror of some thing before I see a shape. She heads out the driveway, turns toward the lake, disappears in the direction of the cabin in the woods.

*

I lie awake for a long time, staring at the ceiling, listening to the rain on the roof, listening for Mom coming home. A cool breeze passes through the screen in the open sash window.

Here in the dark, Cathy's face won't leave my head. I see the flash of expectation again on her face, a flinch of muscle shifting under her cheek bones, the lifeguard passing her by, choosing her friend. The way the water absorbed her hurt, freed her weight, how she swam out past the buoys, the angle of her chin tilted toward the sky.

I don't remember entering sleep, but all at once I am on the beach; it is dark and empty. The leaves shake on the tree near the beachfront. Rain dashes pockmarks into hundreds of footprints. Down the way, a towel wrenches and twists itself under the sand. Pages of a book flutter in the breeze. Something grabs at me, grows over my legs. I pull away and hack – hack at the milfoil.

3

SUNDAY MORNING, THE DAY after the drowning, Mom doesn't get out of bed. Sammy is staying at Aunt Rita's, and Hare hasn't come out of her room. Dad's truck is gone from the driveway. He is usually at his mother's farm on weekends; this is where he has been every weekend for the past two years, since his father died unexpectedly. He bled to death in a farming accident, his leg getting caught in a combine harvester. Now, Dad does whatever needs doing.

But not today. Today, he left early, when the sky was still pink, to meet his cousin Freddie. He is helping him launch his boat, trawling the coast for the body.

When the cobbler has cooled, I wrap it in a dishcloth, place the bag in the basket of my bicycle. The bicycle is too small – it was even too small last summer, with its basket and its banana seat. The tyre is flat, and I find a pump on Dad's shelf in the pole barn.

The professor's car is in its space at the edge of the woods. I shudder to think of him on his screened porch with a pair of binoculars, watching our house instead of the lake, seeing all that is us: watching me pedal along the road on my too-small bike, my knees jutting out at the angle of a cricket's, pedalling slowly up the coast road.

The humid strangeness of late spring lies over the town, a pulpiness that wasn't there yesterday; it moved in during the night, bringing its own mouldering concoction of lake water, silt and the sunken smell of last autumn's dead leaves rising from the earth's clammy grip. At the halfway point along the road – the verge where Mulberry Point is visible to the left and the curve of the shoreline at Kettle State Beach to the right – there is a string of boats trawling the coast-line, probing the coves and shores. One or two belong to the coastguard, but most are private boats, yachts, trawlers, like Freddie's speedboat. Some boats have crossed the Great Lake from Milwaukee, Escanaba, Mackinaw City, even Chicago, converging on this bay for one purpose: to recover the body of the missing teenager.

A grainy, resized inset of a girl taken from a yearbook photo confirms what I already know. The girl who drowned is Cathy. *Eighteen-year-old Catherine Allen*, the headline reads; the lines are pushed up against the glass front of the metal newspaper box outside Kitty's Korner grocery store. Cathy's hair is styled to her shoulders and heavily feathered. She stares at the camera with an intensity, not even a trace of a smile, as though she had a premonition she was posing for this fate.

Nearly all the tables at the diner are empty, even the ones nearest the door, overlooking the front window, the ones usually occupied by the volunteer firefighters. Everyone is out on the lake, helping in the search.

I cross through the square and take the coast road until it meets with the turn-off for McCarthys'. The county road is flat, moving inland away from the shore, irrigation ditches running either side. A blue heron screams and rises out of a ditch, flying over a field of corn stubble.

The McCarthys' home is a white clapboard farmhouse set back off the road, nearly identical to every other house along this stretch: a barn, a silo, fields of corn and sugar beet. There is an old farm windmill in the driveway; its blades are still.

I park my bike out back near the kitchen, expecting to find Mrs McCarthy here, supporting herself against the door jamb, a handful of children pressing their faces to the screen, staring out at me. But no one is here. The farm is empty.

I walk around to the front of the house and stand at the screen door. There is the buzz of a television from within. The bright sunshine makes it difficult to see inside from the front porch. I push my nose against the dusty screen. It smells of rainstorm. Karl McCarthy sits on the couch, the curtains drawn behind him, his knees spread wide, a can of beer open in his fist and another one tucked into his crotch. I pull back, thinking I'll slip away, but he spots me.

'Who's there?' he calls. 'Where's your manners? Show yourself.' He slurs his words.

I bring myself to the screen door again. 'Hi, Mr McCarthy. I'm looking for Lucinda?'

'Luc – what the – you one of mine?' He leans forward, squinting as though he, too, is peering into the dark. 'Get inside here.'

I open the screen door, holding it with my knee, but I don't step inside. The front room smells like a bowling alley.

'God damn, Danny Kennedy's kid? Why didn't you say? Come on in, honey. Lucinda!' he bellows into the house.

In the corner, a small man perches on the edge of an armchair. He is skinny like a teenager, with long, stringy yellow hair, though his face is aged. He stubs out a roll-your-own and shrinks back into the chair, sliding his hands back under a dirty leather coat clutched on his lap. The coat reminds me of the hide of a dog. His eyes dart around the room now and back to me standing at the screen door. He gives me a wormy feeling in my belly.

The red bulbs flash across Karl's radio scanner, then stop; the speaker crackles. A voice tunes in from amid the static, doling out numbers like a bingo caller.

Lucinda comes into the room, shouts for him to turn down the television so we can hear the scanner.

'They got a body?' she asks Karl.

'Nope.'

There is more crackling and number-calling.

Karl sits upright and leans forward, shushing everyone, even though we are listening with the same eager attention.

'I've heard enough,' he says, waving his hand at the scanner, dismissing the voice. 'They aren't going to find a body anyhow, not now. You either find it right away or you don't. That lake is too big. Bet you Daniel Kennedy is out there this morning, called to his noble duty.' Karl laughs so hard he starts to cough.

Lucinda rolls her eyes and beckons me to follow. We move out into the kitchen.

29

Mrs McCarthy has taken the other children to church.

'I'm in trouble,' Lucinda says. 'I refused to go. Let's get out of here before she gets home.'

'Does he mind?' I ask.

'Does he look like he minds? He's half off his head. And Martin, the war veteran. Good God, did he tell you yet? He's a soldier. *Please.*'

I shrug.

'He drinks and wets himself on the couch. Wasted, both of them, since Friday. Edna McCarthy is kicking Martin out the minute she gets home from church. She already told him. Wait here,' she tells me. 'I'll get some money and something to swim in.'

She leaves before I can tell her the beach is still closed.

A small breeze comes through the kitchen window; it barely raises the curtains. Someone is standing behind me. I expect to see Mrs McCarthy, but it is Martin, the veteran with the yellow hair and the dog coat. He doesn't have his dog coat and he doesn't smell of urine, just smoke and beer. He holds an empty glass. He seems frail, small from this close up.

He freezes when he sees me, and I freeze, too. He has the look of someone about to be carsick. We stand here looking at each other until Lucinda comes back into the kitchen, wearing a bikini top and shorts.

'Beer?' Martin asks us, holding out an empty bottle.

We break into convulsive laughter. Lucinda rushes out the door; I follow. We fall on the ground, laughing until it hurts.

She pedals my bike with her bare feet, and I cling to the back of the banana seat, riding double, my legs stretched out to the air. The cobbler, still wrapped in its dishtowel in the front of the basket, bounces down the road with us. We stop at the top of the beach, watching a helicopter hovering low over the water. The parking lot is empty apart from emergency vehicles and boat trailers.

Lucinda pedals into the town and keeps going, riding up the hill.

It is her idea to go inside the laundromat, a cinderblock building at the edge of town; the door is propped open but offers little relief from the humid blast of the dryers.

We watch soapy water sloshing in the big drums. Lucinda is cheerful to the small children hovering around their mothers' legs, so the mothers don't mind that we are here; they might even be grateful for the distraction. They move between washer, dryer and folding table with a single-mindedness, breaking dollar bills in the machine, the coins rushing down the shute with a metal *ting*. Gathering them in their fists, they plunge them back into the service of the dryers with the urgency of someone taking a chance at the slot machines. Lucinda pokes her fingers around the return hatch, searching for unclaimed coins.

We barely both fit into the bathroom, but we squeeze in anyway and Lucinda turns off the light. She spins me around thirteen times in front of the darkened mirror.

'Do you see her?' she asks.

I don't know who I'm looking for, but I like the feel of her hands on my shoulders.

'Try again,' she says when I tell her I can't see anyone.

'Who am I supposed to see?'

'You don't know about Bloody Mary?' she asks and begins to spin me again.

When she stops I am dizzy, but I don't see the bloody face of the woman who is supposed to appear – still, we squeal and push toward the door with the same thrill as when Martin was standing there asking for a beer.

It is a relief to burst back into the open, airless room, laughing and falling over one another.

The laundromat has emptied out. One woman remains, sitting on a plastic chair along the wall, waiting to transfer her clothes from washer to dryer. She doesn't have any children with her. She is probably only around twenty or so, which seems like a great leap to us at our age. Her transistor radio is playing hard rock, and she drums her fingers on the pages of the magazine she holds. She looks up and scowls when we fall out the door.

Lucinda walks past her with an air of indifference and pretends to busy herself with a washing-machine. The woman loads her wet clothes into a dryer and feeds the slots with coins, then leaves. Lucinda walks to the window and watches her get into her black car, rolling down the tinted windows, lighting a cigarette. She starts her engine and pulls out, her wheels squealing.

The moment she is out of sight, Lucinda turns from the window and opens the woman's dryer. She takes towels and uniform pieces – white, like they belong to a waitress or a nurse's aide. She pulls them out one by one, layering them over her arms. A wet sock and a bra fall to the ground. I walk behind Lucinda, picking up these smaller things that drop behind her. She opens the cold doors of unused dryers, the clothes lifeless, still warm, lying there at rest. She tosses in one piece each and moves down the line to the washing-machines. Lifting the lid of one, she holds a white skirt in her fingertips, feigning nonchalance, then drops it into the agitating waters below.

I am full of wonder watching her. The mischief feels wicked and fun and strangely natural all at once, like I am wide awake.

She closes the lid on the last piece. 'Time to go.'

I follow her out the door.

Outside, I breathe in the steamy air, which is fresh in comparison. Lucinda runs along the warm pavement in her bare feet. I get the bike and pedal after her. We go downhill this way; I cycle beside her all the way to the inlet.

At the bottom of the hill, Mrs McCarthy is waiting in her truck. She has been searching for Lucinda. She lays on her horn when she sees us.

'Get in this truck right now, lady, and don't give me any lip. No one gave you permission to go anywhere.'

'Karl told me.'

'His name is Mr McCarthy. Marching out of the yard without permission!' Mrs McCarthy is furious. She turns her glare on me. 'Your mother and Rita will be worried sick. You go straight home.'

'Only reason you knew I was gone was you needed someone to clean out your chicken coop,' Lucinda is saying as they pull away.

'See you,' I call to Lucinda.

She turns her face and presses it to the back window as they pull away; she shows me her middle finger, placing it behind the driver's seat, and I know this is for Mrs McCarthy. For me, she blows a kiss and gives me the peace sign.

4

MARYLOU'S PREDICTION IS RIGHT. Monday's parade is cancelled. Families pour into the square anyway, and set up lawn chairs, staking claim to patches of ground with their coolers and blankets. Some haven't heard the news about the parade; others come to pay respects. The body of the drowned girl has not been recovered. Cars park along the four roads leading into town; their occupants walk the rest of the distance, snapping stems of lilacs, elderflowers, early meadow rue – a garland of tributes raided from fields and shrubs and hedges, intended for the drowned girl.

Dad sent Hare and me ahead into Kettle Lake on foot, while he tried to coax Mom out of bed. He was shouting her name into the silence as we left the house. Now, as we reach the halfway point on the road, Dad's truck passes, and he taps a rhythm on the horn. I wave – with even more vigour when I spot Mom beside him in the cab of the truck. Hare ignores them, marching toward town at a disgruntled pace. I quicken my step to keep up with her, walking into Dad's dust.

When we reach the edge of town, we walk up the inlet side of the square. Across the street, down near the water, a figure slumps against a telephone pole. Martin wears his dog coat pulled over his shoulders, even though it is warm. Mrs McCarthy must have kicked him out after all; he looks as though he spent the night here, cross-legged in his crumpled trousers. I don't expect to see Lucinda; she's probably grounded. Me, on the other hand – no one even knew I was gone when I arrived home.

We hurry past Martin up the road toward the diner, the last red-brick business in town, where the sidewalk tapers down to a single square. The diner's current owners are an elderly brother and sister; they took over from their father when he died. The sister has yellow skin like shrink-wrap. Her hair is stark black, piled high like a tumour on top her head. She stands behind the Formica counter as though it is her cage. It runs the length of the gable wall through three interconnected open-plan dining rooms, all the way to the back-door.

Most mornings, weekends or otherwise, regular customers fill the swivel stools mounted on the floor in front of her, watching her as though she is an endangered bird. She walks from one end of the room to the other, refilling coffee mugs and polishing silverware. Sometimes, when there isn't a rush, she recedes to the screen door overlooking the lake and smokes. Behind her, the waters on the big lake give the illusion of rising and churning against the building, but she never turns her back on the diners. Her brother stands at the grill, flipping pancakes, moving the sizzling bacon around with a long fork; his grim face matches hers. When an order is ready, he taps the bell with the end of his fork and calls her 'Sister'.

'Table four, Sister.'

Today, every seat is taken, both inside and out on the deck overlooking the lake. A line of townspeople wrap out the door and down the steps, waiting to be seated. A small girl clutches a clump of wood poppies, the papery petals drooping in her warm palm. They will be ruined by the time her family finishes lunch and leaves the bouquet on the beach in memory of the drowned girl.

On the sidewalk in front of us Heather and Jessica, two girls from our high school, pass a cigarette. Pedestrians step onto the grassy verge, walking around. Hare passes without acknowledging that they are there. I hold up my hand in greeting; they look past me to Hare, trailing her with vicious eyes.

There is something unsavoury about Heather; she makes me think of cats marking their territory. 'Hello, *Harriet.*' She says my sister's given name as though exposing a dirty secret.

Hare doesn't even glance her way. Heather's eyes look like two dead pools of water. She stares out of them with that cold expression, watching Hare move away.

I give the girls an awkward smile and follow my sister. I am still looking back at them when Hare stops suddenly farther down the street, looking for her friends. I run straight into her, stepping on the tendon at the back of her heel. She crumples, sprawling onto the pavement. She gives a small, pitiful cry as she rights herself, sitting on the sidewalk, cradling her foot in her lap; dots of blood spring from her knee. I squat beside her, trying to screen her from the hideous laugher of the girls behind us.

Hare punches my chest with both fists, and I tumble backward, sprawling onto my bottom.

We sit in the middle of the sidewalk like fallen wires, blazing red with humiliation, both of us wanting to disappear into the ground.

Hare recovers herself first. She limps away, a seam of blood threading down her shin.

I stand and follow, brushing dirt from my hands.

'Get away from me. Freak!' she hollers with raw emotion, raising the interest of passing families.

I stand here, crossing and uncrossing my arms.

'Bitch,' Heather says, watching Hare take refuge amongst her friends, absorbing into them, turning and walking arm-in-arm up the street. She turns her look of disdain on me. Jessica turns on me now, too.

Glancing around, I look for Lucinda, even though I expect Mrs McCarthy has made her stay home and clean out chicken coops. I spot only Dad, standing across the road on the town square with his sister Maureen in her stiff, square-shouldered, electric-blue blazer. The lines of make-up across her cheeks are symmetrical with the sculptured wedge of her perm. She could be an executive or a politician ready to face her constituents. She looks out of place now, grasping the handles of her mother's wheelchair.

Grandma doesn't always need the wheelchair, but Maureen insists she use one out in public. Grandma clutches the Infant of Prague in her lap now, a statue she has taken to holding lately. Whatever she is saying, Dad chuckles, and Maureen rolls her eyes. Jessica and Heather have walked past the diner in the other direction, heading out of town, toward the beach.

Back along the square, on the business side of the street, Mom strolls on her own, looking into the windows of the closed storefronts. I watch her for a moment. Distant, solitary, even detached from the jostling activity around her, she could be a sole person moving along a quiet street on a parallel day.

A cheer rises up in the town square. Men stand, rising from their lawn chairs, saluting a float – a trailer decorated in red, white and blue bunting – turning onto the square. Rows of veteran soldiers in uniform sit atop the trailer on metal folding chairs, each holding a small American flag. Whether they haven't heard the parade is cancelled or came anyway isn't clear, but the float circles the square twice and then mounts the curb, pulling onto the grass near the gazebo. They lay their flags in their laps and take out their lunches, eating them in their folding chairs.

Across the road, Mom moves down two storefronts to the thrift store. She pauses in the doorway. A man has found her and is rubbing her arm in greeting. Mom runs her fingers through her hair, and when she lowers them to her side, he picks up her hand and holds it, giving it a little joggle now and again to emphasise whatever he is telling her so intently.

A gap opens in the traffic, and I cross the street farther down, mounting the steps, moving slowly up the sidewalk toward them. I am not trying to hide. I only want to get close enough to hear their words. The professor's voice has the sort of quality that comes with lecturing students in vast halls. It carries down the street.

'Think about what I told you last night. It's not easy. But you have to make it happen. You know that very well. Say goodbye. It's the only way forward.'

'I can't.' Mom shakes her head. 'I can't. I can't do any of this anymore.' She takes her hand from the professor's and covers her face, turning away.

He squeezes her shoulders and pulls himself close, folding himself around her like a robe. 'Let me help.'

Mom's head shakes back and forth.

'Joanne? Hey!' Aunt Maureen calls, crossing the road at a crisp pace. Maureen always sounds as though she has caught me in the act, accusing me of one thing or another. And this time, she has. 'Your father is looking for you.' She pushes her hands into her blazer pockets; the shoulder pads stiffen. She is a towering presence looming toward me, although I have already surpassed her height. She mounts the steps and awaits an answer. Vic, her husband, follows behind, pushing my grandmother's chair across the road toward us.

Mom moves around the professor and hurries out of the doorway. The professor takes a step toward her, then stops.

'There you are,' Mom says to me, gripping my elbow, the corners of her eyes still wet.

'Rosemary.' Maureen's tone turns cold.

Vic turns Grandma at the curb and pulls the chair backward up the three steps to the top of the sidewalk to join us. The professor stands behind us, watching us with a clinical eye. No one else notices, though Mom resonates with his presence. Her hands shake. She grips my elbow tighter.

'Hi there, honey, how you keeping?' Vic leans in and kisses Mom's cheek. She smiles. He tussles my hair as though I am twelve, then exaggerates my height, pretending to have to look up into my face even though my forehead only reaches his chin.

'You're even catching up with me,' he teases. 'You've the pirate genes – Maeve, warrior queen of Ireland!' He always says this to me, and it has the same effect every time: I smile dumbly, not knowing what to say. Vic could say anything; I like having his attention turned toward me. It feels cold when it is turned away.

'Geez, hello?' Grandma hollers from her wheelchair.

Vic gives me a knowing look. 'Go on, kiss your grandma before she flings herself out of that chair and dances a jig.'

I giggle at the image. Grandma lifts her cheek and I brush my lips close to her papery skin. She smells of onions and Oil of Olay.

Dad crosses the road with Freddie, his cousin. Freddie carries two bags from the diner, grease seeping through the brown paper. Mack and Cass, old-timers – that's what Aunt Rita calls them – stroll up the street, stopping to say hello. The professor walks slowly away, his hands in his pockets, looking into the storefronts, as though the meeting with Mom never happened. Farther up the street, I see him stop outside a shore, contemplating the soaped-up windows: another business closed.

'Locals respect the water, am I right?' Mack rehashes his version of events on the drowning.

'They'll never find a body,' Cass agrees.

'You're not out there, Freddie?' Mack asks.

'Heading out again now,' he says. 'Had to get me some lunch.' He nods at Dad.

'I'll catch up,' Dad tells him, and Freddie continues on up the street toward the marina.

'They've trawled the waters along the beach and the coast,' Cass says. 'Nothing.'

'Canadians will keep a look out now,' Mack says. 'The way these waters drift.'

'Only outsiders drown on our shore,' Cass adds.

'You reckon?' Maureen asks, a hint of sarcasm in her voice.

'Yep. All these blow-ins,' Cass says with confidence, then, sensing he is being challenged, he looks around at the other faces.

Mack is gesturing toward Mom.

'Last person I recall drowning lived not too far up the road,' Maureen says.

'Oh . . .' Mack looks uncomfortable.

'Not sure you'd call them local,' Maureen says.

'I hardly recognise a face today. Too many outsiders trying to buy up this town,' Mack says, trying to change the subject.

Vic looks incredulously at Mack, as though he has just run out of patience. He sees me watching him and winks.

'How dare they?' He pretends to lend support to Mack's argument. 'Buying our houses and our women? How much for this girl?' He grabs my shoulders and pulls me into a bear hug. The others ignore him, except Maureen; she sticks her elbow into his ribs. He lets me go and pretends to be in trouble, as though he's now resolved himself to behave.

I try to repress a smile, or next he'll be counting my dimples.

'Why do we let people from elsewhere buy our businesses, anyhow?' Cass asks.

'Because it's a free country?' Vic turns sober. He isn't from Kettle Lake, either. He and Maureen have a house out past the city, in the country above the bay. Vic is a prison guard in the city. Dad always says his intelligence is wasted on the job – and on Maureen. Together, they have two daughters who are nearly finished with their high school in the city. Vic drives them in every day on his way to work. I once overheard Dad call Maureen a snob for sending her girls to private school.

'Nothing's ever good enough for her.'

'Nothing wrong with trying to give your children every chance,' Mom defended.

Maureen glances at Vic now, giving him another warning look.

'I don't really mind the business owners,' Maureen says. 'It's the lowlifes moving in, the spongers giving us the bad name.' She turns to Mom. 'There's something about people trying to take what doesn't belong to them. You agree, Rosemary?'

Mom startles when Maureen speaks her name. 'Sure.' She hasn't really heard the question.

'Though we should be careful what we say,' Maureen says. 'Rosemary's not from here, either.'

'I've lived here a long time,' Mom says, guarded.

Mack starts to chime in, but Mom interrupts.

'And my father's people lived here, too – they go way back. You know that.' There is a waver in her voice.

Vic nods in agreement. 'You girls went to kindergarten together, didn't you?' Vic asks Maureen.

'Second grade,' Maureen says tersely.

'You know, it takes five years for a foreigner to become a US citizen? After all these years in Kettle Lake, Rosie? I'd say you're not quite a blow-in.'

Mom gives him a grateful smile. Maureen glares at Vic. Dad wears a pained look; he doesn't seem to hear the conversation. I feel Mom's discomfort, her inner being curling like the cellophane of a fortune-telling fish, writhing under the slightest change of heat.

'They might be citizens, but they'll always be outsiders. Not *one of us*.' It is rare to see Maureen ruffled. 'They don't share our DNA.'

'That's a good thing, Maureen,' Vic laughs. 'Incest breeds strange creatures.'

The old-timers laugh, and Dad shifts his feet and smiles, fetched back from some distant place.

Mom's face remains blank.

'You know what I mean,' Maureen gives Vic a look, ending the conversation – but it is clear she will be raising it again, later, in private. I feel we are glimpsing life for Vic behind closed doors.

'We'll keep moving,' Mack tells no one in particular; he and Cass move off up the street.

Maureen turns to Mom with a renewed sense of triumph. 'You heard, then?'

Mom takes it with as much caution. 'Heard what?'

'We're back.'

Mom is puzzled.

Dad shakes his head, warning Maureen.

'I'll explain later,' Dad says.

'Back?' Mom asks.

'At the farm. At Kettle Lake, to help with *our mother*,' Maureen stresses, looking at Dad. 'We knew it would be left to us.' Maureen points a look at Vic, daring him to contradict her.

Vic looks away.

'Back for the weekend?' Mom asks, looking from Dad to Maureen, and back to Dad. 'No.' She answers her own question. 'You're living at the farm.'

Vic presses his lips together.

'Did you know this?' Mom asks Dad.

'Of course he knew,' Maureen says. 'He helped us move.'

Mom turns to Dad, stunned. 'How long have you known?'

Grandma, sensing the change of mood, lifts the statue on her lap. 'I brought your Irish ancestor.'

'You knew about this?' Mom asks again.

Maureen makes an attempt to smile warmly at her mother. 'That's not Grandad, Mother. You know he's missing.'

'Who's missing?' Grandma studies our faces, worried for some reason, though she can't figure out why.

Maureen tries to hide her annoyance at Grandma's confusion. It comes out like a smirk. 'He's been missing, Mom, since Danny's wedding. Remember?'

'Is this necessary?' Dad asks.

The Kennedy family used to keep an old marble urn, patinated with age, containing, supposedly, the ashes of Daniel Kennedy, the first resident of the farm and, as they liked to say, of Kettle Lake. The urn travelled to every Kennedy wedding down the generations, taking its place as a centrepiece on the head table. The Kennedy men inherited the ashes, took them home the night of their wedding, then passed them along to the next Kennedy in succession.

When Mom and Dad announced their engagement, however, our grandmother also announced that she wouldn't allow the urn to pass on. It would sit at the head table at the reception, and then return to the family farm. Dad assumed it was because he would be living at the Kennedys' farm one day, taking over from his father.

But Maureen had set him right. I heard it at a cousin's wedding, at the bonfire that went on into all hours. I disappeared into the shadows and listened to their drunken chatter, learning more than I wanted to know.

'You knew Mom didn't approve of marrying into *that* family. What did you think she would do? Bring the urn on a golden cushion?'

'It serves her right it went missing,' Dad told her. 'It's a foolish custom anyway. The man should be buried in the ground.'

From what I could make out, the urn had gone missing at Mom and Dad's wedding.

Grandma looks as though she is remembering something of this now – not exactly the *what* of the story, but the *who*. She glares at Mom with the same withering look Maureen has inherited. She clutches the statue tighter to her chest. 'Don't think you're getting your hands on this!'

Mom tips her head sideways, ready to flee.

'Be nice, Mom,' Maureen scolds, not trying to hide her amusement.

'Get me a sherry,' Grandma says, forgetting the conversation.

'We're in town, Mother. Behave yourself.' Maureen turns to Dad, her amusement fading. 'See how bad she's gotten? You probably didn't even notice. We'll find her body in a cornfield, stiff and dead, if we leave her on her own any longer.'

Dad ignores the accusation. 'You could have passed it by me first.'

'Dee and I decided it was best.'

Dad's younger sister, Dee, lives out east. Of the two sisters, I wish she was the one who stayed.

'Don't bring Dee into this. Dee says what you want her to say. It's basic courtesy to pick up the phone.'

I don't like conflict, but it feels good to hear Dad push back. He usually folds, like everyone else, in the face of Maureen.

'I did pick up the phone—'

'For help moving furniture.'

Vic grimaces and shifts apologetically.

Dad opens his hands and shrugs. I feel like slugging him. Giving up so easy on himself – on us all. Maureen nudges

Vic aside and grips the handles of Grandma's chair. She takes the brakes off. The chair shudders and Grandmother gasps as Maureen lurches ahead.

'I do everything for this woman, and you ride in and tell me how you want it done,' she calls back toward Dad.

I look at Mom. Dad has just finished dragging Grandma's fields, arriving home smelling like the nitrogen fertiliser he has laid on her sugar-beet field. He has shovelled her snow all winter and will still mow her grass all summer when he gets home from work, even if Maureen is living at the farm.

'Well, good to see everyone,' Mom says, forcing a cheerful smile. She turns to Dad. 'I'll walk. I need the air.'

Dad looks at the ground. Mom's back is trembling as she walks away, alone up the street. Maureen has taken something away from them both – something greater than a house.

Dad remembers something; he puts his hands in his pocket and takes out the car keys, handing them to me. 'Give these to your mother. I'm heading out with Freddie.'

*

I slip away, unnoticed, and follow Mom. She spots Mrs McCarthy in front of the diner, talking with Aunt Rita. She heads toward them as though they are safe harbour. I am disappointed that Lucinda is not with her; she has left her behind. I consider riding out to their farm again; I am trying to think of an excuse when someone falls into step beside me.

'Hey,' Lucinda says, 'I've been looking for you everywhere.'

And like that, everything shifts direction, and we are heading toward the lake shore, toward the beach.

5

THE BEACH HAS REOPENED, but no one is swimming. Families drop fresh bouquets of flowers near an altar that has grown since morning, radiating outwards from the lifeguard tower.

We make our way down the hill. Lucinda removes her boots, and I take off my sandals; we carry them, tiptoeing across the warm sand.

All along the beach, freshly painted signs spring out of the sand. Lucinda reads them as we pass.

'"Rip tides happen. Don't get carried away." Bummer. "Know the signs,"' she reads. '"Children under eighteen must be accompanied by an adult."'

The young lifeguard has been replaced by a man about Dad's age. He has cleared a path through the flowers and sits in his tower, watching the empty water.

Lucinda walks through the crowd, nodding at strangers as though she knows everyone.

There are plenty of kids I recognise from high school, but they are not the girls I take refuge with on the periphery of the lunchroom, near the condiments table, which no one has gone near since two boys dropped the eyes of a dissected frog into the relish container. We have little in common, those of us who make up our lunchtime refuge, apart from mutual isolation: one girl reads murder novels all through lunch; a reverend's daughter eats stewed tomatoes out of a thermos; another girl, with questionable fashion sensibilities, wears bowling shoes to school. These aren't the girls you expect to bump into on the beach.

Heather and Jessica are here, sitting on an oversized blanket, their legs stretched out in front of them. They each hold a bouquet of flowers in their lap, roses plucked from someone's garden. They look out to the water with a solemn expression over their faces. For years I thought they were twins – but it turns out they aren't even sisters; just best friends, inseparable since kindergarten. There is, of course, a rumour that they are lesbians, which is what everyone says about girls who spend too much time together.

The boys from the football team hover around Heather, hanging in her orbit. My trajectory aims to give a wide berth to the group, but Lucinda spots them and makes her way shamelessly along the beach toward their blanket. She squats down beside Heather. Heather looks at Jessica; Jessica shrugs. They make room for her. I stand behind them, like a tree, casting a shadow on their sun. I feel every bit of my awkward height. Lucinda motions for me to join them, but there doesn't seem an easy way to transition the gap.

Jessica covers her buck teeth when she laughs, but her face is otherwise pretty. Heather is undoubtedly beautiful; she could have been a model – this is what she is telling

Lucinda now, the story she always begins with. It is her way in.

'I was hanging out at the mall, and this woman gives me her card.'

'She *lost* the card,' Jessica finishes for her.

'I have no way of contacting her. My mother says there is plenty of time.'

Jessica nods and tells her she'll get discovered again for sure. 'You're so beautiful,' she crows, covering her mouth.

Lucinda's eyes are shifting back and forth between the two girls.

'I'm from Detroit,' she tells them, as though this is something entirely more interesting. She says she is staying out at McCarthys'.

'Are you fostered?' Jessica asks, looking toward Heather for reassurance.

'No.' Lucinda laughs. 'She's my aunt. I've come to help with the kiddies for the summer.'

I sneak a glimpse at her, knowing she is lying.

Heather giggles, relieved. 'Unfortunate to end up in Kettle Lake.'

The boys revolving around Heather and Jessica suddenly begin moaning – they sound like a herd of cows.

'Moooooo, moooooo . . .' Their moans turn into a chant. 'Mooo-ssse, Mooo-ssse, Mooo-ssse.'

The lifeguard turns and blows his whistle.

'Moose, Moose, Moose!' the boys call.

Heather laughs out loud. Jessica puts her hand over her mouth.

52

'What's all this?' Lucinda asks.

'It's the mating call of the Moose,' Heather tells her, and then collapses into Jessica's arms with mortified laughter.

A girl is walking down the hill wearing her team swim-suit, towel in hand, a sheen of black trimmed with red around her muscular shoulders, her biceps, the tops of her thighs. Her cheeks are red in her ruddy face; her broad smile doesn't hide the fact that she is alarmed and then embarrassed by the outburst she expected to hear at school but not on the beach.

'What are they doing?' Lucinda asks.

Moose is a champion swimmer; she wins gold medals for the school and brings home perpetual trophies our county hasn't seen in years. I know her because the lunch-room erupts whenever she comes through the door. She is the PE teacher's favourite. But this isn't why the boys taunt her. It's not even because she has an accent and is from northern Europe – both her parents are scientists with the pharmaceutical company in the city. None of these things are the reason the teens torment her. Moose is the tallest girl in the school, taller than me, even taller than most teachers.

'Man, that's harsh,' Lucinda says. 'This town is a joke. I'm already fed up.'

The smile dips off Jessica's face; a tight corner turns up on Heather's mouth.

Moose is absorbed into the team waiting at the side of the water, and the calls fade away. The team wades out, waist-deep, swimming past the buoy line. They are the first back in the water since the drowning.

'I've got to get out of this town,' Lucinda says, standing up. She picks up her boots, tips out the sand and walks off without so much as a goodbye.

I gather my shoes and follow.

Jessica and Heather watch us walk away; they put their hands to their mouths and whisper. Heather laughs out loud.

We walk barefoot over the hot sand.

'Wake up, wake up, wake up!' The coach raises a megaphone and shouts to the swimmers. 'Where do you think you are? A field trip to the zoo? You're here to train. Go go go!'

And the swimmers break hard against the surface, cutting the water like blades with their strokes.

We walk to the edge of the sand, where the dunes give way to black, silty marsh. We drop our boots at the end of the beach and wade out onto the mudflats. Black silt slides between our toes. The water is shallow here; as far out as we walk, the water comes up only to our knees.

In the far distance, a helicopter hovers near the shore. It is difficult to know how close it is to the hook at Mulberry Point, or if it is farther up the coast, beyond our part of the woods. Lucinda follows my finger as I trace the coves and peninsulas, the finger of land and the cut of the trees where you can only make out the hook if you know where it is.

It is Lucinda's idea to walk from here back to our house along the coast.

'How long could it take?' Lucinda says.

'No longer than walking the road – maybe even quicker.'

We wade past the town. By the diner, we are up to our thighs; our shorts have wicked through, soaking us up to the pockets. The water begins to deepen.

Lucinda doesn't want to turn back, even when we realise that she is not carrying her boots and that I have left my sandals beside them, back at the end of the beach.

We pass the inlet and follow the shore, walking into the knee-high seagrass when the water becomes too deep, when it churns dangerously in swift currents. We march through manicured backyards, through curtains of cattails already up to our waist. Trailers, mansions with wraparound views, crossing docks and decks, and then out onto the rugged coast-line, nothing but woods and seagrass anchoring the sand, the sound of waves and the cry of gulls. We gain and lose sight of the hook; it doesn't look like it is coming any closer. My nose is beginning to feel tight under the sun. Lucinda's bare shoulders are reddening.

We come to a cove that I think shouldn't be too far from the coast road. Here, an uprooted tree trunk is partially buried in the sand, its bark smooth and bleached by the sun, a tangle of roots protruding like fossilised bone. Two turtles, sunning themselves, lift their necks at the sound of our approach. They drop off into the water and swim out. Lucinda stretches herself out on the trunk while I root around in the undergrowth at the edge of the forest for early wild strawberries. I don't find what I'm looking for, but I pick a stem of Michigan lily, a stem of black-eyed Susan. I snap off the blossoms and place one in my hair, one behind Lucinda's ear. Small mayflies nip at our ankles, our necks. We scratch and swat them away.

'What do you think it's like to die?' Lucinda asks.

A snake emerges from under the trunk, escaping our vibrations. We watch it mark a trail in the sand, slithering toward the water.

'Maybe this,' I say, sitting at the edge of the trunk.

And I mean it. I feel happy and free, walking along the coast with Lucinda, going home in a way I have never gone home before.

6

THE BUDS ON THE mulberry trees at the edge of the peninsula are thick with glossy leaves; clusters of white berries, hard and tight, cling like larvae to the stem. A small flock of late-spring tundra swans land on the hook; they rest along the shore of the Great Lake on their way from the south-east to their breeding grounds in the north. They come quietly in the spring, in dribbles, but in late autumn, hundreds – possibly thousands – return, filling the sky, guiding the newly young home. I envy their inner compass, their sense of knowing: when to rise, when to fly.

Lucinda doesn't want to stop to hear about the tundra swans. She is too interested in the bay house. It should be falling down after all these years. The lawn is tidy and the windowsills painted, garnished with carefully planted boxes. I think we have come up the wrong peninsula of land onto someone's property.

Lucinda steps onto the cement steps of the screened porch and tries the door. It is locked. She shivers and holds her arms close to her body.

'Something bad happened here.' She comes down the stairs and grips my arm. 'I'm cold in my bones. Do you feel it?'

I can't say I do; the humidity has only increased with the heat of the day. She walks around the house, peering into the windows. I listen for the sound of the professor coming through the woods. I hear only the wind lifting the trees and the lake water lapping the shore.

'They say I have *the gift*,' she calls.

I giggle.

She stands in front of me, sullen. 'I've been called to crime scenes.'

It is outlandish, and I don't believe her, and I think she is trying to be funny, but I can't be sure. I bite my tongue to keep from laughing.

To one side of the house, heading toward the lake, something catches my eye. A figure roosting on one leg, like a sandhill crane. Moving closer, I see that it isn't a crane but a sculpture, attached to a rusted reinforcement rod and stuck deep into the earth.

There is no mistaking the sculpture: it is a Great Lakes cargo freighter, a common feature passing across the horizon, ships moving in and out of Port Ojibwe, carrying ore pellets from the north in their hulls. At dusk, for a time, they appear suspended on the horizon, in another world, between the steely mauve of water and the lavender of the sky.

The bridge and main hull on the sculpture are constructed of scrap iron: a rim of a barrel hoop, a segment of a cast-iron gutter, rusted engine parts. The finer details – an anchor, portholes, lines, railings – are formed out of odds and ends: bicycle chains, cogs from a timepiece, spark plugs, the wheel off an outdoor faucet, the plug from a bathtub, nuts, bolts – easily identifiable curiosities. On either side of the bow and stern, a name is etched in metal. It seems a prayer, a memorial, a sailor lost at sea. BILLY. BILLY. BILLY. BILLY.

'Who's Billy?'

Lucinda is standing beside me, examining the fused seams of the sculpture.

I shrug. 'I think we better get back,' I tell her. The freedom I've felt all day is beginning to constrict, the looseness I feel around Lucinda already beginning to close. I'm hungry. It is time to go back to the house, find the others, face any trouble we may be in.

Lucinda backs away from the sculpture and screams.

I shriek, too, when I see him. The professor is leaning out of a dormer window in the upstairs of the bay house, holding a pair of binoculars. He waves when he sees us – not a friendly hello, but something frantic, like a signal, like he is angry, warning us away.

Lucinda runs back toward the water, along the strip of land jutting out to the Point. I follow her. We are a streak of buoyant laughter now, spectacles of hysteria. The bank of swans rise in a frenzy and depart to a stretch farther along the shoreline. When we reach the water's edge, we bend over, clutching our sides, trying to catch our breath.

'Who the fuck was that?'

'The professor. He thinks he owns this land, but he doesn't.'

'Sick fuck. Did you see how he was looking at us, up close, through binoculars?'

The cold in her bones – and even the professor as a potential audience – doesn't stop Lucinda taking down her wet cut-offs, kicking them into the middle strip of land at the edge of the lake where the wash over the pebbles won't reach them. She shimmies out of her bathing-suit bottoms.

'You're coming?' she calls, pulling the tank of her bathing-suit top off, throwing it back behind her with the rest of her clothes. The skin underneath, protected by clothing, forms a negative space: bluish white in contrast to the freckles and burn from the sun, which spreads down her legs, arms, across her shoulders. Lucinda tiptoes into the water, gentle waves lapping her feet. The waves reach her knees, her thighs, cover the curve of her bottom, nip at her waist.

The waters are unpredictable here, Dad has warned me; suddenly they can become a river, taking hold, carrying a person away.

The wind picks up, and Lucinda turns to me. Stretching her arms behind her, she lifts her chin to the sky. Her breasts are full and round; her nipples float under her collarbone like brown petals on stone. Stratus clouds have moved in and covered the blue sky; they have fallen to the horizon and blend with the grey water of the Great Lake. The white lines of the waves break before they reach the shore, forming an axis, breaking against the vertical of Lucinda's body rising out of the water.

I don't trust myself to move; to look away will give myself away.

'Will you save me?' she asks. 'I can't swim.'

She sits back into the water, immerses her head in the waves.

I walk to the edge of the water, put a toe of each foot into the cold, closing my eyes. The wind comes off the lake, separating the strands of my hair, cooling my skin. It smells of rain.

I take off my shorts, stretch my T-shirt to hide my greying underwear. The waves roll at my hips for much of the way out. The cold stuns my thoughts, takes the heat out of my thighs.

'Just do it,' she tells me. 'Get it over with.'

I let myself fall. My breath catches with the cold. I am glad I have this distraction. I swim out toward her. My muscles have always known what to do in the water; I don't understand the concept of not knowing how to swim.

Lucinda lets herself be carried backward by an oncoming wave. She lifts her chin to the sky, quickly sinking again.

'Teach me,' she says when I reach her side.

'I learned on a smaller lake.'

'Teach me here.'

I move toward her, pretending her nakedness has no effect on me.

'First, float,' I instruct, fanning my hands out to show her. 'Lie back.' Her nipples, in the cold, tighten like an iris turned to light. I concentrate on holding the small of her back, my fingertips barely supporting, not taking her weight.

She scoops water like she is bailing out.

'Relax,' I say.

She grabs my waist. 'Who taught you?'

'My dad.'

He taught us to swim, many years ago, on the kettle lake in the woods behind our house, the same lake where his own father had taught him to swim, in the same way: throwing us into the deep end. I buoyed to the top, stretched out my arms and felt the need to move them like a blade through the water. He threw Hare in behind me. She floundered and shouted, then sank like a stone. Dad let her sink and then, exasperated, went in after her. When he reached Hare to drag her back in, she beat out at him with her fists flying.

'My dad started to teach me,' Lucinda says, '. . . but he died.'

'I'm sorry,' I tell her. Mrs McCarthy brings new children around with her all the time, extensions of herself; it never occurred to me to ask why she was living with the McCarthys, even though I knew she was fostered.

She holds my waist tighter. The water covers my breasts now; it rises swiftly to my shoulders. Our heads are only just sticking out of the water. The shelf slopes; we are approaching the drop-off. We shouldn't be out here at all.

She lets go of my waist and holds out her arms, letting my fingertips take her weight, stretching her toes and arms in opposite directions. On the underside of her arm, round scars, tan-less and taunt, mark the line below her elbow; another sits at the folds on her wrist.

'Don't be sorry,' she says to the sky. 'They're all dead. All of them. Mom, Dad, my sister . . .'

'How?' I expect her to say a car accident, something awful and disastrous. I press my palm into the small of her back as she lifts slightly out of the water. I feel the pull underneath, an undertow of water on its return from the shore.

She closes her eyes. 'They died in their sleep. Poisoning from the fireplace. Carbon monoxide. I'm the only survivor . . .'

I don't know what to say.

'My window was open that night. It was Christmas Eve. When I woke on Christmas Day . . .' Her eyes squeeze tight.

'That's sad,' I whisper. I think of the public service ad running on television not so long ago.

'. . . I'm alone in the world now.'

'What about your grandparents?'

'Dead.'

A gloomy shadow hangs over us. I walk slowly along, parallel to the shore; the waves are becoming frothy now, closer together. My fingertips float her along like a raft on a drifting sea. A solitary sandpiper forages in a patch of milfoil. It bobs and dives, resurfacing, nervously gazing around.

Suddenly Lucinda opens her eyes. 'And now I'm stuck with the McCarthys.'

She wriggles away from my fingertips, paddling forward, moving out deeper into the lake, into the drop-off.

'It's deep out there,' I tell her.

'Can you keep a secret?' she asks, parting the water with small strokes, paddling to stay afloat.

I move toward her, treading water. 'Of course.'

'I'm not staying long. My boyfriend's coming for me.'

'Boyfriend?' I don't know why I feel disappointed.

We tread low in the water.

'Don't tell anyone.'

'Who would I tell?'

'He's not really a boy,' she continues. 'He's a man. His name's Robert. He's *married.*'

A wave lifts us. We drift deeper out from shore.

'What?' I smile, nervously off cue. I don't find it funny, only strange – wrong.

'He has children older than us. He hates his wife. *Hates her.* She's worse than Mrs McCarthy.'

I don't think Mrs McCarthy is so bad. 'He ... was your foster father?' I can't shake an image of Mr McCarthy. I shudder.

Lucinda is beginning to pant; I take her elbow, tow her back toward the shallows, resting our feet down into the softness of the sandbar.

'Yeah. That bitch caught us, and that's why they moved me.' Her face furrows with spite.

'Will he come here, to Kettle Lake, to find you?'

'Probably. We'll run to Florida – Mexico, eventually. He wants to get away from her, too. She's rotten.'

I must look worried, because she lifts her arm out of the water and strokes my forearm, runs her finger along my jawbone.

'Don't worry. I have to finish high school first. I'm not leaving yet.' She thinks for a moment. 'Maybe you'll help me – help me find a way to see him.'

I don't think I want to help with this plan.

She takes my shoulders, turns me around and climbs onto my back. I can feel her breasts against my skin.

'Have you ever done it?' she asks.

'Done what?'

'Honestly? *It!* Have you ever got laid?'

'Like, *hump* someone?'

She laughs now, and I'm glad she can't see my face.

I spin her around in the water.

'Oh my God, it is so nice.' She moves herself around, anchors herself to me, faces me. She lies into the water, her legs wrapped around my hips. Small electric shocks dart through my core.

'Ever been kissed?' She touches the scoop of her own neck. 'What if I were drowning now?' she asks.

The heat off my face feels like sunburn.

'Would you give me the kiss of life?'

She pulls herself upright, stands in front of me, puts her lips to mine. Presses them gently, then slightly opens my mouth with her tongue. She presses harder. When I put my arms around her waist, she pulls away.

'That was practice,' she says, splashing water into my face.

I take her arm, circle a scar with my finger. 'What's this?' I ask.

She touches the mark. 'A burn.'

I'm blank.

'Cigarette burns.'

Her answer astonishes me. 'Who did this to you?'

She doesn't answer. Instead, she falls back into the water, propels herself out into the deep, over the drop-off, out of her depth.

She can hold herself up just fine without me. She spreads her arms out to the sky. Her teeth begin to chatter. Her lips have turned blue.

'We've stayed too long,' I say.

She doesn't answer.

'Was it the father – your boyfriend? Robert?' I asked. 'The burns?'

'No. Nothing like that.' She laughs a little, but the gloom hangs heavy.

She swims in, back toward the sandbar. She stands up out of the water and walks toward the shore.

'Tell me. Who did this to you?'

'I did it to myself.'

'Why?'

'Because it hurts.' The way she says this, softly, full of sorrow, makes my insides ache. 'It hurts, waiting for Robert.'

*

Back on shore, someone is waiting for us, waving his arms over his head. I see his shape, his hands at his mouth; I nearly hear his voice disappearing on the wind. Lucinda thinks it is the professor – she gives him the finger in case he is looking through his binoculars at us. But it isn't him; I know the shape of Dad. I wonder how long he has been standing here.

I touch my lips, feeling Lucinda's still on mine.

When we are close enough for him to know we are coming back in, for him to see Lucinda's nakedness, he turns, crosses back through the woods.

I scramble into my shorts. The wet of my underwear soaks straight through. Lucinda takes her time, sluicing the water from her skin, wringing her hair out until the drips slow then stop. Finally she pulls on her cut-offs over her wet legs; the wet from her breasts soaks into the long-sleeved shirt, leaving damp patches across her chest. She pushes her bikini into her pocket.

My legs are full of scratches and itches. The mayflies follow us all the way through the woods. Neither of us speak. When we pass the bay house, the dormer window is closed. We pass the cabin on the hill. There is no sign of the professor. His car is no longer on the patch of grass at the edge of the woods.

*

Everyone is waiting for us on the driveway. Mrs McCarthy holds Lucinda's boots.

'Jesus, Mary and Joseph,' she shouts. 'The whole town has been searching for you girls for hours.' Her voice rises and she lets out a sob. Aunt Rita puts her arm around her.

Sammy runs to me and holds my waist, crying. Even Hare comes down the driveway, shaking her head. She holds her arms over her chest; she is shaking.

Dad has walked off to the pole barn.

'Your poor father,' Mrs McCarthy cries.

'They're fine now,' Aunt Rita says. 'Look, they're here.'

'Only thanks to Everett spotting you girls,' Mom says. 'If he hadn't, we'd be out looking for you still.' She has dark circles under her eyes. Her voice is flat. 'Do you have the truck keys? Your father says he gave them to you.'

'Your poor mother, stranded in town. They had to send for the coastguard to retrieve your father off Freddie's boat when they discovered this lady's ridiculous boots on the beach.' Mrs McCarthy grabs Lucinda by the upper arm. Lucinda pulls away. 'A search for one drowned girl turns into a search for two fools—'

'It's all right now, Edna, don't make a fuss,' Mom tells her. She turns to me and stretches out her hand. 'Just give me the truck keys.'

I search my pocket, but they are gone; they must have fallen out on the sand.

'Where do you think you're going?' Aunt Rita is appalled at Mom.

'I'm not going anywhere now, am I?' Mom glares at me.

Aunt Rita shakes her head at her, bewildered. She watches Mom as she disappears up the driveway and into the house.

'Come on, honey, let's get these kids home,' Aunt Rita tells Mrs McCarthy.

Mrs McCarthy is crying, seemingly with relief more than anything else. 'Look at your brothers and sisters waiting here, starving.'

The foster children are running around the yard, shouting and laughing with our cousins. Sammy squeezes my waist once more and runs back to them, realising that they will leave soon, too.

'They are not my family,' Lucinda mumbles.

'I was going to keep an open mind about what they told me at her last home,' Mrs McCarthy tells Aunt Rita, as though Lucinda isn't here, 'but I can certainly see some truth in it. She does what she likes. The world revolves around Lucinda! Look at her – what now? You're a wet T-shirt contestant?'

Lucinda walks across the yard and sits on the steps, leaning her elbows back on the deck, staring serenely into the woods. Her breasts are visible under her T-shirt.

'That's her summer done – blown all in one day. She's not leaving the farm now until I can teach her some manners. Sorry, Joanne – I'm afraid you won't see your friend until high school is in session!'

'There were two of them in it,' Aunt Rita reminds her, glaring at me. 'You frightened us, disappearing from town like that, girls, without telling anyone.'

'So?' I say, because I don't know what else I can do.

'Don't you start now.' Mrs McCarthy turns on me. 'You're a good girl, Joanne, and you don't need to adopt this one's mouth.' She glares at Lucinda. 'Close your legs, young lady. Your shorts leave nothing to the imagination.'

Lucinda's power to provoke Mrs McCarthy is quite marvellous and disturbing at once.

Lucinda puts her face to the sky and closes her eyes. Drops of rain dot her cheeks, her forehead. They sprinkle the table, make rings in the glasses of abandoned sun tea.

'Here comes the rain,' Aunt Rita says. 'Joanne, get those clothes off the line for your mother.'

The rain picks up; streaks are already darting across the dry clothes. I run for the line. Lucinda follows, but Mrs McCarthy calls her back.

'Get in that truck, lady. The only place you're going is to a young women's reformatory school if you keep this up.' She throws her hands up. 'There is no hope for this girl.'

Lucinda slips into the truck. She shows me her middle finger, then transforms it into the peace sign. I dash the clothes from the line, pegs still gripping their corners. Mrs McCarthy turns the truck around and drives off, taking all my new hopes up the road with her.

I walk out into the drive with my bundle of clothes, lift two fingers from underneath the towels.

'Peace,' I mumble to the dust rising on the road.

7

I AM SITTING ON the deck. The last gold of the sun sinks behind the trees; the peepers fill the woods. I hear Dad closing the pole barn. I don't know if he has been fixing a car or avoiding us. He walks past me, up the stairs. He pauses before he reaches the door.

'Your mother in bed?' he asks.

'Yes,' I say, in a tone that sounds straight from Hare.

He clears his throat. 'That girl, living out at McCarthys'—'

'That *girl* has a name.'

'Lucinda lives with the McCarthys,' he restates.

'I know.'

'Watch your tone, miss,' Dad warns. He comes back and sits down next to me.

Angry, humiliated tears pool in my eyes. I blink them away. 'That doesn't make her bad.'

'No, it doesn't.'

We sit in silence.

'You know, I helped pull someone's daughter out of the water today.' His voice is soft, almost a whisper.

I feel awful. I'm the most selfish person in the world. I didn't know they found her.

'Sorry,' I tell him, and I mean it. For the girl, for him. For the way I have behaved.

'Yeah. Unfortunately, there wasn't a big fuss because – well, we had to get on with the next search. What possessed you?' he asks.

I shrug. How can I explain this feeling I have with Lucinda?

Neither of us speak.

'Where did they find her?' I ask at last.

'Freddie calculated the waters. He tends to know which way things get carried. We led one of the coastguard boats. They spotted her off the islands beyond the Wildlife Refuge.'

'Sorry. That's upsetting.'

'It wasn't nice.'

The sun sinks; copper smears at the edge – a flash of green, and the light is gone. We sit quietly, listening to darkness settle into the woods.

'The McCarthys are mistreating Lucinda,' I say.

He lets air out his nose. I look at him to see if he is laughing. He is watching the woods, the look on his face sombre. 'You really believe that?'

'I don't know.' I falter. 'Mr McCarthy is disgusting.' I think of him sitting there drinking beer on a Sunday morning.

'Stop it, Jo – that kind of talk is below you.'

My face is burning.

'They aren't bad people, the McCarthys. They aren't perfect, but they aren't bad. Edna's been doing this for a long time. She is tough and expects a lot, but she is decent to those children.'

My throat squeezes, constricting with defensiveness. 'That's not what Lucinda says. The McCarthys use her and all the children for labour. It isn't right.'

A flicker of a smile twitches on Dad's face. It makes me indignant.

'It's a gross thing – to take children in for your own benefit.'

'Edna puts the kids to work, but that isn't a bad thing. Sometimes it's good to have some physical labour to sort out whatever plagues your mind. You have chores around here – we put you to work, don't we? No one's calling social services on us.'

'Yeah, but—'

'Look, I'm not arguing with you on this. I just want to make sure you know there's a reason Lucinda isn't living at home with her family.'

'Of course there's a reason—' My voice breaks. 'Her family is dead!'

Dad laughs, incredulous. Then he covers his mouth when he sees he has upset me again. 'Jo, babe. You can't be so gullible—' But he softens when he sees I am crying for real. 'Look, Lucinda's family is alive but very much in trouble. And your friend, Lucinda, sadly, is also a very troubled girl. I'm sure it's exciting having a new friend, and we're not saying you can't be friends, but we want you to be careful. Aunt Rita is a little concerned—'

'Aunt Rita.' I practically spit her name. I make to stand up.

'Yes, Aunt Rita. Sit back down here – let me tell you something.' Dad clears his throat. He looks back over his shoulder. 'Things are tricky with your mother right now.

73

I'm not going into that, either. But she kind of needs your help – she needs someone around the house. To keep an eye on her, to keep an eye on Sammy. Aunt Rita does us a lot of favours, always taking your brother. I just don't want him on his own with your mother.'

'Are you saying I can't see Lucinda?'

He chuckles again. I am infuriated he is finding this so funny. He holds out his hands to slow my reaction. 'It's just that I don't think Lucinda is going to be let loose any time soon, honey, do you? You saw Edna – she isn't getting over this for a very long time.'

He has a point.

'I haven't seen a child break Edna yet.' He chuckles and then grows serious again. 'But look, we need to be careful. For a few weeks, anyway. Your mother – she isn't well.'

I don't ask. I don't really want to know. All I know is that I want to see Lucinda again. I will find a way.

Dad stands and moves inside. I hear him opening the fridge, hear him pop the cap off a bottle. The television clicks on.

I walk back toward the edge of the woods. The shapes of the trees press in, the darkness amplifying every sound. Red clouds pass the moon. The woods resonate with deep longing, bullfrogs' throating notes low as a double bass. The stars accumulate in a darkening sky.

We need to be careful. I look back toward the house. Music drifts down from Hare's clock radio. Mom's light is off. Sammy has gone home with Aunt Rita. Memorial Day weekend is over.

The whole, bleak summer stretches out ahead of me.

8

WE ARE OVER A month into the summer vacation and nothing has let up. Not the humidity, which leaves beads of sweat on the kitchen cabinets. Not Mrs McCarthy's vow to hold Lucinda hostage at the farm for the summer. And definitely not Mom's restless state.

After her slump over Memorial Day weekend, and after Maureen's coup at the family farm, I hear her long into the night: her wire brush hurrying over wood, the drawers of her toolbox opening, a clatter, a search for missing tools. I wonder if she sleeps at all. Dad urges her to come up out of the basement, to take a break. She moves around him as though she hasn't heard, as though he does not exist.

Aunt Rita brings Sammy home every few days to kiss Mom on the cheek. He doesn't even collect clean underwear – Aunt Rita has everything sorted. It is as though he is being absorbed into her family.

'I'm taking Sammy,' she'll say.

'Suit yourself,' Mom says and brushes them aside, sanding the cabinet with a renewed sense of her own force.

'I'll watch him,' I tell Aunt Rita, trying to keep my promise to Dad.

'No, no. He's easy. The boys play better when he's home.'

I'm thinking I'll slip out the door when Mom returns to the basement, ride over to the McCarthys' farm. But Mom has other plans.

'Not so fast,' she tells Hare, holding a steaming bucket under the overflowing faucet. She turns off the tap and splashes Murphy's Oil Soap into the water, sloshing it around. She hands Hare a pile of dry dust rags. Hare stares at her, incredulous, but she takes them and holds them tight in her fist. Mom opens an oak door and piles stacks of cans onto the counter, calling out a list to Hare and me.

'. . . grouting on the faucet. Make a paste, use an old toothbrush. Kitchen, bathrooms. Vinegar on the windows, wipe with newspapers.' She opens the refrigerator door. 'This needs doing . . .'

'You're kidding me,' Hare says, stamping her foot, tears at the corner of her eyes.

'I need you girls to help out around here.' Mom says this as though it has only just occurred to her.

'I'm late.'

'If they're your friends, they'll wait,' Mom says cheerfully. 'I'm sure they have to help their own mothers out. No one is going down that driveway until your chores are finished.'

'*Please*,' Hare exaggerates. 'Give me a break. You sound like Aunt Rita.'

'You know, Rita might be right. If you want to meet your friends, you're going to stop sulking and start helping.'

Hare walks out the door, still clutching the dust rags.

Mom follows her out to the deck. 'Take one more step, and I'll send you to work for Aunt Rita for the rest of the summer.'

Hare stops. She weighs it up, then turns and stomps past Mom, back inside. She sniffles into the phone, replaces the receiver and then goes to work on the fridge, pulling bottles of salad dressing out of the door. She dismantles the shelves and washes the door with furious strokes.

Mom and I remove the screens from the windows and hose them down until the grey water runs clear. Every door frame, every windowsill. Mom hums as she works. When the dry clothes come in from the line, she shakes them out and irons them, folding them until the seams are crisp. She stacks them away and rearranges the cabinets and dresser drawers throughout the entire house.

I pour lemon oil onto a rag and rub it into the wood of the hutch, the way Mom taught me. I know this cleaning stint won't last – her bursts of energy never do, except with her antiques, and even then, she shifts easily between projects: a set of drawers here, a Kalamazoo range there.

She doesn't lose her resolve as quickly as usual, though, and by the end of the morning the house looks brighter in that way cleaning can shift the light. Hare doesn't lose steam either; she stomps and slams and mumbles under her breath.

'If you don't like it,' Mom threatens from the top of a high stool, dusting the exposed beams, 'Aunt Rita offered you a job at the Bait & Tackle.'

She sends Hare up onto the dining-room table with a vinegar solution, instructing her how to clean the birdcage chandelier, salvaged from a garage sale near the city. Hare has to take all of the glass teardrops off the brass frame, soak them, then scrub them with a toothbrush until they gleam.

'Why bother?' she complains. 'We never eat in here.' But she unhooks the teardrops anyway.

I am sweating and weary from the heat after cleaning screens, but Mom sends me straight to the icebox, an antique she refinished last year – Mom and Dad dragged it down into the workshop, amid Dad's grunts and Mom's terse commands. The top door was crooked and missing a hinge, the wood gummed with years of varnish. It didn't come back up for a long time, but when it did, it was the colour of raw honey, the decorative carvings now obvious through the refinished wood. I love lifting the polished heaviness of the handle, feeling the door move open on its new hinge. It is my favourite piece in the house. I like thinking of the family who once used this as a modern, functioning unit: how they fitted blocks of ice into the bottom door; a family who most likely sewed their own clothes, and ploughed the fields and attended Sunday service and never deviated from what they were meant to become in life.

Now, the icebox stores folded-up brown paper bags from the grocery store, Tupperware, clothes pins, an overflow of tin cans.

Hare comes to Mom in the early afternoon, repentant in tone, helpful and sweet, wanting to know if there is anything else to be done before she leaves to meet the girls. Mom tells her tersely that she isn't going anywhere. I sense a danger in her movements, something fraught.

'I hate you,' Hare screams. She dusts the piano with furious blows to the keys.

'Plenty more jobs waiting for you tomorrow,' Mom tells her.

Mom turns to me, gives a little shake of her head, giggling, as if we are allies and I am having as much fun as she is.

'What else do you expect?' I ask. 'We're not dogs.'

I turn back to restack the brown shopping bags, already regretting the remark. I feel the silent, unstable atmosphere building behind me. When I turn, betrayal burns on her face.

'Don't you dare speak to me like that,' she cries. 'Not you.'

Why not me? I have never spoken back to her the way Hare does daily. I jut my hip out with the injustice of it.

She crosses her arms.

I cross my arms.

We lock each other in a glare, the house gleaming all around us. It has never looked so clean. There is a sense that we are going away, leaving for good. Mom laughs. She brings her hand up to her mouth and giggles. I put my arms down and press my lips together, not wanting to give in so easily. She lifts strands of my hair, twists the ends together, brings the pile up close to my chin, surveying me as though seeing me for the first time.

'Get in the truck,' she says. 'We're going to Carol's.'

*

Hare storms out of the house and sits down hard on the passenger seat, slamming the car door, the hatred rolling off her. There is no arguing.

79

'Haircuts, girls.' Mom claps. 'Let's go get you some smart summer styles.' She sings her words. She sings to the radio, all the way to Carol's.

When we pass Maureen's farm, Mom lays on the horn. Hare startles. I startle, too – but then I laugh, a nervous laugh. Hare's bewilderment, though, quickly turns to tears. She turns her head and watches the fields move by in a blur, wiping her eyes nearly all the way to the city limits.

Carol lives and works in the last rural farmhouse before the city. A wooden sign hangs off the front porch; her husband hand-painted it: THE VILLAGE BANG. We walk around back to an addition that connects to her house with a screen door. Carol is surprised to see us.

'I was about to close up shop,' she tells Mom. She is finishing smoothing the blue-rinsed strands of an older lady's hair. Mom gestures to the chairs, anyway, and we all take a seat. 'How've you been?'

Carol is Mom's friend – sort of. That's how I think of her anyway, the way they are friendly with each other. Carol never stops by our house, and Mom never goes through the door that leads from Carol's beauty parlour into her kitchen, but they speak to each other like they have known one another a long time. Carol does most of the talking and Mom listens, flipping through magazines from the coffee table.

Hare slumps in the chair beside me. Something like a dishpan rattles in the other room, through the open door of Carol's kitchen. The customer stares dully at her own reflection while Carol teases her short, tight curls into volumes of fluff orbiting her scalp. All the while Carol speaks at Mom through the mirror about the price of gas. Mom half-listens, half agreeing with a disinterested smile. When Carol turns on the hairdryer, Mom leans over and shoves a magazine under my nose.

'What do you think about this?' she asks, excited.

The picture is a famous skater, Dorothy someone-or-other. Her dark, shiny hair is the same colour as mine, but hers is hewn in a wedge below her ears. Hare shifts in her chair to get a better look. She shoots me a warning look. Hare always says Carol is a hairdresser for old ladies.

A girl comes out the doorway that leads from Carol's kitchen, carrying combs and brushes in a towel. She organises them back onto their hooks on a pegboard by the register. Carol is perpetually training a new girl; we never meet the same girl twice.

The girl sweeps the fluff from underneath Carol's feet. Carol shakes her head and sets her mouth; she catches Mom's attention, rolling her eyes.

'Sonia will take one of the girls,' she says sharply, which makes me look again at Sonia.

I feel sorry for her and like her at once, with her long hair, shiny and straight and tucked behind her ears, like mine – only hers is so blonde that it looks white. I can sit on my own hair, even when it is tangled. When I was still in elementary school and Mom would remember to come up out of the basement to watch us leave for school, she'd look at my hair as though the knots and tangles were there purposely to annoy her. She'd tear a comb through the strands, catching the snarls in the teeth.

'It's full of rats' nests,' she'd tell me.

She'd work it backward then, pulling the strands into two tight lines of braids that made the skin behind my ears pinch all the way through lunch.

'Well?' Mom asks now.

I shrug. Mom tells me all the time that I need to learn to say *no*. Now would be a good time to practise, but while I hesitate, she decides.

'Let's do it.' She taps the page off her knee.

'You girls are getting tall,' Carol says, walking the lady to the register. The bells on the door rattle when she leaves.

'She has terrible psoriasis on her scalp,' Carol whispers, watching the woman get into her car. She shudders. 'Poor woman.'

Once the lady has closed her car door, Carol's voice returns to its normal volume.

'Three grandchildren – they never visit. They live a couple blocks away and it seems they go out of their way to avoid passing her house – unless her daughter needs something.' She waves to the lady's car. 'And she is so nice. I don't understand. It's very sad.'

Carol pats the chair, signalling for one of us. Hare bolts out of her seat and sits down. Carol spins her around to face the mirror.

Sonia smiles at me from across the room and pats the chair on the opposite wall. Mom follows me over and shows Sonia the picture. I hardly register the look of concern on Sonia's face. I am beginning to think how closely the look resembles Lucinda's cut, which is short, though her hair flips up at the ends and this one tucks under.

'Are you sure?' Sonia asks me, when I settle back into the chair. It almost seems she is willing to conspire if I say the word. She pulls my long strands through her fingers.

'She's sure,' Mom answers from across the room. She has opened the magazine before Carol can start talking again.

Sonia washes my hair, and I imagine walking into school in the fall with my new hairstyle and my new friend. She wraps a towel around my head and rubs; some drips fall down my back. She combs all around so that a curtain of hair falls across my eyes. I can see through the parted strands into the mirror: straight black rows, like a field harrowed in spring.

She measures with the tips of her scissors and the point of her comb, brings her scissors to the ready for the first snip, measures again, hesitating as one calculating their entry into a moving skipping rope. Finally, she makes the first snip, and then another. Long black strands fall limp into my lap. Sonia shrugs her shoulders as though shaking off her conscience.

I close my eyes and feel the weight of my hair fall away from my head.

Behind me, Carol attempts to have a conversation with Hare, telling her how her own daughters graduated, how they had been cheerleaders back in high school, when they were Hare's age.

'Had the time of their lives.'

Hare stares blankly at herself into the mirror.

'Are you a cheerleader?' Carol asks.

'Nearly,' Hare answers flatly. 'Don't take too much off,' she adds, 'just a trim.'

Sonia spins me around so that I face the back wall. I watch their exchange in the mirror. Carol raises her eyebrows and looks pointedly at Mom, who smiles sheepishly and picks up a bottle of lotion on the table beside her.

Carol pumps the pedal on Hare's chair vigorously, misting the ends of her hair with brisk pulls on the water bottle. She turns her attention to Mom.

'Any news from your parts?' Carol asks.

Mom has none.

'How's Rita?'

'Rita's good.'

'And Edna? Have you seen her?'

Mom nods. 'Edna McCarthy? Yes, she's fine.'

Mom glances down at her magazine, turning the page on her lap.

'You sure about that?' Carol has paused, mid-snip, a smug curl to her lip.

'What about her?'

'She's got a new girl staying with her. I hear she is quite a handful.' She leans down to Hare and evens up her bangs. 'She's about your age.'

Hare doesn't bother telling her we've already met Lucinda.

'I have never seen one hair out of place on Edna – have you? But this girl has Edna positively possessed.'

'I saw Edna on Memorial Day,' Mom reports. 'I'll have to get out to the farm for a visit.'

'You do that,' Carol instructs. She brushes Hare's long strands, separating them down the middle.

'Hey, what about that girl drowning in the lake near you?' she asks. 'That was terrible.'

'Yes, it was.' Mom glances at me, sensing me tense.

'They cancelled the parade.'

'Yes, they did.'

'She was a cousin of one of my clients. You know Josey Stephens? They came in before the funeral, the family all distraught. Imagine losing your child – any way would be horrible, but drowning?' Carol's scissors stop mid-air; she presses her lips together. 'Oh, Rosemary, I'm so sorry – I'd forgotten.' She puts her scissors down to her side, and her face drops.

Hare looks up at Mom in the mirror.

Mom stares down at her magazine.

'That's tough . . .'

'It's all right,' Mom says firmly.

Carol takes her scissors back to the ends of Hare's hair, snips crisply. She talks faster, not stopping for breath.

Mom occasionally mumbles 'hmm' in response. Soon I lose interest; Carol's voice becomes like a washing-machine spinning out in the background: loud and annoying and something to ignore.

'Jack and I are driving to Elvis country for the Fourth.'

'Hmm.'

'We can do that now the girls are grown up. Taking the convertible. It'll cost a fortune in gas, but when will we ever do it if we don't do it now?'

Mom doesn't have an answer for this.

'Are you going anywhere yourselves?' Carol asks Mom.

'Maureen's having everyone over to the farm,' Mom says.

Hare looks up at her then; for the first time, she seems interested.

'I hear she's back home now.'

Mom straightens, then shifts, in her chair.

'You're practically on each other's doorsteps.' Carol isn't ready to let up. 'How nice.'

Mom turns the page, bows her head back down to the magazine.

Hare shoots me a look in the mirror. She does a double take, squints.

Sonia swivels the chair and concentrates on my bangs, clipping a little here, then a little there. She brushes them one way, then the other. Her brow wrinkles, puzzling something over, then measures again as she takes another little snip.

Carol decides to change the subject. She lowers her voice conspiratorially. 'You heard about the Shirey boy?'

'Hmm,' Mom says. I am not sure if this means that she has or she hasn't. But I am hoping Carol will say more so I can hear about the Shirey boy.

'Caught.' Carol puts her tongue in her cheek.

I have no idea what this means. Mom doesn't confirm or deny that she knows or doesn't know exactly what happened with the Shirey boy. She lifts her eyelids and tips her head back a little, showing mild shock, but her distant smile never fades.

'There's something for you,' Carol says, catching Mom looking at the products displayed on the table.

'Hmm,' Mom says again, turning a bottle over in her hand, reading the ingredients.

'That's my new line. It's the three-step cleansing process. You've got your cleanser, your toner, your clarifying lotion.' Carol's voice changes from conspiracy to commercial, like a cheap ad on television selling salad-chopping instruments.

'I'll take your order if you want to think about it. Usually takes three weeks to deliver. Or I've a few sets in the back if you want to take some home today, give them a try. They're moving pretty quick. It'll change your life.'

I very much doubt this and hope Mom won't fall for it.

'Oh, really?'

'What are you using at the moment?'

'Ivory soap.'

'Oh, dear.' Carol's voice takes a dramatic turn. 'That's OK for now – you're young – but give it a few years, hon, and that soap will turn you to leather.' She shakes her head, concerned, and looks at Mom in the mirror. 'It's an investment. But you're worth it – I would hope Danny sees it that way.'

'Hmm,' Mom says again. She seems so small, there, at once – and beautiful, with her legs crossed underneath her. Her hair is natural and soft with curls – curls Hare inherited. Mom trims it herself to keep the split ends away. She pulls it back or pins it up most of the time, but I love when it sits on her shoulders, like now. Her eyelids are plump and rounded, rosy on the lids when she closes them, squinting to read the print on the bottles.

She looks from Carol to the beauty products. Her consideration of the bottles gives me a swollen ache in my throat. I look at Carol in the mirror, her scissors clipping furiously at the ends of my sister's wet hair, and I think of how much more beautiful Mom is than Carol, with Carol's sharp nose and jet-black hair, dyed and chopped too short so that it sticks up like a bird on the crown of her head.

'Head down,' Sonia instructs, tilting my head forward. She doesn't seem as gentle now.

'I'll give it a try,' Mom tells Carol. She sounds unsure or a little embarrassed – or both.

'You won't be sorry,' Carol tells her authoritatively.

Sonia clips closer and closer to my ear. She turns the chair toward herself and tells me to look up while she clips across my bangs again. She looks terror-stricken now; she moves my chin abruptly and clips above the other ear. I am terror-stricken, too, afraid to look.

Carol pats Hare's shoulder, and she climbs out of the chair, slumps into a seat by the register; she picks up a magazine. Carol sweeps up the clippings. There are so few that they seem like a light pile of feathers, like the ones that come out so easily from the corners of my pillow. Below me, my own dark pile of hair looks like the long tails of dead rodents. When Sonia swivels me back toward the mirror, I can't bear to look.

Mom pays at the register, asking for the price of the bottles along with our haircuts.

Sonia turns me toward the mirror and moves my head up, trimming here, moving it down, trimming there. I keep my eyes on the strip of lights running along the table under the mirror.

Carol takes the money and picks up the broom again. She follows the long strips on the floor up to my face.

'What in the world have you done to this child?'

When I finally look up, I watch Sonia, not my own reflection: her face crumpling, lips trembling, tears streaming down her face and onto the back of my neck.

Carol hands Sonia the broom. She swivels the chair around one way, and then the other. I feel as though I am the styling-head doll that I didn't ask for but received one year for Christmas; I never even pulled it out of the box. Carol pulls her fingers through what remains of my hair.

I bring myself to glance at the mirror. My bangs, wet, look like the serrated cardboard in a book of matches. Mom and Hare stalk up beside me; their faces look as though they are registering a car crash or a puzzle or both. Hare's puzzlement quickly turns to mirth. She tries to supress it, but this only makes it worse. She hisses like the opening of a shaken bottle of pop, effervescent laughter escaping from behind her hands.

Mom shoves her out of the way and lifts the magazine, shifting through pages for the image as though this will change the outcome.

'This is not what we asked for,' she is telling Carol. 'Her bangs are like a ski slope!'

'It's only her second haircut!' Carol barks.

'Look at her.' Mom sounds confused and angry.

'What did you expect?' I'm not sure if Carol is saying this to Sonia or Mom or herself.

When I finally look full in the mirror, it is not me but one of Aunt Rita's boys staring back – the way their hair looks at the end of the summer once the buzz cuts grow out. And Mom is right: my bangs slope to one side. Shards of hair prickle the nape of my neck.

Fresh tears stream out of Hare's eyes; she shakes with laughter.

I push the hair to one side, then the other; finally I push it back off my forehead altogether. This makes Hare laugh even harder. Tears fill my own eyes.

'Oh, Rosemary, I am so sorry . . .'

I don't know why Carol is apologising to Mom. I am the one stuck looking like a boy now.

Sonia is crying, too, standing by the register. Carol shoves her through the kitchen door and tells her to get herself together. 'It's only hair,' Carol tells her viciously. 'It'll grow back,' she tells Mom, stepping back inside and taking up the scissors. She puts her face, beaked like an eagle, near mine, and begins to make quick, furious snips at what is left of my hair.

'It'll grow back,' she says again.

But Mom has already sat down and is turning the pages of her magazine.

9

AFTER THE HAIRCUTS, WE drive the rest of the way into the city to the grocery store. Low-lying clouds have moved in off the lake while we were at Carol's; now, they lie like a grey blanket covering the fields. Fine droplets of rain mottle the windshield, the wipers clearing it over and over again in a soft sweep.

I catch my reflection in the rear-view mirror. My freckles have darkened under the new July sun; they are no longer defined points but clump together, forming a brown swath across my nose and cheeks. I am already ugly, I think, and the only thing this haircut does is show up my gapped smile.

In the store, I watch Hare's reflection behind mine in the freezer door. She giggles again when she catches sight of me. Her own hair is unchanged. Dad will say it is a waste of money; Mom could have done it herself. Mine, on the other hand – I can hear him sniggering – he has gotten his money's worth.

Hare pushes past me and rummages around in the freezer. She takes up a pack of frozen waffles, the kind we see popping out of toasters in the commercials on television – the kind we are never allowed. She stuffs it into the cart under a box of no-brand cornflakes. Half of our cart is full of the plain black and white labels that Hare hates.

We follow along behind Mom into the next aisle. She calculates the best-value coffee tins, even though she will buy the same two-pound can she always buys. The shelves in her workshop are lined with them, filled now with solutions and fluids, used to store hinges and screws, the weights off old clocks, the hands that once turned along the faces, dresser knobs, door-handles and all matter of sundries that she doesn't have a use for yet but dips into now and again when the need arises.

I remember once making a pair of stilts from these coffee cans. I poked holes in the bottom and the sides with a can opener and pulled strands of rope through, looping them up to my hands. I was wobbly, like a toddler walking in a first pair of shoes, moving up and down, my feet taking great effort to lift and move forward. But soon I got used to them and I raced across the yard, and Hare laughed, and Sammy chased me and cried until I let him try them. He was only about three at the time and could barely stand on them – and only then with help – but I made him a pair, too. They were easy to make. I learned how to do it by reading the crafting edition of the World Book encyclopaedias that Mom had ordered from a door-to-door salesman. Dad wasn't happy about the cost of the set and said we had to walk only a mile to the library, where they were free. But we did get some use out of them – especially the craft edition.

'Hey!' Hare's voice brightens, beaming down the aisle.

Maureen pushes her cart slowly toward us, surveying the list in her hand. She hasn't noticed us yet. She dresses sharply, even shopping for groceries, wearing an Oxford button-down, khaki shorts – and, despite the heat and humidity, she has the arms of a navy sweater wrapped around her neck as though a small child is piggybacking. Mom, when she sees her, reaches down and fixes her own hem, straightens her hair. Maureen looks up, a wide smile on her face, anticipating the greeter. Seeing Mom, her face turns down slightly; her ice-blue eyes sharpen. She turns to Hare and manages a smile, but it changes into a full-blown frown when she recognises me.

'Good God, who did your hair? They should have their licence revoked.'

'It'll grow back,' Mom says, smoothing my hair, pushing what little is left behind my ears. She looks at Maureen eagerly, like she is trying a new approach. 'You should have given me your list – we didn't both need to come into the city. Next time.'

Maureen gives a little shrug. 'Oh, that's not necessary.' She pushes her shopping cart forward.

Mom lays her fingers on the edge of the cart. 'I've been meaning to ask – we're shopping for the Fourth – what should we bring? What do you need?'

'Oh.' Maureen mouths a note of surprise.

Both Mom and Hare wait with anticipation.

'Yeah, well, it's just a small thing. I didn't think . . .'

Hare's shoulders slump.

Mom stutters; her face turning red. 'Danny said . . . I thought the Fourth – a barbeque?'

Maureen throws her hands up then. 'Sure, fine, come if you wish.'

Hare smiles and her shoulders lift. Mom seems apologetic now. I want to smack them both.

'Well, I want to make something.' Mom flicks her hair, settles her shoulders. 'Is it a potluck?'

Maureen sets her chin, glances into our trolley, roving her eyes over our groceries. 'Oh, don't bring a thing.'

Maureen has this way of speaking – I notice it more regularly now – depending on who she speaks to, it can sound both upbeat and unhappy at the same time. I never know which to believe.

She picks up a can of coffee from the shelf to read the ingredients. I could have told her what it contains: coffee. She turns the can around and puts it back.

'We've got it covered,' she says, when she notices Mom still waiting. She selects a smaller, gourmet brand from the shelf, turns it over and reads the label. Mom waits. I read the price. It is three times smaller and twice the price of our usual can. Maureen places the bag into her cart and looks at her watch.

'Well, I better get home. Vic's on his way back with the girls.'

'See you in Kettle Lake.' Mom laughs nervously.

Maureen raises her hand and wiggles her fingers as she walks away, not bothering to look back.

'Send the girls over for a visit,' Mom calls after her, but Maureen is turning the corner.

Hare rolls her eyes. Mom stands in the aisle, as though she has forgotten what she was looking for. She picks up the brand Maureen selected, staring at the label, but I don't think she is reading it. She replaces the bag and moves on a way up the aisle, pulling out her list, stopping to study it, crossing off items and totalling up numbers. Hare takes a bag of coffee beans from the shelf – we don't even have a grinder. She places them underneath the no-brand toilet paper and puts her fingers to her lips. I supress a giggle and follow behind as Mom pushes the cart ahead.

'I should have thought this through at the house,' Mom mumbles to herself.

We make another round through the store while she decides what to make for the party. She surveys the frozen meat section. 'I wonder if Maureen already has sweet and sour meatballs?'

Something tells me that no matter what Mom brings, it will be the wrong thing.

We pass by the ice-cream section again. Hare motions for me to put something in the cart. I make a face at her, then catch a look at myself in the glass, feel the back of my hair. I study the frozen cakes, and finally open the door, quietly, taking out a strawberry cheesecake from the shelf. The glass fogs up. I hide the thing, dragging two boxes of saltines over the top. Hare giggles, and I am beginning to feel mean, wanting to call off the game. We make our way around the store like this, sticking in cosmetics and magazines and rows of candy bars. In the peanut-butter and jelly aisle, Mom picks up a jar of grape jelly. 'You can use this for the *sweet*. I remember reading that – and ketchup for the *sour* side of things.'

It sounds disgusting, but Mom catches me laughing at Hare as she slips in a glass jar filled with stripes of mixed peanut butter and jelly, which we always think is a silly thing, anyway. Mom echoes my laughter, mistaking it for a judgement on her dish.

'You're right. Maybe not. Let's make a dessert.'

We follow her down the next aisle.

'Have I ever made a Jell-O salad for you kids?' Mom asks.

I don't think so. She explains how the fruit is suspended into the Jell-O in a mould, and once it is tipped out, you surround it with lettuce and whipped cream. I think it sounds nice.

'It's kind of a retro thing,' she is saying. 'From the sixties, maybe the fifties.'

'Nope, never had it, let's do it,' Hare encourages her.

'I know! Red Jell-O, blueberries and white whipped cream.'

'It's a grand ole flag . . .' Hare mocks. 'Crazy. Go for it.'

Mom finds a box of strawberry Jell-O. She sends me off to find blueberries; Hare doubles back to find whipped cream. Mom is focused now, charged up about her decision. We meet her as she is heading toward the counter. Maureen is at the check-out at the end. When she sees us, she puts her head back down and watches the conveyor belt move her groceries down the line.

'Let's get out of here so you can get started on your masterpiece,' Hare declares.

I know the game has gone too far when Hare shoves the *National Enquirer* into Mom's hand.

'We'll do this for you, Madame,' she tells her, curtseying. 'Read your magazine.'

I think for certain Mom will hear the unkindness in Hare's words – but she suspects nothing. Instead she amuses herself, turning the pages of the magazine she sometimes buys; it hasn't been in the budget now all summer. Mom opens it, hunting for the celebrity marriage story from the cover.

I'm not sure why I am letting this happen: maybe it is the warning look Hare shoots me, or maybe it is punishment for the haircut – or maybe I just don't know how to stop it. Whatever the reason, before long, it is too late. The belt moves forward and Hare stuffs the stowaway items under the loaves of bread and economy-size toilet-paper rolls. It isn't funny any longer, and the total on the register surpasses our usual weekly grocery bill, rising higher and higher, even though the belt is still full. Hare puts the last brown bag into the shopping cart and walks away, over to the window near the penny-horse rides. Mom closes the magazine and sighs, throwing the cashier a guilty smile.

'You can't believe everything you read,' she says.

'No, you can't,' the cashier agrees.

Mom rummages through her purse for her cheque-book; the smile that is still on her face makes me saddest of all as she carefully writes the store name and poises her pen, waiting for the total. When the cashier tells her the amount, Mom's face falls. Her eyes shift to the register. Her fingers stiffen over the amount box on the cheque, as though she doesn't know how to reverse the action. A little sound escapes her throat.

The cashier shifts on her feet and stares at the total box; it seems they are both frozen here in this moment.

'That can't be right.' Mom's voice wavers.

The cashier looks back to Mom and at the digits on the register. She lifts her hands slightly, as though she couldn't care less either way. Mom rummages through the closest bag in the cart and pulls out a box of Drumstick ice-cream cones.

'What is this?' Her voice rises. She pulls out shoelaces and polish, magazines – all the extra things we have shoved into the cart.

'Kids?' Mom turns to me. 'What is this?' Her face flushes bright red.

Over by the window, Hare looks away, crossing her arms, as though she can't believe Mom is embarrassing us again.

Mom's lip trembles. She reaches into another bag and takes out cake mixes, tubs of pink frosting, expensive shampoos.

'I'm so sorry,' she tells the lady. 'I don't know when this happened—'

'Overring on check-out seven,' the cashier calls over the PA.

Mom glances around then, looking for Maureen.

'I need a manager on seven,' the lady calls again. She turns to me then, her eyes alert with annoyance. 'That wasn't a very nice thing to do to your mother, young man.'

I touch my hair in shock.

'Everything OK?' Maureen is standing at the end of the counter, her groceries neatly sorted into two paper bags.

'Sorry, Mom. Sorry . . .' I dig through the rest of the bags, rooting out the unwanted items. I feel a deep sickness.

Mom is frozen, looking down at her cheque-book. She can't even turn around, face Maureen.

'Fine, we're fine,' I say.

'You sure?' Maureen doesn't look too certain, but she walks away. I see her stop and speak with Hare.

The manager arrives.

Mom has to hand me the cheque-book. I write the total into the box where a watery droplet magnifies the digits, then smears.

Maureen leaves her shopping cart with Hare and comes back.

'Let me lend you the money,' Maureen is saying. 'You should have said – it's no problem.' Her voice is genuine this time, even warm.

But Mom pushes past her, walks toward the car. Hare pushes Maureen's shopping cart all the way to her car, helps her load the bags into her trunk. She rejoins us, climbs into the back seat. Mom gets into the truck as I put the groceries in the trunk.

On the way home, she is quiet. Occasionally, she wipes tears on her sleeve, blinking so that she can see the road, but mostly she doesn't bother; she lets them fall, dripping down her cheeks. They hang from her nose.

It has stopped raining by the time we reach the edge of Kettle Lake, and the sun has come out. The tail end of storm clouds rise high above the diner, over the lake, like the bright florets of cauliflower.

Hare is unrepentant in the back seat. I can feel her frustration building. She reaches over the divide and turns the dial on the radio. It blares into the car.

Mom slaps her hand away and turns it off.

'Why can't we listen to the radio?' Hare whines.

I hate her in this moment.

Hare throws herself against the window, her arms folded on her chest, pouting. She kicks Mom's seat.

'Stop it,' I tell her, my throat thickening.

We wait at the crosswalk in front of the diner for a mother and her toddler to cross. The mom pushes the stroller and holds the little girl's hand. Steam rises off the road. Hare kicks Mom's seat again. When the pair have crossed and Mom can pull off, she doesn't move; instead, she throws the car into park right there in the middle of the road.

She whirls around to Hare.

'Don't.' Her voice is pressed and angry and frightening. 'I'm warning you—'

'You're so stupid,' Hare yells. She looks at me, expecting me to join her. 'We are the shittiest family – we can't even buy a box of nice cereal. Everything is no-brand and cheap.'

I shake my head, disagreeing. I am pleading for Mom to turn and look at me; I want her to know I am on her side. She stares at Hare instead. Her eyes are wild and frightening.

She starts low and shaky – fragile and furious at the same time, as though she is trying to wrestle down some-thing dangerous and ugly before it breaks free. She turns in the seat and points her finger at Hare. 'You have no idea—'

Hare interrupts. 'Ha! I think I have some idea. What a joke. You're a joke.'

'Stop it,' Mom whispers, her voice hoarse.

But Hare doesn't stop. It is as though she supressed her vicious streak through all those hours of cleaning, and now it has come out here in the back seat of the car.

'You are ruining my life.' She kicks the back of Mom's seat again. 'You ruin everything. No wonder everyone hates you. No wonder Daddy's sisters hate you. You're so stupid. And you embarrass the hell out of us—'

'Get out . . .' Mom says through gritted teeth. 'Get out before I kill you.' The way she says it, I believe that she can, in this moment, at least hurt Hare very badly.

'Go,' I plead with Hare. '*Please*. You can walk home from here.'

Hare sits back and laughs. 'Oh, what? Like your brother? Are you going to take me out to the lake and drown me, too?'

Mom is stunned. I am stunned.

Hare laughs harshly.

I shake my head at her. I can't make her stop.

'You don't have to read old newspapers to know about you. Everyone knows what you did.'

Mom mouths something.

'What are you saying, Mother? Speak up.'

'Who told you this?' she is mouthing, but Hare still can't hear.

'Who told you this?' I shout. 'She wants to know who told you this.' I am sobbing. 'Why are you doing this? Stop it. Stop it.' I put my hands over my ears.

'Maureen?' Mom's voice breaks. 'Is she putting you up to this, too?'

'I know you're looking for a reason to hate Maureen, but it isn't her. It doesn't matter who told me.'

'Who told you this?' Mom's voice is becoming more audible.

'Grandma, OK?' Hare is screaming now, leaning into the front seat with her shoulders and her red face, yelling. Mom is trying to compose herself, trying to catch a breath. I am pushing Hare into the back seat. She is pushing me away.

'Grandma, Mom – Grandma told me. She's not lying. She showed me the newspapers. She showed me who you are. But it doesn't matter who – everyone knows what you did.'

'Get out,' Mom shouts. Her voice is out of control. She hits the steering wheel with her fist and the horn fires with the force of each blow. 'Get out of my car,' she screams. She turns then and lunges over the back, but the seats catch her, and she flies her fists at Hare instead, smacking what she can reach of her.

The mother walking up the street turns back toward our car; she picks up her toddler, puts her on her hip and pushes the stroller quickly up the road.

The door of the diner is open in the steamy heat; faces at the front window peer toward us, and I know they can hear us. I roll up my window. Hare sits all the way back, trying to avoid the open palms flying at her. She scoots away toward the door, her eyes wide, stunned by Mom's violence. My throat clenches up so tight I can't swallow.

Mom gets out of the car. She pulls Hare from the back seat, throws her into the road and hits her with her fists. Hare pulls away and cowers, blocking the blows with her arms.

Hare manages to crawl away. 'You're crazy!' she shouts. She looks like she will rush at Mom, but instead, she goes to the car and pummels the roof with her fists. Then she gathers herself, her laughter frenzied.

'Fucking crazy woman.' She walks up the road, away from us.

The tables in the diner are full. A small crowd of firefighters, the police chief, all watching us on main street.

A slim man steps outside; he isn't in uniform. It is the professor.

He walks toward our car.

Mom doesn't see him; she puts her hands to the side of her face, watching Hare walk away. She leans against the car, her hands holding the roof, and sobs. The sun above the town puts a glare on the wet streets. Mom climbs back into the car, turning the key, but the engine is already idling, and the starter chews at the flywheel. She puts the car in gear and rolls slowly down the street, past the diner, following after Hare.

'Why can't you be nice?' Mom screams. 'You have to be nice.' Her voice is a mixture of anger and raw agony. It pulls more tears to my eyes.

Hare walks up the street, disdainful of us, her chin in the air even while tears pour down her face. She wipes them angrily with her sleeve.

The professor catches up to the car and reaches into Mom's open window. He places his hands on the door panel and walks along beside the moving car, a deep focus on his brows.

'Hey, hey . . .' he soothes. 'Rosemary, can I help?'

Mom doesn't look at him. 'Oh God,' she mutters, then slowly puts her foot on the gas and accelerates away.

The professor removes his hands from the door frame and watches us pull off. I can see him moving toward Hare.

We both sob all the way home. Mom throws her purse onto the counter. The bottles, the three-step process she bought from Carol, spill out, roll across the floor. She runs down the hall and into her bedroom and slams the door. I hear her alternating between throwing things against the wall, screaming and crying. I stand at her door, unsure what to do next.

After a while, Mom grows silent in the bedroom. Her sobbing stops. I wait for her to come out. I wait for Hare to come home. When neither happens, I walk to the phone, wondering if I should look up the number and call the diner; the firefighters are there, the police, not far from our house. Then I think of calling Dad to tell him what happened. I open the telephone book to the back, where Dad's number is written in pencil. I lift the receiver, then put it down again. Instead, I dial Aunt Rita's number. No one answers. I imagine it ringing out in her kitchen, imagine her empty table by the back-door. I hang up and ring the phone number for the shop. Roy, Aunt Rita's helper, answers; I hang up.

The groceries are still in the trunk of the car. I bring the bags into the house and put everything away, the frozen foods, the dry goods – everything. I find a rubber dog bone at the bottom of one of the bags. I open the trash can and throw it in, burying it deep under the papers. I fold away the bags, trying to collapse them at their creases the way Mom does. I place them into the wooden icebox.

At the bottom of the driveway, a pair of sandhill cranes have wandered over from the Wildlife Refuge, picking at the wet dirt on the road, softened now with rain. They stretch their long necks and call to one another with a rattle-like squawk. There are small movements around their feet: two chicks, picking for food through the discarded piles. They aren't newly born – they are too grown for that – but they are still fuzzy and have not yet gained their caps. They walk up the road then, the two young birds between their parents, their skinny hind legs wheeling like scrawny chickens as they walk. They turn into the woods.

I bring my hands to the back of my head and rub my neck. My fingers touch the shock of bare skin where my hair was this morning. I rise and follow the birds into the woods.

10

THE SKY CATCHES THE apricot fire of sunrise over the field behind our house. It casts around the house and sets behind the trees, over the lake. Mom and Dad argue. Dad leaves the house for work, for his sister's, for his cousin's. He comes home, pops the cap off a bottle of beer. Mom returns to bed. Mom is up, all night, with boundless energy. Aunt Rita stops in with Sammy. She leaves again, in the red bus, taking him with her.

On the Fourth, Mom, Hare and I watch Grandma's field light up from our deck. The pinwheels spin and shoot sparks and flames into the darkened sky. Approval rises from the crowd. Sammy watches from the other side of the field, from Aunt Rita's driveway. The visitors dissipate. Dad is the only one to go to Maureen's party, and he doesn't come home until dawn, walking sideways.

I ride my bike to the McCarthys' farm. Mrs McCarthy tells me, kindly, that Lucinda is busy, that she'll be around again in a few weeks. I ride away, disappointed, slowly following the streaks of clouds along the county road.

This is how the summer passes.

And every day, I swim. I don't care if the professor is in town or not. These are my woods.

*

His car is here today. I pass by, the weeds poking up through the fender. The cattails are as tall as me now. Their long blades tickle my calves, their velvety heads like corndogs on a stick this time of year. I rub the velvet fur with my thumb. The deeper into the woods I walk, the farther away from home I feel. Somewhere up ahead, a woodpecker knocks against a tree. Cicadas buzz like powerlines coming alive in the summer heat. I tread through the weave of reeds until they give way to the glassy surface of the kettle lake. This spot lacks the expansive feel of the Great Lake beyond, with its chaos and weather and indifference.

Here, the water is calm and unfussed, the surface still and black, a metallic blue sheen of lights on the water like the feathers of a grackle. In the still heat of the day, there is not a single ripple of disturbance. I feel the pull of the water. You have to be very still to feel it, but it is there.

Across the kettle lake, a bird warns of invasion; its shrill call from high up brings the woods to life. A red-winged blackbird rises out of the reeds and crosses the lake, the tips of its wings barely skimming the surface. I slip out of my shorts, lay them over the saddle of the misshapen tree. I step into the cool water. Circles radiate from my knees, rippling across the lake.

Piece by piece, the cold detaches warmth from my skin, dissolves the drum of thoughts, draws them out with its chilled sting. The water severs my feet, my legs, my belly, the spot in the middle of my chest – until finally, I dive under and resurface, swimming for the dead birch that breaks the surface. I lap the lake, then turn on my back and float. I am a husk on the water, a seed dispersed on the wind. All that comes before, all that will come after, disappears: the birds, the sun, the clouds sheering across the sky like the hands on a timeless clock.

Later that day, I chop the legs off my jeans to make cut-off shorts. The strings hang down my thighs; the lining of the pockets poke out the edges. Mom is not in her bed; she arose, sullen, and left the house for the woods. I root through Dad's closet and find an old pair of cowboy boots.

I stand in front of the long mirror, thinking about Lucinda.

Hare left early this morning for her new part-time job. She works the breakfast shift and then has a break until the lunch rush. It came out of nowhere, this job, the day after Mom's breakdown on the street. That's what Dad calls it: her *little* breakdown. The day after, there was a knock on the sliding door, early in the morning when the sun had just broken above the horizon. The sister from the diner stood there with her grim face, demanding I deliver a message to Mom's bedside. Either she was to come downstairs, or the sister was going up. Mom came down. She looked smaller than she should have under her light cotton gown. I wondered what was so urgent. When she asked Mom if she had a free pair of hands, I expected Mom to start rummaging through her coffee cans for the severed hands wrapped in newspaper sleeves – wooden, with traces of tree rings visible on the surface, pulled off mannequins Mom has collected at flea markets. All these strange curiosities that fill our house. But Mom went straight up to Hare's bedroom, got her out of bed and told her to get dressed; she was going to work in the diner. Hare knew the choice: it was this or the Bait & Tackle. By the time she climbed into the front seat of the sister's truck, closing the door softly, her petulance was already subsiding. Reverence for the sister's predictable austerity was already influencing her composure.

I turn this way, then the other. I look at my bottom in the mirror. The seat of the jeans hangs differently on me than it does on Lucinda. I squat, looking at myself from behind, then push my bottom high into the air, examining it from the window between my legs, wishing to see plump flesh skirting the fringe, the way Lucinda fills her own shorts. But I am all bones.

Hare is standing at the door to the bedroom we share, watching me.

I jump when I see her.

'Something's wrong with you,' she says.

I kick off the boots and follow her downstairs. Ever since the day of the haircut, it has been on my mind to ask Hare what she said to Mom in the car. The thing about a brother drowning. But I haven't had the nerve until now.

'What were you saying about Mom?' I blurt.

'I said you're a freak.'

'In the car, that day—'

She pops bread into the toaster for her lunch. She turns and looks at me as though she believes I am stupid.

'I have no idea what the hell you're talking about.'

'You said Grandma told you something about Mom.'

'That? Seriously? You don't know about her brother—'

'She doesn't have a brother—'

'Or a mother or father? What do you think – her and Aunt Rita sprang out of the lake, like a myth? Why do you think Mom and Edna McCarthy are such good friends?' She tilts her shoulders to one side, her neck to the other, posing with the butter knife in mid-air, curious at my naivety, enjoying this knowledge she holds over me.

'I don't know – they've always been friends.'

'They were foster sisters. Mrs McCarthy's mother started the little prison farm. That's where Mom and Aunt Rita went to stay, after their little brother died. Surely you knew *that.*'

I shrug and pretend I knew. Hare throws her eyes to the sky when she sees that this is the first I've heard of these secrets. Her toast pops; she puts the slices on a plate, scrapes butter across them.

I've known of the shape of these secrets; I have felt what I cannot name.

Hare points out that these things haven't been so easily hidden, despite our family's talent for keeping secrets. 'You need to go spend time with Grandma. She'll tell you everything. There's your freaky friend now,' she adds.

Lucinda is walking up the driveway, wearing long sleeves on this warm day, her feet tucked down into her boots.

'Grab your boots. You two can play cowgirls,' Hare jokes. She takes her toast out onto the deck and calls to Lucinda. 'You escaped from the cuckoo farm?'

Lucinda smiles and runs up the drive. I want to run toward her, jump off the deck, hug her, tackle her. Instead, I wait for her at the top of the stairs, touching the short strands of my hair, but she doesn't seem to notice. I stand aside and let her pass. She sits on the rail of the deck, locking her boots between the spindles. She and Hare talk as though they have always known each other. As though I am not here.

I'm surprised to hear Hare tell Lucinda that she loves her job. She makes her laugh with stories of customers, of the volunteer firefighters, the way they make fun of themselves, how eager they are to attend an emergency. Hare makes fun of everyone, especially the sister and brother who own the diner. I wait for her to finish, willing either one of them to look at me, even once, bring me into the conversation, include me in their banter.

'I don't care, though,' Hare says. 'I make a ton of tips.' She empties a wad of dollar bills from her pockets and unfurls them onto the table. Lucinda sits down next to her and helps her count. I come back inside, pour myself and Lucinda a drink. I hear them laughing, Lucinda's voice animated, now lowered. Hare gasps with exaggerated shock at the things Lucinda tells her.

I set the glasses of juice down heavy on the table.

'Don't you have to get back to work?' I ask.

Both of them look at me in surprise.

'Whatever,' Hare says, but she lifts her plate and takes it inside.

'Your hair,' Lucinda says, noticing.

I touch the back of my neck.

'I like it. You're cute, Joey.' She hits the side of my leg. 'Why'd you run your sister off like that?' she asks. 'She's cool. You're lucky to have a sister.'

'I hate her.' My fury immediately turns to regret. I forgot what she told me about her family, her sister. 'I'm so sorry, Lucinda—'

'I wish I had a sister,' she says. 'What do you want to do? I'm bored.'

We hear Aunt Rita's Volkswagen bus knocking up the road before we see it.

'Oh God,' Hare calls from the screen. 'The hippy van is coming.'

Hare hates the red bus. She won't let Aunt Rita drop her off anywhere near town or high school. I don't mind so much. It is practical for Aunt Rita, ferrying crates of worms and life jackets and bait for her shop, and it still has a nice cherry colour that hasn't faded the way other buses from that era have.

Mrs McCarthy's truck is pulling up behind them.

'They're coming in caravan,' Hare commentates from the window.

I look at Lucinda.

She holds her hands up. 'I swear, she knows I'm here. She told me she'd collect me after she finished her errands.'

'On parole, huh?' Hare calls.

'I've been a good girl.' Lucinda raises her eyebrow and winks at me.

Even when they hear Mom isn't home, they continue advancing, Aunt Rita takes Mrs McCarthy's elbow, helps her up the stairs.

'No, I won't stay,' she is saying, all the while pulling her weight up the handrail. Aunt Rita signals for me to get the special seat. I run inside and drag the strong wooden chair through the door before Mrs McCarthy makes it up the stairs, sliding it underneath her as she lowers herself down in the full sun with a groan.

'Gone again?' Aunt Rita asks, which sounds like she is accusing us for Mom's absence. 'Joanne will put the kettle on. Come on, wait with me.'

'I guess I'll stay for one,' Mrs McCarthy says.

The children have piled out of the vehicles; they run around, chasing a dog that has escaped from the back window of the McCarthys' truck.

I return to the kitchen to put the kettle on and get the teacups ready.

Lucinda leans on the counter, looking out the screen. 'Here's your mom now.'

Mom is walking up the driveway, carrying a bouquet of wildflowers. Her sullen mood from this morning has changed; she seems light and free.

Mrs McCarthy calls to her. 'There you are, honey. We were worried about you.'

'Why worry?' Mom laughs. 'I'll get tea.'

'Joanne has it. Sit down.'

'Where have you been at this hour of the morning?' Aunt Rita snaps at Mom.

'Don't treat me like a child,' Mom snaps back.

'This heat is relentless again,' Mrs McCarthy says. 'We've got to get some rain soon. This is the worst drought on record – Lord knows about the apples. Speaking of which—' She calls Lucinda out to the deck. 'Go get those bags from the trunk.'

The kettle whistles. I leave the window and scoop leaves into the cups. I don't like tea much, but Mrs McCarthy reads our leaves once they settle to the bottom and form a pattern. Mom steeps her tea to dark amber, then clouds it with milk. I like mine weak without milk. I watch the leaves, their silhouettes like birds flocking black against the white of the bone china.

The three women seem so different in the morning light. Mom is pretty and delicate, sunk down in her chair, holding the bundle of wildflowers on her lap. She crosses her legs underneath her, her flowing skirt tucked around her golden calves. Mrs McCarthy and Aunt Rita tower over her.

Lucinda returns with two brown paper bags of apples, leaves remaining on the stems. She drops the bags at Mrs McCarthy's feet. Mrs McCarthy eyes her with impatience.

'You'll bruise those, child. Take care.'

Lucinda sits down. She takes an apple, bites it. They are crisp, and juice dribbles down her lip.

Hare looks me up and down as I watch the scene out the window. She goes out onto the deck in a snit.

'I'm late,' she tells the table of women. They all look up. 'I have to get back.'

'Harriet has a job at the diner,' Mom tells them.

'Relax, I'll drive you after a cup of tea,' Aunt Rita says.

Hare collapses into a chair.

I put on another cup.

The children run across the deck, carrying long sticks. They try to run into the house. Aunt Rita rushes them out again. 'It's too nice to play inside, go away,' she tells them.

114

'Don't sit there watching these people work.' Mrs McCarthy swats at Lucinda's leg. 'Make yourself useful.'

Lucinda comes into the kitchen and looks at me with her eyes wide with impatience. I am overcome with the sense that Mrs McCarthy and Aunt Rita are here to take Lucinda away. I wish they would disappear, dissolve into the air, leave Lucinda standing in our kitchen, rolling her eyes to the sky. I feel that a change, indistinct yet inevitable, is coming, sooner or later.

'Can you stay?' I ask.

'Maybe she'll let me stay – I doubt it. I picked every single one of these apples.' She takes another crisp bite. 'But I've been good. She thinks I have been *reformed*.' She smirks.

'Tell her we're going to the library.'

She tilts her hip and crosses her arms. 'Truly?' she says with contempt. 'The library? Edna will think it's code for smoking crack.'

We burst out laughing.

Then she thinks for a moment. 'Maybe not if you ask.'

We bring the tea out together; we can't dispel our giggles. Tremors of laughter shake our hands, rattle the cups. No one seems to notice. Both women are watching Mom. We pass out the steaming mugs. Lucinda and I squash together onto the remaining seat.

'What are you thinking there, Rosemary?' Mrs McCarthy asks Mom.

Mom smiles to herself, lines appearing on her forehead. Her mouth turns down. She appears to shrink further, sitting between the two women.

'I need to get out of here,' Mom announces.

Lucinda presses her thigh against mine.

Aunt Rita and Mrs McCarthy look at each other. Mrs McCarthy pretends to misunderstand. 'Well, you just got home, honey – where do you want to go now?'

Moms pushes her tea away. 'I'm leaving Kettle Lake.'

'Does Danny know?' Aunt Rita asks.

I sit very still at the table. I know if you stay quiet, the adults forget to send you away.

'I'm going to the city.'

Aunt Rita's chiding tone gives way to a tentative statement. 'You're a dreamer, like our father.'

'I should have known.' Mom knocks the table as she stands. Tea splashes over the edges of our cups and drips down the sides, pooling into the grooves of the decking. No one moves to wipe it up. 'You never listen. No one takes what I say seriously.'

'What are you saying, dear?' Mrs McCarthy asks gently. 'What are you trying to tell us?'

'Don't get offended,' Aunt Rita says. 'You're so sensitive.'

Mrs McCarthy puts a hand out to Aunt Rita, all the while addressing Mom. 'Come sit back down,' she coaxes.

Mom gasps, holds her hands to her mouth. Her words are barely audible. 'I'm a prisoner.'

'I know how you feel,' Lucinda mumbles.

Mrs McCarthy shoots her a look. I press my shoulder into hers. Hare watches the back of her own hands, folded in her lap.

'Rosemary,' Mrs McCarthy says sharply.

Mom shakes her head. Her face is anguished now.

116

'Come on and sit down here with us,' Mrs McCarthy says, more gently now. 'Drink your tea. I'll read your leaves.' She exchanges glances with Aunt Rita. Aunt Rita watches Mom sideways.

I feel a tug of fear.

Hare looks up from examining her hands. 'Read mine!' She pushes her teacup under Mrs McCarthy's nose.

'OK, child, OK. Give me a minute. I have to get into the space.'

Mom sinks back into her chair; she closes her eyes and sits very still. Moments before, Aunt Rita and Mrs McCarthy's presence felt threatening. Now, they are like ballast to our rocking boat.

Mrs McCarthy gazes into Hare's empty teacup. Hare and Lucinda and I lean over to peer at the remains. The leaves form a gritty swath across the bottom. I can make out the shape of a harp.

'Go away, girls, give me space,' Mrs McCarthy demands, settling back into her chair. 'You've the bird,' she announces. 'You'll take care along your way.' She glances deeper into the cup. 'You may travel. You will journey to far places. Your guiding spirits will bring you home.'

Hare sits back, satisfied.

'Mine,' Lucinda insists.

'You'll have only trouble in those leaves, lady,' she tells her, but accepts her cup anyway. A mass of leaves clump at the bottom. Mrs McCarthy peers in. 'Think before you act, or you haven't seen the worst of your troubles.'

Lucinda sits back, miserable. Hare looks at her sideways, pleased at her own outlook in comparison, even though it is nearly the same version we hear every single time.

I don't move or ask her to look into my cup. A line of leaves wavers across the bottom. She looks anyway, glances down into my leaves without taking the cup. She shakes her head, and I swear it seems we have a secret between us. I am not asking, and she is not telling. I shift in my seat. Lucinda elbows me.

Then Mom sits back in her chair, staring into the middle of the table, her eyes wide with fright.

'Mom?' I can't separate her look from what Mrs McCarthy reads in my cup. It seems they all know something about me – secrets of which even I am not aware, here, naked to their eyes, twining up through the blackness of the leaves.

'I'm leaving Danny,' Mom announces, as though she reads this there in the middle of the table.

'Read Joey's,' Lucinda commands, ignoring the enormity of Mom's declaration.

'*Joey*?' Hare mimics.

'You call her "Joanne",' Lucinda declares. 'But her friends call her "Joey". Suits her better, don't you think?'

Hare rolls her eyes.

Lucinda pushes my teacup closer toward Mrs McCarthy.

'Some leaves are better left unread,' Mrs McCarthy says.

Aunt Rita shakes her head. 'I told you this would happen from the very beginning.'

'I'm going to Italy,' Mom announces.

'Italy?' Hare snorts. She shakes her head, looks around the table. Only Lucinda smirks.

'Rosemary, there is no travel in your leaves, I hate to tell you.' Mrs McCarthy lifts her teacup with whimsy and looks deeply into the bottom. She means to be comical, but I feel the tension growing. 'You're staying put, honey.'

'I've already decided.'

'You're off your medication,' Aunt Rita says.

'You're off your rocker,' Hare mumbles.

Lucinda snorts.

Aunt Rita shoots Hare a warning look.

'I can't do this any longer. I should have never tried.' Mom sits taller. She seems to grow, to gain strength through her words.

Mrs McCarthy reaches out and takes Mom's hand. It remains limp in her own.

'Sometimes it's a battle to stay. I know that with Karl.'

Lucinda raises her eyebrow at me.

'Do you want to lose everything?' Aunt Rita scolds.

'Maybe I do,' Mom says, her voice a whisper.

'There is no better world out there,' Aunt Rita starts. Mrs McCarthy holds up her hand, but Aunt Rita finishes anyway. 'And if I can't remind you of that, who will?'

Mom pulls her hand out from Mrs McCarthy's grip. She stands up and takes her teacup inside. It bursts into shards as it hits the sink. The door to the basement opens and slams.

Mrs McCarthy blinks her eyes and then holds them closed.

Aunt Rita turns to Hare. 'Why didn't you girls tell us?' she asks. 'You should always call when she starts spiralling down.'

'How are we supposed to know today is different from any other day?' Hare defends, but she sinks down into her chair, a look of guilt on her face.

'It's that drowning. It brings it all back . . .' Mrs McCarthy says.

'It's not just that . . . it's everything – with Maureen and *that* family, the farm. . .'

'It's all a lot for her right now. Too much. Maybe she should go away. We could all use a nice trip to Italy.' Mrs McCarthy gives a harsh laugh at the absurdity of the idea, but Aunt Rita remains sober.

'I wish she'd snap out of it. I'm worried now.'

'I'm always worried. Ladies—' Mrs McCarthy sits to attention, as though only just realising we are here, witnessing something we shouldn't. 'Take these cups inside.'

Aunt Rita dismisses her. 'Everything has been secret too long. They have to know. They're old enough. There is no hiding any longer.'

Mrs McCarthy sighs and shakes her head. She sits back into her chair, resigned.

11

THE DARK SHAPES WE navigate are no less terrifying when the day brings them to light.

Aunt Rita leaves and takes Sammy and Hare with her. Mrs McCarthy lingers, as though she wants to try to solve something, figure out what is needed. She agrees, to our surprise, to let Lucinda stay. We don't even have to pretend we are going to the library, but we go anyway. Lucinda borrows Hare's bike, and we ride into town.

Lucinda has three crumpled dollars in her pocket; we stop and buy two glass bottles of cola and a bag of sour cream and onion potato chips. I tell her we can't bring them into the library, but she puts her bottle behind her back as though it is no big deal.

We don't have to hide them, anyway. The bells on the back-door don't wake Miss Hughes, the librarian; she is napping in her armchair behind the partition of bookshelves.

Dad remembers Miss Hughes as an older woman even when he was a boy. She was the only one left on her family's farm out on one of the back roads from town, around the curve of the Great Lake. In the old days, she used to pass by the farm on horseback on her way to work, skirting his family's property along the trail, joining up with the main road and riding the rest of the way into town. When she grew too old for the horse – or maybe the horse died – Dad told us that Miss Hughes relied on the goodwill of the town to get her where she needed to go. She never had to put out her thumb; the townspeople knew to stop and pull in to give her a ride, usually to and from the library.

Once, when Dad and I ran into the grocery store for a gallon of ice cream, we spotted her on her way back out of town. It was the end of the working day on a bright summer evening. She locked the library and was walking up the road toward the diner, pulling a bag on a frame behind her as though it contained the weight of many books. I imagined that she had more than our book limit of four.

She didn't appear grateful when Dad turned the truck around and stopped, offering her a ride. He put her bag in the flatbed and helped her climb in beside me. I pushed myself as close to Dad as I could, my legs curled up over the gear shift, trying to avoid touching her knees, which I couldn't help looking at. They had come out from under her print dress like the knuckled scales of a chicken's foot.

We drove away from our own road and continued, but when we reached the crossroads that led to her house and Dad turned on the blinker, she hollered at him.

'Go straight.'

The way she said this, all Dad could do was turn his blinker off and drive. They weren't books in her bag, it turned out, but clothes. She was going to her sister's house in the city for a week of annual vacation. Our ice cream had turned to soup by the time we returned home.

'What could I say?' Dad told Mom when we arrived home. 'She's an old woman.'

And I had to agree. There was no telling that woman no.

*

Here in the library, the scent of the written word – decaying pulp and dust – loosens the tension I have felt all morning. Lucinda disappears straight away, navigating toward the romance section.

I sit down in an alcove full of old newspapers. A filing cabinet drawer is partially open, a microfiche reader dusty in the corner. I wonder how far back I would have to go to find out about Mom's brother, to read the papers Hare said Grandma showed to her.

Lucinda comes back with a stack of books. She opens *The Other Side of Midnight*.

'Mrs McCarthy has this book on her shelf, the dirty woman! Listen to this.' She opens to the pages with the steamy bits and reads. We giggle and sip from our pop bottles.

Miss Hughes shuffles into the alcove on a mission; she startles when she sees us. We hide the pop bottles between our legs and lean over the table, hoping she doesn't spot them. Mrs Hughes takes the book out of Lucinda's hand.

'Too old,' she shouts. 'Don't read.'

'It wasn't us, I swear,' Lucinda insists. 'It was sitting here—'

We snigger when she shuffles away.

'Let's get out of here,' Lucinda says, but then Miss Hughes comes back carrying a library membership card and a pencil. She hands it to Lucinda then moves away. Lucinda looks sideways at me; she picks up the pencil and draws faces on the side. I grab it from her. I rub out her drawings and write her name. I feel something on my calf.

Lucinda is watching me. She is slouched in her chair, rubbing my leg with the edge of her boot. She turns the pop bottle slowly between her legs.

I try to take a swig from my bottle but find I can't swallow.

'You like my boots?' she asks.

'Of course.' I laugh, pretending that the movement of her boot up my calf, resting the tip on the inside of my thighs isn't sending a wave of tingles through my privates. 'I love them.'

What I love, though, isn't the boots but how she fills them. How she fills the doubt that is around her with clear, definitive lines. I don't know how people do this. It seems like everyone else manages – Lucinda, Aunt Rita, even Hare, certainly Maureen; they inhabit their own space, guard it.

In comparison, I feel so utterly lacking – in detail, in personality; it seems I have no defining lines at all, only those which are on the outside of others. I have a sense I am filling in the space that isn't them. Knowing what others are seems the definition of me, defining me by what I am not.

I could smudge this line, this separating line between Lucinda and me: make it permeable, crawl inside – draw the bareness of myself into her borders.

She has reached my shorts. I think I might fall off my chair with the rigidness of trying to act normal in the face of the intensity her movement invokes. I put my head down, pretending to read.

'Come with me,' Miss Hughes interrupts.

I can breathe again when Lucinda reluctantly follows her out of the alcove. She glares at me while I try to hide my laughter. I can hear Miss Hughes reading her the rules of the library, telling her how many books she is allowed, insisting she not dog-ear the pages. And now Lucinda is following her to the stacks for young people. She is told to choose something suitable for a young lady: *Little Women*, *Anne of Green Gables*, *Pippi Longstocking*, *The Black Stallion*, *A Tree Grows in Brooklyn*. 'Pick two,' Miss Hughes tells her.

I gulp down the rest of my pop and place the empty bottle under the table.

On the table in front of me is a file box of microfiche films. I take off the cover and run my fingers along the cardboard frames. I don't know exactly what I am looking for, but I lift each film and hold it to the light, knowing that if I find it, it will be about us.

Lucinda returns to the alcove with her books and a newly issued library card. Miss Hughes points at Lucinda's glass bottle sitting on the table.

'No food,' she shouts.

Lucinda, who has worked out that Miss Hughes isn't shouting – she just can't hear herself – yells back, 'It isn't

125

ours!' She shrugs and drinks the bottle dry. 'Empty. Ten cents return,' Lucinda tells her. I think Lucinda is enjoying this mutual antagonism.

Miss Hughes looks hard at the box, then at me. She takes the film out of my hands and picks up the file, carrying it away. I hear her rummaging around at the back of the library. She soon returns and throws a scrap-book in front of me. I turn the pages slowly. It is filled with car accidents, killings, accidental drownings. I soon realise that it is a collection of every tragedy that has happened in Kettle Lake in the last many years. The most recent pastings are newspaper articles on Cathy's drowning: first the search for the missing body, next the recovery and then the death notice.

Lucinda slams *Little Women* closed. 'I'm leaving.'

'One minute,' I beg.

I turn back through the pages. They become worn and yellow the further back I go. I know what I will find. Miss Hughes knows it, too.

'Fine,' Lucinda whispers. 'But we're going to the beach after this.'

I don't argue. She has pulled out her chair and is crawling underneath the table – she must have dropped something.

I scan the article quickly and then read it a second time, slowly, taking it all in.

Body of Child Washes Ashore at Kettle Lake

KETTLE LAKE, MI – Police identified the victim of a drowning in Kettle Lake as eight-year-old Mulberry Point resident William Johnson. The child's body was recovered yesterday along the shore of the Wildlife Refuge by a local resident. A search and recovery operation for his father, thirty-five-year-old Charles Johnson, is ongoing.

The discovery comes one week after the alarm was raised of a child entering the water in a rowboat off the Mulberry Point area of Kettle Lake. Police said the boat was swept out to sea by a combination of strong currents and offshore winds. A second juvenile involved in the incident received treatment for non-life-threatening injuries.

The father of the victim entered the water in an attempted rescue but was unsuccessful, after which he also got into difficulty and witnesses claim they saw him struggling to stay afloat. Police alerted the coastguard, and the boat was found capsized, but the child and father were missing and presumed dead. The search was called off at nightfall but resumed at daybreak.

No remains were recovered until yesterday, when a local resident discovered the remains of a juvenile one week after the incident and alerted the police.

Captain Healy of the Kettle Lake Fire and Rescue Department said that they have turned the remains over to the police for further investigations and that the family have been alerted. The events leading up to the incident are also subject to an ongoing investigation. Meanwhile, two juveniles have been removed from the home while investigations are in progress.

There is a hollow fear, an old familiar feeling, travelling through my blood.

Something brushes my leg, pokes at my shorts. Underneath the chair, Lucinda has taken up the empty glass bottle. She is pushing it up through my shorts.

'Stop.' I stand up, knocking over my chair.

We hear Miss Hughes shuffling in the back.

'Don't,' I whisper harshly, shoving her away.

'So you don't like dick?'

'What?' I laugh. I pick my chair up and sit back down.

Lucinda comes closer. 'You don't mind me touching you, but the bottle is a no-no? I can't figure you out.'

'Stop,' I whisper. 'That's just weird.'

'It's not weird. I think you like me touching you.'

I bite my bottom lip and try not to look caught.

Her face is serious. 'It's OK,' she tells me.

I giggle. I want to ask her if she is this way, too, ask her how Robert figures into all this, but my knees are shaking, and I think my voice will tremble if I speak. She knows what she is doing to me. I close my eyes and accept the way her finger feels now skimming my shorts. She finds the edge of my underwear and runs along the centre.

'You are who you are,' she whispers. 'And I think I'm falling for you, Joey.'

Miss Hughes has moved back into the alcove. I push Lucinda back under the table. She bumps her head and snorts.

'I dropped my pencil,' she shouts from underneath the table, laughing. She scrambles out on all fours.

Miss Hughes stops, perplexed, watching Lucinda run for the door, leaving her books and library card on the table. I leave the scrap-book open and follow her.

Cycling home, the air around me feels weightier, as though it has something to push against. The shape of me shifts, filling out the void, shoring up the boundary of where the world stops and I begin.

12

IT IS THE WEEKEND of the annual balloon race. Though the launches are spectacular, the big event is the beer tent.

Everyone is surprised when Mrs McCarthy shows up in the driveway with Lucinda. She stays in the truck while Mrs McCarthy hoists herself up the deck stairs, speaks with Dad at the screen door.

'I know you have your hands full, Danny – I hate to ask you this – but will you take her? Just for the night? I can't trust her enough to leave her at home.' Mrs McCarthy's voice isn't angry; it is tired and a little fraught.

'She'll be all right with Joanne,' Dad tells her. 'Joanne is sensible.'

'And I suspect Rosemary's not going to town.'

'You suspect correctly,' Dad tells her. He sounds tired, too.

'How's she doing?'

Dad just shakes his head.

Lucinda comes through the door wearing jeans and the boots. She wears a denim jacket over a tank top, even though the night is sultry.

'Go tell your mom Lucinda's here,' Dad tells me. 'Tell her she's staying the night.'

He doesn't know that Mom isn't in. Just after Hare left for her friend's house, Mom had come to me. She told me to say she is sleeping – she said this like she was a teenager and I was someone she could confide in. She giggled and left the house with the last of the evening's rays illuminating her yellow silk dress, the one with the dainty buttons, spun in yellow thread. I have only ever seen this dress hanging in her closet.

'She's sleeping,' I tell Dad.

'Well, wake her if you need her.' He kisses my cheek and grabs a ride into town with the McCarthys, since they are going that way too.

Lucinda pulls out a palette of blue eyeshadow and informs me that we, too, are going to the beer tent. She digs in Mom's closet until she finds a pair of clogs. She turns up my cut-offs – they already feel like they are riding up my backside – and I try the clogs. She tells me that my legs are sexy, but I can't even lift my feet; I can only clomp. Instead, I put on a pair of canvas tennis shoes. She smears blue eyeshadow above her eyes and takes Hare's rouge from her table to rub into her cheeks. She comes at me, then, with the colours, and I let her apply a light shade.

'You look eighteen years old,' she tells me, but I don't think so.

At dusk, we hear a blast of heat before we see the balloons; they are followed by silence. The woods appear to breathe and come alive. We run down the stairs and out the door in time to see the hot-air balloons lifting above the house, like stars reaching their zenith, colourful bulbs like Christmas ornaments, liquid bubbles. They are suspended in the red heat of the late-July night. Arms, small as sticks, wave back at us from the baskets; voices drift down as though coming through a stratosphere between ours and some hidden world.

It is Lucinda's idea to climb the fences between our house and the farm, to chase the balloons through the open fields. They quickly outpace us and shrink into dots beyond Grandma's farm. We can see their fires glowing, lightening bugs in the red sky. We follow their fires toward the main road, walking into town along the busier-than-usual route, cars coming in from farmlands farther down the road.

A marquee tent rises out of the square, transforming the town, shrinking the gazebo to a doll-size feature. A truck arrives, unloading kegs of beer. Women and men stand together in small groups, laughing and jeering one another; they wear jeans, cut-offs with frayed edges, the women in sandals and tank tops, the men with more hair than the women. Deeper into the fringes of the tent, tables line the perimeter of the dance floor, claimed with half-full pitchers of watery gold beer, empty plastic cups stacked beside empty pitchers. Strings of light thread across the tent; the faces are animated in the eerie glow. When the band finishes warming up and kicks out the first tune, a handful of women come tentatively to the empty space in front of the stage. They lift their arms and sway with the music.

We watch from the shadowy edges; Lucinda's certainty wanes. She crouches near a tent pole, and we watch the dancers instead of joining them as she planned. We duck low when we see Dad carrying two pitchers of beer toward a table close to the dance floor. He sets them down in front of the McCartys. Maureen and Vic are arriving, Freddie follows behind them.

The dancers gain confidence and begin to swing. Men join the ladies and before long, two of them lift a woman into the air and carry her around on their shoulders. As though this is their cue, entire tables rise and join the dancers. They abandon half-drunk beer cups and full pitchers.

Lucinda grabs a rag from a crate nearby and pretends to bus a table. She comes back with a half-pitcher of beer and two full cups. She hands one to me. She closes her eyes and gulps a glass back, then belches, not bothering to cover her mouth. We giggle. My cup has a ring of red lipstick on its edge. I turn it around to the other side and sip. It is warm and salty but not entirely disgusting, so I take another sip. And another. The beer disappears quickly, and I begin to feel light-headed.

The darkness envelops us, the music comes closer and throbs in my chest. I feel happy and warm, sitting on the grass against this tent pole. We wrap our arms around one another and giggle at nothing. Lucinda points to the dancers embarrassing themselves; I point to the ones I envy with their beautiful moves.

The music changes beat and a tall lanky man about Dad's age crashes into a ring of dancers as he jerks wildly about the dance floor. We put our hands over our mouths and laugh until our sides split. Dancers move out of his way when he comes near. He takes off his shirt and slings it around, throws it into the audience to cheers, jostling – and calls of distain when he knocks the side of a table, sending a pitcher sideways.

Two dark figures sneak up behind us; they squat at our level.

'What the hell is this?' Heather gives Lucinda a friendly punch on the arm. She looks at me and gasps. 'Your hair!' She rubs it with her knuckles. Lucinda offers her the dregs of the pitcher, then goes off to steal another. She comes back and fills their plastic cups. I am happy to see them, it feels like we are all old friends. Jessica is surprised when I crawl over and hug her.

She pushes me away.

'She's drunk.' Lucinda laughs.

I deny it. My head reels to the beat of the dancers, and it feels like we are all one big pulse.

A cheer rises up from the back of the tent. A woman stands on top of a table; she walks barefoot, turning small moves, circling her own world.

'Isn't that your mother?' Jessica asks.

And it is. The table tilts like a see-saw toward the ground, and it feels like we all collectively hold our breath. We cheer when she recovers.

Dad rises out of his seat. He walks to Mom and reaches out his hand, offering it to her. Before Mom can respond, the wild man arrives; he lifts her over his shoulder and runs with her to the dance floor. She reels when he sets her down, regains her balance, stumbles again, confused. Dad's table stands, watching the unfolding scene. Maureen looks on with scorn. Dad follows Mom to the dance floor.

The man grabs Mom's waist; she pulls away. He reaches out and fingers a silk button on her dress, oblivious to Dad approaching, reaching for Mom, grabbing her elbow to bring her away. But Mom regains her bearings. She is already swinging; she hits the man square in the jaw, pushes him level in the chest so that he stumbles off the dance floor and lands on a table. Beer pitchers spill everywhere, onto the laps of the group sitting at the table. Dad follows the man, pushes him again while he is still trying to regain his balance. Vic and Freddie are making their way toward Dad. The first group nearest the dance floor lift their table and move it straight out of the tent, pitchers and all. Everything and everyone are mixing, the crowd closing in, the tent spinning, and I realise it is actually me – I am spinning and going to be sick.

In the shadows outside the tent, when all the beer has come back up, I lean against a tree for balance.

Mom strolls past. She doesn't notice me. She walks through the square, smoothing her hair out of her face, adjusting her dress. Some of the buttons have popped off. She moves away in a dreamy state, as though she has no idea of the trouble she has left behind in her wake. She puts her hand against a tree, too, and I think she will be sick, but then she begins to caress it, holding a branch in her hand as though it were a child's wrist, pressing her cheek to the cool trunk, looking up to the stars. I remember her as the stranger once again, when we were young, in the woods behind our house.

Someone follows her out of the tent. Mom tenses when he puts his hand on her back, ready for another fight, but she sees who it is and takes his arm to steady herself.

'Everett, oh goodness, Everett. You have no idea. I was hoping to see you.'

The professor lets Mom lay her head on his shoulder, and he strokes the back of her hair.

'How are you, my dear?' he asks.

I haven't realised until now how foreign he sounds – as though he comes from out east, not New York but a city in New England, such as Cambridge or Princeton, one with a fancy university. He has a precise way of speaking, like the voices I hear on NPR radio. I listen to it some-times, pretending to land the dial accidentally rather than admit I like the way it feels: as though some gate surrounding Kettle Lake lifts and lets me sail out of its boundaries.

'Oh, Everett. I'm making mischief again.'

'I believe you are, Romy. I believe you are.' His face is grim in spite of the humour in his words.

'It's awful, it's so awful,' she says, and I think she is laughing, but her laughter becomes tears. 'Take me out of here, Everett.'

'Would you like to come back to the cabin, sober up a bit? Is that the best thing?'

'Just take me home.' Mom sounds defeated. A man comes up behind Everett – I have never seen him before in Kettle Lake. He has a different accent altogether, from another country, tense and clipped.

'All right, Everett?' The band has stopped playing, and he looks back toward the tent when he speaks.

I keep watching the tent, too, waiting for Dad to emerge. I don't know why he hasn't followed Mom.

'We'll drive Romy home, if you don't mind, James. Come on, dear. Let's walk across the park and see if a bit of air will help.'

Mom and Everett walk off, and James follows at a distance, pulling the car keys from his pocket.

'Take me away from here,' Mom says. 'Won't you take me, take me with you to Italy?' She puts her head on his shoulder and weeps softly. He holds her around the back lightly, guiding her toward the car. Her voice becomes firm. 'You promised me Italy.'

'One day, my dear, we shall go to Italy.'

James isn't amused, but he takes Mom's other arm, and the two men walk her across the square. At one stage, she lets her weight fall across their arms, giggling until they half drag her across the road, to where James's car is parked in front of the diner.

Inside the tent, there is the sound of breaking glass.

The DJ has stopped playing and the lights are turning on.

Lucinda is walking around the outskirts, hunting for me. She holds two cups, each full of beer.

She spots me. 'I think your Dad and his friends are leaving.' She hands me one of the cups. I sit it down near the tree and follow.

We walk out of town, back across the fields. The moon is full and neither of us speak. We don't have to climb up to the roof; the sliding door is wide open.

Downstairs, something crashes in the basement. Dad's truck pulls in. Lucinda and I shrink into the shadows behind the couch and wait for him to come through the door. He strides through the room.

Hare has come down the stairs. 'What the hell is going on?' she asks.

'Go to bed,' Dad tells her. His voice doesn't leave room for argument. She backs up the stairs, then turns and runs back to Sammy's room, where she sleeps when Lucinda stays the night. She slams the door. I am glad Sammy isn't here in this house, glad he is tucked up safe at Aunt Rita's.

'Where the hell are you?' Dad calls.

My nerves stand on end. Lucinda grabs my arm.

His heavy footfall hits each of the basement stairs. I rise from our hiding place and follow him to the door, ready if Mom needs me.

Lucinda follows.

'Honestly, Rosie,' Dad yells.

Another object drops in the basement; it sounds like it is swiped off a table.

'Don't you dare—' Mom shouts.

'You're drunk,' he accuses.

'Well, that makes a change.'

'What are you saying, Rosemary? What the hell is wrong with you? You made a fucking mockery out of us. We are the laughing stock of the town. '

'This is what you're worried about?' She is laughing dangerously. 'I've embarrassed you?' Glass crashes. 'I've humiliated *you*? In front of your sister? Don't make me laugh, Danny.' But she does laugh – a long, sinister laugh. And then her voice becomes very quiet. 'Listen – you can hear Maureen laughing, too. Hear that? All the way across the field, sitting in *your* armchair, eating *your* dinner. Don't worry about the town – they were already laughing at me. Now, *you* make us all laugh.'

'Shut your fucking mouth—' Dad doesn't yell this; instead it comes out in a hoarse sort of whisper, full of restraint, a sound of struggling.

I don't know whether to go down the stairs or flee, return to bed and put my head under my pillow, pretend this isn't happening to us. The kitchen begins to spin.

'Get off me,' Mom says, through strained teeth. 'Let me go.'

Dad explodes. 'Don't make me do this, Rosie. Don't push me too far.'

'Listen to me. Listen to me!' The way Mom says this makes my arm hair rise. It makes Dad stop roaring.

Lucinda grabs my hand; we clutch each other.

The basement is still.

'I need help,' Mom whispers.

'No. No. Don't start this again.'

'Listen to me. I'm not well,' Mom says.

'You're imagining it.' I know by the weight of Dad's voice that his anger has left him, that he is trying to convince himself of something else.

Mom laughs weakly. 'I'm not, Danny, I'm really not. Something is wrong in my head. You know what they all say about Billy—'

'Ah, Billy,' Dad says, and his tone moves to sorrow. 'What do they say?'

'You know what they say. Everyone watches me. I can't even look after my own son. They can see my head is not right. I am not right. I even sometimes think—'

'Don't—' Dad tells her.

'I think I did it – do you think I did it?'

'Whose thoughts are these, Rosie? They aren't yours. They aren't mine. Who is putting this shit in your head? You know you didn't do it – Billy drowned, for God's sake. This has never been a question—'

'They say I did—'

'Who says this?'

'The town – everyone. I've got to leave. I've got to get out of here.'

Dad explodes again. 'It's that man, isn't it? Putting things in your head.'

'I'm leaving,' Mom continues. 'He's taking me with him.'

Dad laughs bitterly.

'Hear me, Danny. Just hear me. This could kill me. I can't think – I can't love. I'm either numb or everything looks so wrong, so ugly, I can't bear my own children—'

Her words, the rising emotion in them, fill me with dread.

Dad raises his voice. 'Whose ideas are these, Rosie? Whose ideas? These aren't your own ideas.'

Lucinda squeezes my hand again; I squeeze hers back.

'Please, understand.'

'He is filling your head with this shit – his psychoanalytical bullshit.' He hits something hard in the basement with his fist – the workbench.

We jump.

'Stop,' Mom says.

'What about the children?'

'Rita will help. And your sister.'

'You want Maureen in on this craziness? What the hell will she think? Oh yeah, after tonight, I guess she already figures something is so fucking wrong in your head.'

Mom is silent. I hear her sniffle now. Her voice regains control when she speaks. 'What do you care? You'll be sitting here visiting your sister and your cousins and watching the fucking birds and doing your fucking cross-word. I am so alone. I am so *lonely* here in this house – in this town. What am *I* supposed to do for the next thirty years? Sit around and think about and dream about and have nightmares and hallucinations about my brother getting in a boat and floating off into the fucking middle of nowhere? Walking out to the Point and watching him float away again – every single day.'

Dad's tone softens. 'I'm sorry. I'm *sorry*. What happened to you, what happened to Billy happened a long time ago. Rita moved on. I moved on. Look – I'm losing the farm, so what? Life moves on. *Move on*. Don't let that nut job pull you into believing there is something wrong or some-thing that needs fixing – you do that, and you are fucked! We are all fucked!'

Mom speaks through gritted teeth: there is a harshness, a determination to her voice. 'I. Am. Not. Well. This is the last time you will hear me say this.'

There is a stunned silence both upstairs and down in the basement. Lucinda's mouth opens to speak, then closes.

I have to strain to hear Dad. His voice is full of fear. 'What are you saying, Rosie?'

'I'm just trying to stay alive here,' she whispers.

141

There is a long pause. Whatever this thing is growing between them downstairs in the silence, it churns its way upstairs, wraps itself around me. Lucinda watches; there is pity in her eyes.

'Don't leave me,' Dad says, and I know, the way he says it: this is the course we are already on.

*

Upstairs, Lucinda doesn't go to Hare's bed. She lies at the end of mine; we lie head to toe under the covers, our arms wrapped around each other's legs.

'She's not well,' I say.

'There are many ways people become unwell,' Lucinda whispers back. 'And there are many ways people become sick.'

She tells me about her father, the way he sold just about anything, how her mother knew. 'He's in prison,' she admits. 'Just as good as dead.'

When she whispers, I don't care anymore which are truths and which are lies. It is her closeness under the covers, the comfort of her voice filling the void. I want to be closer. I move until I am facing her.

The air changes. It feels as though I have known Lucinda all my life, like we have been in this darkness together before. My border closes around her, and I can't tell where my body starts and her voice ends, and we merge into each other. I don't mind, then; she is wrapping one leg around mine, and then the other, and she comes in close and moves her body until our breathing becomes heavy, and I am not afraid. I feel the intensity of her; I let her lips meet mine as I am overcome.

And it is over nearly before it has begun.

We lie here, breathing, intwined, so quiet we can hear the crickets out in the yard.

'That's it, Joey.' She sighs. 'That's all there is to it.'

I smile into the darkness.

'Well, how does it feel?' she demands.

'Normal. My whole life I have felt strange, abnormal – but now—' I smile even wider.

'You're beautiful, Joey.' She yawns. 'Don't let anyone tell you different.'

I feel safe lying here and warm. I am beginning to drift off to sleep when Lucinda calls me back.

'Tell me something,' she says. 'Tell me something you've never told anyone before.'

I roll over on my back, put my hands behind my head, thinking. Nothing comes to me. I strain, wanting to find something to say that will keep her here, keep us as close as we are now. It comes to me, then: I see Cathy's face crossing mine in the darkness. I tell Lucinda about Memorial Day weekend, every detail about the beach. The way the girls tiptoed across the sand, the sound of the waves, the hurt on Cathy's face. I wonder aloud: was I the last to see her alive? Did I watch her swim or struggle against an unseen tide? Drifting, breathing, not breathing.

As I talk, a weight lifts, and I feel as though I am flying, here in the darkness. Lucinda listens in silence; only her light breathing tells me she is here, too, drifting off this way, together, toward sleep.

13

WE ARE STILL SLEEPING the next morning when Aunt Rita calls out below my window. Mom comes out of her bedroom, moves around downstairs, slides open the door, inviting Aunt Rita to come inside, like nothing has happened. She is sleepy but bright.

Lucinda stirs and turns toward the wall, drawing her knees up to her chest. The sheet has come off in the night, and it is already stuffy in the room. My tongue feels thick, my head, throbbing. She stretches and sits up, and I move across the room and sit on Hare's bed. I don't know which way to hold myself. Lucinda rolls out of bed. Crossing the room, she rubs her knuckles over my short hair.

'Don't look so worried,' she says.

I breathe out.

I watch the wall while she stands in front of the mirror, brushing her hair. I wait for her to dress. She doesn't. We tiptoe downstairs. Aunt Rita and Mom talk in the kitchen; Lucinda and I wait on the other side of the pass-through. They are talking about us.

'I was surprised when Edna told me she dropped that girl off here. I'm not so sure – send Joanne to me at the shop, I'll put her to work—'

'The job sounds more suitable for Hare,' Mom said.

'Hare already has a job. Sister is happy with her. I would like Joanne, just for a few hours, in the shop – that is all I'm asking.'

'What about that boy who helps?' Mom asked.

'Roy? He's at band camp for the rest of the summer. I could use the extra hands. Joanne is perfect.'

'I'll take a job,' Lucinda says, bouncing into the kitchen.

Aunt Rita is taken aback. 'How long have you girls been standing there?' she asks.

'It's not nice to eavesdrop, Joanne,' Mom says, looking at Lucinda's bare legs. Lucinda is wearing only her T-shirt and underwear.

'I was just telling your mother that I need some help in the Bait & Tackle.' Rita looks purposefully at me.

'No, thank you,' I say.

'We can do it together,' Lucinda says.

Aunt Rita isn't quick enough.

'That's not a bad idea,' Mom says. I think she is hiding a smile.

'OK,' I say. 'When can we start?'

By the time she finishes her coffee, Lucinda and I have a part-time job, together, at the Bait & Tackle, starting tomorrow morning.

'On a Sunday?' Lucinda asks.

'Do you want the job or not?' Aunt Rita scolds, then softens. 'It's a busy weekend with crowds attending the balloon festival. You girls can stock the shelves to start.'

145

Lucinda looks at me and shrugs. It's not the way I want to spend my Sunday, but I don't complain.

'Just for a couple hours during the week,' she tells Lucinda. 'I know Edna needs you out on the farm. See you tomorrow, kids. Nine o'clock sharp.' She rinses her mug and puts it in the drying rack. 'Come on, Sammy,' she calls. 'We're leaving.'

Lucinda is eager to get out of the house, away from Mom.

'Do you need anything while we're in town?' she asks Mom.

'Town?' Mom looks up from her coffee, puzzled.

'From the store.'

Mom doesn't have the energy to argue – or she doesn't care.

'No. Nothing. Hang out the clothes before you go,' she tells me. 'Strip the beds and start a load.'

Lucinda helps me strip the beds. She is quiet as we hang out the laundry.

It is late morning by the time we finish the chores. Lucinda borrows Hare's bicycle and we ride into town. I expect to see James's car at the edge of the woods, but only the professor's is in its space.

The cloud streets move sideways from the direction of the lake; they run parallel to one another, parallel to the road. We ride toward town underneath them, serrating cumulus clouds like small vertebrae in the upper atmosphere – a spinal column lying across the soft, blue flesh of the sky. I point this out to Lucinda, how the clouds pull away like muscle off bone.

Lucinda takes her feet off the pedals and coasts. 'You're deep,' she calls.

I sit taller and smile, taking my hands off the handlebars.

'No one says things like that,' she says. Something about the way she says this makes me put my hands back on the handles, swerving to avoid a pothole. 'You say nothing, and then you say things like that.'

I gather she is not talking about my meteorological observations any longer. My throat squeezes, and I slow down, letting her catch up.

'How will you break it to her parents?' she wonders aloud.

I try to glimpse her face and also watch the road. There is nothing in her voice to give her away, but I feel the shift, sensing the undertone in her question.

'The girl's parents – they deserve to know you saw her drown.'

I slow down and let her ride ahead. I feel stunned in this moment.

Lucinda slows down so that I can catch up and ride beside her. She is watching my face with a curious detachment.

'I didn't say I saw her drown. I saw her swim. I didn't mean—' I feel muddled now, unsure of where this is going, unsure of why she is twisting my words, twisting what I have told her.

'You said you saw her drown. What are you going to do about it?'

'There's nothing to do,' I say.

'That's not what you told me last night.'

I am too stunned to answer, too uncertain how to pull us back from this brink – but she isn't looking for a response now, anyway, because she stands up on the pedals and rides so fast into town that I can't keep up with her.

14

THE BEACH IS MORE crowded than usual. Throngs attending the balloon festival vie for space with the usual weekend sunworshipers. Lucinda rides down the hill and leaves the bicycle up against the only tree on the beach. She kicks off her boots. I leave my sandals beside them.

Lucinda walks toward the bathrooms behind the concessions and leans against the warmth of the breeze block beside the payphone. She doesn't seem to notice I am here at all – or doesn't care. She picks up the receiver and dials the operator.

Out across the water, the swim team is at it again: back and forth, then back and forth across the horizon – moving in the last place I watched Cathy swim.

'I'd like to make a collect call,' Lucinda is telling the operator. She calls out a number and waits. 'Lucky,' she tells the operator. 'Tell him Lucky is calling.'

She waits while the phone rings, waits for an answer. She waves me away then turns toward the wall, resting her shoulder against the phone box, twisting the coil in her finger. I walk a few steps off and watch the swimmers on the horizon. I can't hear what she is saying, but I know by her tone, the shift, that she is pleased to hear the person accepting the charges and then answering on the other end.

'Hello, Robert,' she says. 'It's me.' Her voice drops, becomes conspiratorial, then seductive. Suddenly, that all changes, and she is defensive, disappointed; now, back to eager. Robert, the married father, her ex-foster father, is on the other end, letting her down more than she wants me to know.

Muffled admonishment travels through the receiver. She holds the phone away from her ear; his end is quiet. She twists the armoured cord and raises her voice, falsely cheerful. Her voice doesn't break, but I detect something I haven't heard in Lucinda before now: something vulnerable, naked, deeper than anything she intended to expose. She glances at me and continues the one-sided conversation without pausing, even as a dial tone feeds a steady pulse down the line.

'OK, bye,' she says cheerfully. 'Love you, too.' She hangs up and marches down the beach.

I watch her walk toward a group of teens. Instead of following her, I turn into the cool dampness of the bathroom block. When I come out she is standing in front of the group, I spot Heather and Jessica in the middle. The sun is high in the sky, it is just after noon and Lucinda's body casts virtually no shadow, even though she towers over them, animating a story with wide gestures. She puts her hands up and falls onto the ground in front of them. They begin to laugh. It looks like Lucinda is rubbing herself into the sand. Jessica places her hand to her mouth; some of the boys begin to wonder what is so funny.

When I come up beside the blanket, the girls turn silent.

Lucinda sits up and looks straight ahead, hugging her knees. She pretends to look out to the lake, but I can see she is holding her breath to keep from cracking up with laughter. Jessica and Heather don't even pretend; they are giggling, and Jessica holds her mouth as though she is holding back her teeth.

I stand behind them, frozen. I want to flee but my feet feel planted, like a tree, holding one elbow in the opposite hand; then I switch elbows, and switch again. My face burns. Tears sting at the corners of my eyelids. My mind races, trying to figure out what I have done wrong, why the tide has turned on Lucinda's tolerance of me.

If this is about last night, I want to say, *it's OK if you think we made a mistake.* But Heather and Jessica are looking back at me with their false smiles and giggling.

Lucinda begins to hum, a tune I know is meant to provoke. Heather and Jessica join in, singing the lyrics to 'Darling Nikki', a song I've heard on Hare's *Purple Rain* album.

It's too much for Lucinda; she stands up and walks off, laughing like she can't contain herself any longer. Heather looks at me and shrugs; her lips tremble and her shoulders shake. I follow Lucinda because I don't know what else to do. Because I don't know *what* just happened, even though I know something did.

'Our bikes,' I call after her.

She ignores me. She is wiping her cheeks.

I follow her up the hill and into the parking lot, along a row of cars, keeping my distance. Neither of us are wearing our shoes, and the pavement burns.

The parking lot is full; a steady stream of cars, shirtless drivers with radios blaring fill the parking lot as the day continues to heat up.

Somewhere up the row, a radio is turned up; I feel the bass in my chest. Lucinda follows the sound to a dark green van. The side with the double doors is airbrushed with a scene of a full moon hanging over mountain peaks; two wolves howl in a valley below. The van is parked against a dune; empty lawn chairs are scattered in the sand and grass beyond it. A group of men sit in the sun, the pungent scent of weed drifting into the parking lot, the smell making my mouth water.

Lucinda stops at the front of the van and calls to a man who is leaning into the open van door, shaking ice off a can of beer he has pulled from a cooler. He is at least thirty, probably older. He is shirtless, darkly tanned; a line of hair rises out of his cut-off shorts, running toward his navel. A twisted gold horn hangs on a chain above the hair of his bare chest. He walks toward Lucinda; she juts her hip out and they talk like this, while I wait a short distance away, holding my elbow with my other hand. He hands her a beer. He looks over at me and waves.

'Tell your friend to come over, too,' he says.

Lucinda looks at me, beckons with her head for me to follow. 'Come meet John,' she says.

She seems easy again. I'll do whatever it takes to have her go back to being herself.

Behind the van, two other men sit on the grass, smoking a joint. Lucinda sits down in their circle, and they hand her the roll-up. I stand behind her and she hands it up

152

to me, pats the ground beside where she is sitting. I put it to my lips, pull on the ends and cough. The men laugh, though Lucinda doesn't. She pulls the tab of the beer John hands her. It cracks with a whoosh of air.

'You sure you girls are old enough for that?' one of the men ask.

Lucinda clucks her tongue against her teeth and cocks her head. 'What do you think?'

'I think no,' he laughs.

'I'm eighteen,' Lucinda tells him.

'Like I said. Not old enough to drink.'

'So?' Lucinda says and guzzles the beer.

'You're old enough for this,' one of the men says. He puts a glass tube in front of me; smoke fills the chamber within. 'You cover that, and then you suck this,' he says.

'Suck this,' John says, holding his crotch, and they snigger.

Lucinda scoffs, then she laughs. 'I'll suck it,' she says. She takes the contraption from me.

John makes a soft groaning sound and rubs her shoulder while she sucks on the pipe. She holds her breath, closes her eyes. When she lets the air out, she does it slowly, in rings.

'You try,' she tells me. Her mood has passed.

I take the pipe and do what she did, but the smoke hits my lungs like water. It hurts. I let it out and cough. They all laugh again.

One of the men shows me how to do it, and I try again. We are all laughing by now. I can't stop myself – nothing is funny, but everything is funny. Lucinda stands up; John is taking her by the hand, and they disappear into the van. The doors are closing. I lie back on the grass. I feel like I am plastered to it, as though I couldn't get up if my life depended on it. I'm thinking that it must be hot and dark inside the van, with its tinted windows, and this thought sobers me up a little.

Someone is being pushed out of the van now. A man falls onto the hot pavement beside it. It is clear the man has been sleeping in the darkened van. He is stunned to find himself lying like a beetle on his back on the ground. He sits up and rubs his eyes. I laugh again now, so hard I think I will pee my pants.

'Shit, Martin,' John calls after the fallen man. 'Get a life.'

I recognise Martin, the veteran, the man with the dog coat from the McCarthys' house that day. He stands up off the pavement, rearranges his T-shirt. He stumbles over to where I'm lying in the grass. He smells potent with drink. He doesn't recognise me.

'No one light a cigarette,' the man with the bandana across his forehead says, waving his hand at the stench. 'He'll catch fire.' He looks at the other man, nods to the van, indicating that he knows what is going on in there. 'Go for a swim?' he asks his friend. The two men walk down the hill together, leaving me alone with Martin. I lie there, very still, hoping he'll follow the men and go swimming, hoping I will sink into the ground.

Martin rummages through his pockets, pulls out a cigarette. 'Got a light?' he asks.

I shake my head, sitting up.

'That your friend in there with John?' he asks. 'They're going to have a little fun.' He sniggers. He finds a matchbook, tears one off, strikes it against the cover. It doesn't light. He tries again; this one lights and burns out in the wind. His hands shake. He gives me the book.

I sit up and take a match and strike it against the sulphur. It lights first time. He leans in and draws on the cigarette. He keeps drawing in, his face coming closer to mine, so close he is leaning over, until he falls into me. We both keel over; he is on top of me in the grass.

'You like to have a little fun, too?' he asks.

I feel a hand on my thigh. I pull away. He launches toward me and runs his finger along the edge of my shorts; he dives his hand under my tank top. I freeze. He takes this as encouragement and puts his mouth to mine, chuckles as though we've both decided this is fun. His small body is heavier than I imagine it should be against mine. I manage to loosen my hands. I push his hand away and catch the ember of the cigarette he is holding in his other hand. The ember falls onto his thigh.

'Holy shit,' he hollers and stands, slapping at his stomach. 'Sorry, darling. You just had to say no.'

He begins to laugh, but then he steps on the ember that has fallen to the ground; he leaps backward, hops away, toward the van. He opens the doors, reaches past the occupants, into the beer cooler. He takes out a can, ice from the cooler flying everywhere.

'What the hell is going on?' John yells. 'Can't I fuck in peace?'

The doors of the van are fully open, and the seats are collapsed into a bed. Lucinda lies across it; I can see the back of her hair falling toward the door, her knees bent upwards. John is positioned between her legs; he is wearing only the twisted golden horn around his neck.

Lucinda turns her head and looks out through the door, smiling smugly at me. Her face changes when she sees Martin.

'Holy shit,' Martin says. He sobers in an instant.

'Martin!' Lucinda's face holds the full horror contained in Martin's voice.

'Christ, John – She's Karl McCarthy's foster kid. What are you? Like in tenth grade?'

John jumps off Lucinda and backs away to the corner of the seat-bed.

Martin turns to me, suddenly recognising that I'm as young as Lucinda. He pulls the can of beer away from his chest. He holds it in one palm; his other palm he holds out toward me, as though surrendering. The can falls and hits the ground. It bursts a leak, hissing air and foam onto the black of the pavement.

'I didn't know.' Martin's voice is sincere, aghast. 'On my word, I didn't know.'

'What the fuck?' John is cowering in the back corner of the bed, hollering at Lucinda. It is the first time I have seen a hard penis, a man's penis – he is covering it with one hand. I can't look away. He pushes Lucinda away with his other hand, closing her knees. 'You're a high-schooler? You told me you were eighteen!'

'I am soon,' Lucinda insists. She glares at me, warning me not to give her away.

'Holy fuck!' John has Lucinda out of the van; he is throwing her clothes at her, throwing lawn chairs into the van, starting the engine.

Lucinda struggles into her shorts.

I walk away. Martin follows.

'Ma'am,' he calls.

I keep walking.

'Ma'am,' his voice is shaking.

I turn back to him.

'I'm a soldier,' he says, holding palms turned up.

'I know,' I tell him.

'I'm sorry—' he stutters.

'Shut the fuck up, Martin,' Lucinda tells him viciously.

I turn and run, all the way back to the bicycles. I put my hands to my knees, fighting to catch my breath. Saliva fills my mouth; I swallow it down and try not to get sick all over the road.

Heather and Jessica are stretched out on their blankets, tanning oil thick and shiny across the back of their legs and backs; the boys form a circle to the side of them, bumping a volleyball between them. One of the boys spots me and begins hooting.

'There she is,' he yells. 'Pop-bottle JoJo.'

The group of boys scream with laughter. The girls sit up to see who they are calling to. Jessica covers her mouth; Heather turns away as though she can't bear it. I don't know what this is about, but I feel the shame of whatever they are accusing me of. I slip into my sandals and throw

Lucinda's boots to one side so that I can lift my bicycle. One of the boys picks up a glass bottle of cola; he runs toward me, waving it in my face.

Heather and Jessica roll over and stand up from their blanket.

'Leave her alone,' Heather calls to the boy, but the half laughter in her voice only encourages them.

'Here, don't forget this,' he screeches. 'Go have some fun with your pop bottle!'

'Look at her banana seat,' another one jeers. 'That's got to be fun.'

'I'll give you a ride,' a boy hollers.

Lucinda has come down the hill; she stands next to Heather and Jessica now, her arm lightly draped across Heather's shoulder.

'Don't bother with her,' Lucinda calls. 'You're not her type. She doesn't like dick.' She is walking toward me now. Her voice is tinny and remote. Heather and Jessica cackle behind her. 'She's a lesbian!' Lucinda announces.

'A lesbian who loves her pop bottles,' one of the boys mimes what he is implying

'That's not right,' I say.

'Yes, it is. That is exactly right,' Lucinda says sharply.

I stare at her desperately. 'What the fuck?'

One of the boys begins to chant, vicious and taunting. The others join in; they holler after me, following me as I begin to pedal my bicycle, hollering after me the way they'd hollered after Moose. 'One bottle of pop, two bottles of pop, three bottles of pop – POP!'

I pass Lucinda.

'Lesbo,' she mouths. Her lips turn up in a smirk.

I am on the bicycle now, pushing the pedals as fast as I can. Lucinda lifts her middle finger, raises it to me. I turn my back and ride away.

*

I ride up the road. I am shaking with fury and fear – and humiliation. I pedal back toward the woods, toward the kettle lake. One of my sandals falls off. I keep pedalling, kicking the other one off into the road. I am nearly blinded with tears. They streak down my face, red and hot.

I throw my bike down at the edge of the woods. I stalk through the weave of undergrowth, barefoot; every inch of the wet ground touches the skin of my soles. I can't go home this way: out of breath and crying and shaking with fear and anger.

The air is heavy, and the water on the kettle lake has lost its glassy sheen; it is still and opaque and looks as though it is set into the woods like onyx stone. I stop at the edge of the water, put my hands to my knees, try to catch my breath. I drop my hands into the water, bring a handful to my face, splashing the coolness onto my swollen eyes, my throbbing head.

I hear them now, notes, wooden and sharp, music floating down from the cabin on the hill. They are slow at first, then like footsteps – swift and impish, making their way to the water's edge.

159

This is *my* lake, I think. This is *my* country. This is where *I* belong.

I remove my clothes, not caring if the professor is watching. The music from the cabin becomes plucky, like the drops of rain that have begun to appear, disturbing the lake with perfect circles. I walk out into the water; the cold stings the back of my knees. I spread my arms and thrust myself into the water, welcoming the shock. I lie on my back and float. A plop of rain wets my nose. I turn and swim for the birch tree breaking the surface. I swim back toward the shore. I stop when I am halfway back, suspended in the water by my own will, treading water over the deepest part of the lake. I let go and descend, deep into the darkened waters. I let my weight sink down into the endless passage. I know I should be afraid, but I am not. I only feel a lowering, a settling into a final resting place. If I can sink so far, I know I will not return.

And just as I decide this, something else kicks in – an unnamed knowing – and this knowing propels me skywards. I break the surface and gasp for breath.

It must be after three. The time of day storm clouds often gather out of nowhere. The sky has darkened. A gnarl of thunder shudders the woods. I swim to the bank; the sky between the trees is bruised to cobalt. I hold out my arms and open my mouth. The rain is now rapid as it darts in.

Something moves in the undergrowth, all quiet like the deer I see in these woods.

I am naked, exposed, and I lie still; it seems my beating heart sends ripples out into the water. A shape moves out from the deer track. Walking straight, it stands alone, looking out over the water.

She does not see me; she is looking over my head at the storm moving off of the Great Lake beyond. It is Mom, coming from the direction of the cabin on the hill.

The clouds move quickly across the storm-darkened sky, devouring the sun. She wears the dress from the beer tent again; she has repaired the missing buttons already. She is barefoot. Her hair hangs loose around her shoulders. She holds an armful of wildflowers: goldenrod, Queen Anne's lace, knapweed.

A surge of violin strings pour from the cabin, filling the woods with clear, fluttering notes. Mom lifts her eyes to the clouds and lets the rain fall on her face. She looks back up toward the cabin. There on the hill, the professor stands at the edge and waves his arms as though he is conducting the music. She waves and then turns, running, like a girl, shouting and laughing through the cattails, back to the house.

15

THE HOUSE IS DARK with the passing storm. Mom puts a Fleetwood Mac record on the turntable and sings. She doesn't notice that my hair is dripping wet. A cabinet door bangs in the kitchen; she pulls out pots and bowls.

'Mrs McCarthy called,' she hollers. 'Lucinda's staying another night – you girls can walk to Aunt Rita's together in the morning.'

'I don't think she wants to stay,' I call back.

She doesn't hear me. 'Your first day of work!' She pulls out a packet of Jell-O.

'I'm not sure Lucinda wants—'

'Mr McCarthy will pick her up after the shift.'

'She is probably cycling home—'

She sings into the whisk, grinning at me. She dances into the living room, turns the volume up full dial. I wonder if the professor can hear our music. I imagine his feet up on the window ledge, a book in his lap, watching our house, our lives.

Mom's calves are splattered with mud. She spins around the room; her dress lifts and swirls. I walk into the living room, curl up on the couch, hugging my knees to my chest, watching her.

Hare moves around in the kitchen. She brings in a bowl of cornflakes in one hand and turns the volume down with the other.

'Hey, I'm listening to that,' Mom calls, dancing over to turn the volume back up.

'What?' Hare yells, cupping her ear.

She dances around Hare and sings.

Hare rolls her eyes, but she brings her bowl of cornflakes and sits down beside me, watching Mom turn around the room. Mom resembles Hare in this moment, the way Hare surprises me when her mood lifts and something between us connects.

'Dance with me!' Mom shouts above the music.

'Hippie!' Hare yells back, but she is laughing.

'Did I ever tell you what your father said to me once?'

Hare slaps herself on the forehead. 'Only every time you play this song.'

I feel outside of myself, watching a scene unfold across an invisible barrier. I want to cross, but I cannot join. The sun comes back out; the storm has passed.

Dad walks through the back-door. He has been in the pole barn all day, working on a friend's car. The music assaults his ears; annoyed, he shouts for us to turn it down. Mom spins toward him. She takes his grease-soiled hands in her own. He pulls away. He has not forgiven her for yesterday. He walks across the room and turns the volume down himself. Mom turns it back up, grinning, daring him to remain angry with her.

'Tell them,' she commands. 'Tell them what you said.'

She takes his hand again, this time he doesn't let go. He reluctantly allows her to spin herself around the orbit of his hand.

'Tell them what you said to me the first time we heard this song.'

'Please don't,' Hare grumbles.

Mom can see Dad isn't playing along. Her voice deepens. 'Anyone ever tell you . . .'

'. . . you look the way Stevie Nicks sounds,' Dad finishes. He pulls her into his chest and they put their hands together, slow-dancing this way.

'Charming,' Hare mutters.

'Smooth, so smooth . . .' Mom laughs. The album changes tracks and he puts his hands around her waist. He reluctantly moves along with her, grinning, self-conscious.

I have a hard time imagining Dad behaving so romantically, dropping this line, paying attention to Mom in this way – but then here he is, looking at Mom as though something of the night before has reset their transgressions, sent them back to the start. She reaches her mouth up to his and kisses him. Sammy has just returned home; he runs through the door and stops in the middle of the room, alarmed.

'Gross!' he screams, covering his ears. Mom scoops Sammy up. Dad crushes him between their bodies as Sammy laughs and squirms to get away.

I want to believe in this moment, believe this is us.

Aunt Rita sounds her horn from the driveway.

They put Sammy down and Mom sticks her head out the door.

'He's getting clean underwear – send him back out,' Aunt Rita instructs.

Mom looks at Sammy. He shakes his head. He doesn't want to miss this rare fun.

'He's not coming,' Mom says. 'I'll send him with the girls tomorrow.' Sammy comes to the door, standing behind her.

'Are you sure, darling?' Aunt Rita calls to him. He nods again. She pulls away, waving out the open window.

Mom and Dad tickle Sammy until he falls on the floor and is rolling back and forth. Hare and I look at each other and smile.

My stomach drops when I turn and see Lucinda standing at the sliding door, her face blank, her arms folded across her chest, watching us, unamused. She steps through the door, and the moment is broken.

Dad strides to the stereo, turns down the volume and goes upstairs to clean the grease off his hands, his arms, to change.

Mom returns to the kitchen to finish the dish she is making. She stirs a pot. Cabinets close, the fridge door is opened. There is a clatter of bowls being rearranged. Now she is wiping her hands and gathering her car keys and wallet.

'Well,' she says. 'I'm off.'

Sammy looks disappointed.

'Where are you going?' I ask.

'Into the city,' she chirps. 'I'm signing up for a college course,' she announces.

We all look at her, confused.

She smiles, waiting for someone to ask her questions. When we don't, she says, 'It's all about *love*.'

Hare raises an eyebrow.

'Love what?' Dad asks, coming down the stairs. He looks really nice in a pair of shorts and a white shirt rolled up at the sleeves.

'Mom's taking a college course,' Sammy says.

'It's a class on *love*. I'm auditing it – it's not for a grade. But it's fun. It's philosophy.' Her laugh makes her sound young.

Hare rolls her eyes.

'Oh, for God's sake,' Dad says. 'Study nursing or teaching. You don't study *love*.' Mom deflates a little. Dad is trying to be funny, but I wish he would go sit on the deck. 'That's no college course.'

'Yes, it is,' Hare says, disgusted. 'That weirdo who's always at the diner teaches a course on love every fall at the community college.'

Mom rummages around in her wallet. Then she clears her throat.

'Which weirdo?' Dad laughs. 'They're all weird up there.'

'The creep who owns the property.' Hare shudders.

'Everett?' Dad asks, the amusement leaving his face. 'He doesn't *own* the property.'

Mom's face turns red. 'Well, I'm off,' she says.

'He eats at the diner and tries to talk to all the girls about *love*,' Hare continues. 'He tries it on me, too. But I pretend I don't hear and ask him how he wants his eggs.' She wrinkles her nose in disgust. 'He never talks to the firemen. Just the girls. Creep.'

Lucinda clucks her tongue.

Hare looks at her and says, 'I know.' Then something dawns on her. She looks at Mom with fresh disgust.

'Professor Love, huh?' Dad scowls. He is eyeing Mom with suspicion again.

Hare turns back to Mom. 'Will he be your teacher? Holy shit, not you too.'

Mom ignores Hare and turns to me. 'I'll be back shortly. Watch your brother?'

'Isn't the college closed on a Saturday?'

Mom hesitates, glances at Dad. 'It's their open day. I'm in a rush now.'

'Shouldn't you take Lucinda home?' I ask.

Mom looks from Lucinda to me. 'I already told Mrs McCarthy she could stay another night – if she wants to?' She turns to Lucinda.

'I want to.' Lucinda smiles. 'Thank you very much for having me.'

Her falseness both sickens and worries me.

'I'm coming with you,' I tell Mom.

She seems surprised, but shrugs. 'Suit yourself. But hurry up. I'm only going to make it before they close.'

'Watch your brother?' Mom asks Hare.

'Can't he just move in with Aunt Rita?'

'Watch your brother,' Mom says flatly.

'I'll watch him,' Lucinda says. 'Come on, Sammy.' She takes his hand, and they go out into the kitchen. 'Want to make some Rice Krispie treats?'

'That's nice of you, thank you,' Mom calls after her. She walks out the sliding door and I follow. We climb into the truck.

'Something happen between you and your friend?' she asks.

'We just need a break from each other.'

Mom looks at me for a moment, then starts the engine.

Dad runs out the door. He leans into my window. 'Drop me at my mother's on your way.'

'What's on at your mother's?' Mom asks, eyeing his shirt.

'Just a few friends coming by. I promised Maureen I'd help them set up.'

'I take it I'm not welcome.' This is a statement, not a question.

'After last night?' His voice is full of scorn. He jumps in beside me, and I scoot into the middle while he slams the door.

'Why don't you walk?' Mom asks.

'It's hot – I don't want to arrive sweaty. You're passing anyway.'

Mom doesn't say anything. She puts the truck in gear and drives up the lane. Dad smells of sweat already, camouflaged by cologne.

Bunting is strewn all along the porch and wraps around the pillars of the farmhouse. Red, white and blue balloons are tied to the centennial sign. There are cars and pickup trucks lining the driveway, and some have parked on the lawn. Mom pulls off onto the side of the road, onto the shoulder. Her knuckles are white on the steering wheel.

'Just a few friends? Is she throwing *another* party?' Mom says dryly.

'It's the sesquicentennial. Mom just wanted a little celebration.'

'Did she?'

'See you, kid,' Dad tells me and squeezes my nose. His eyes are level with Mom's when he closes the door. I can see what the ride is all about now. There is a moment of triumph, savouring her hurt, retaliating for her behaviour in the beer tent, his humiliation in front of his friends.

Mom is quiet all the way into the city. I glance at her from time to time, but her face gives nothing away. She doesn't drive to the community college to sign up for the course. Instead, she pulls into the parking lot of a super-market. Her movements are hurried. She takes small squares of posterboard out of the glovebox. She has already written on them with permanent marker. It is a handwritten ad. She is selling the wooden icebox.

'It was junk when I bought it,' she tells me, taking thumbtacks from the glovebox. 'And I turned it into some-thing special.' There is a strain in the veins along her neck. 'I'll make a hundred bucks off this. That's nearly half a one-way ticket to Italy.' She opens the door of the truck and climbs out. She sees I am still sitting there. 'Let's go.'

Inside the supermarket, we find the notice board. She removes the ad at the top of the *For Sale* column, a listing for a motorcycle, and she pins it over the top of an ad for a *camper van – hardly used.* She pins her own listing at the top and brushes off her hands. She faces the aisles.

'Now. That is that. What else do I need?' she asks as I follow her up one aisle and down another. 'I'll make that Jell-O salad I told you about a few weeks ago. Is it enough? I could make some spare ribs . . .' Her voice is shrill, and I look around to see if anyone else notices. By the time we reach the condiment aisle, I am shushing her. She is loud and angry, demanding someone help her find the barbeque sauce. She forgets to get the ribs, and I don't remind her.

On the way home, she drives fast, her entire body rigid. I grip the edge of the seat near the door.

'I hope that Jell-O sets quickly,' she says. 'We are going to that party.'

The Great Lake comes into view. The road winds closer to the shoreline. Every now and again, especially in earlier years, we have taken this scenic route home and passed an old clapboard farmhouse, its parklands rolling up to the front-door. Ancient trees tower across the yard on all sides. An enclosed porch wraps around the entire house, but the special thing about this house isn't the enclosed porch room, but the crab-apple tree that grows straight out the top of its roof, its crown shaded by a railed-in roof deck. We always used to holler for Mom to slow down when we passed this house so that we could crane our necks to see the tree. Every season brings a change of colour: the pink blossoms of spring, green of summer, the reds, golds and oranges of fall. And in early winter, Christmas lights outline its stark branches. Even Hare, whether she was in a good mood or not, used to peer out the window, appreciating the novelty of a tree growing right out of a roof.

Passing it now, Mom slams on the brakes; I tumble toward the dashboard. She reverses up the middle of the road. When I recover my bearings, I spot an orange sign sticking into the gravel beside the driveway: YARD SALE.

Mom's mood switches again, from furious to girlish. 'We have sourced this sale,' she tells me, rubbing her hands together. She has lately developed this belief that if she puts things to the universe, good things will come to her, as though the universe is some sort of gumball machine not requiring a quarter. 'We've hit the jackpot! I hope we're not too late.'

I spot piles of furniture laid out on the lawn. Mom sings *thank you* to the sky as she pulls onto the side of the road. The junk is disorganised – jumbles of mismatched items laid out on a table without a common theme: family board games, their boxes faded from age, sit beside tools, a pool ball set and cues, a pile of blankets, tarnished silver spoons, some appliance that looks like a denture bridge without the teeth. Mom walks straight toward a heap of furniture. There are patches of rain from the earlier storm, but they are evaporating quickly.

A woman comes out the garage. She wears a big straw hat and seems surprised to see us.

'I was starting to close up shop,' she calls. 'I was busy earlier but I didn't think anyone else would stop with those storms passing through.'

'Hmm,' Mom mutters, uninterested, and so the woman smiles at me, her eyes crinkle, and I think she looks familiar, like the way you might recognise a clerk you see time and again at a supermarket, but out of context, you forget how you know them.

'Rosemary,' the woman says warmly.

Mom jumps.

'Don't you recognise me? It's Marylou.' She walks across the lawn toward us.

I smile at her, not just to make up for Mom's rudeness and stony face, but because I remember her now, and

I like her instantly. She is Aunt Rita's special friend. Mom is pulling at a headboard in the pile, lifting it to reach a hat stand at the bottom.

'You looking for anything special?' Marylou asks Mom.

'Just looking,' Mom says coldly.

Marylou winks at me. When the breeze blows, strands of grey hair lift in the wind. 'Well, take your time. I'm not in a rush, if the weather holds.'

Mom ignores her and runs her fingers over an oak headboard.

'Do you like my tree?' Marylou asks when she sees me looking toward the house. She has big horsey teeth when she smiles.

I nod vigorously, and she beckons me over, offering to show it to me while Mom looks around. We walk around the glass-enclosed porch to the other side, where a wooden staircase slants up the side of the house. She climbs the stairs, and I come up behind her, onto the wooden roof deck.

'Believe it or not, once upon a time this tree was in the front yard. Someone took the notion to build a porch and someone else must have taken the notion to save a tree. And here you have the result.'

The trunk of the crab-apple tree seems to break out of the tongue-and-groove boards; the tree is completely floored in with boards but its canopy spreads low and wide over the deck. The tree is in full leaf. The flowers are gone now, replaced by small clusters of crab apples beginning to swell on their stems. I imagine the blossoms must have buzzed for weeks with bees and left a fine dust of pollen, which Marylou had to sweep away with a broom. The residue remains between the boards. If this were my house, I think, I would climb up here every day and hide under the low branches. I'd spend the entire summer looking out at the lake. From here, I can see for miles.

'I reared my boys here. Now they're grown, but they made their forts up here, all summer long, when they were young.' She looks down at me and sees my eyes welling up. 'Hey,' she says softly, and it is enough to make the tears spill.

I don't even know why I am crying, but her voice touches something in me.

'Joanne,' she says. I am surprised she knows my name. 'You need to have a good chat with your aunt. I know Rita comes across as tough, but she understands people. Your mother is not doing so good, is she?'

I shake my head, and my throat now swells with the tears. Marylou places her hand on my shoulder. 'Ah dear.' She produces a tissue from her pocket and smooths circles around my back as I wipe my tears. 'This is all going to come out OK – you know that, right? All will be well. Come on – I bet we can find you something you didn't know you were looking for.'

I am sad when we move back down the stairs, away from the tree. This is the kind of place I could stay in forever, under the comforting arm of Marylou, who believes all will be well.

Instead of going back to the yard sale, Marylou walks through the open wooden doors of the garage. 'See anything you'd like in here?'

Beyond the tennis rackets, golf clubs and old wooden frames, my eyes go straight to a ten-speed bicycle. It has a bar across the front, like for a man, but I am tall. I look at her and smile.

Mom has pulled a pair of nightstands out of the pile and is opening and closing the little drawers at the top when we rejoin her. She sees me wheeling the ten-speed.

'How much is that?' Mom asks.

'This is for Joanne. She's doing me a favour, taking it away. My boys don't even live here anymore.'

'And these?' Mom pretends she has little interest in the stands. She talks Marylou down: twenty bucks, fifteen, twelve dollars each.

'You take care,' Marylou tells me as I wheel the ten-speed toward the truck.

Mom lifts each stand from underneath like a waitress carrying trays, delivering them to the truck. I turn back to see Marylou watching me warmly. She tips her hat, and I take one hand off the handlebars and return her wave.

Mom remains indifferent as we cross the lawn, over the long shadows of the oaks that fill Marylou's yard. Mom loads the truck, as though she is doing Marylou a favour, too, taking the stands off her hands. We lift the ten-speed into the flatbed. She maintains this air of haughtiness until we pull away, driving erratically as though we have committed a robbery. Once down the road, Mom whoops and hollers, banging the steering wheel with her palm so the horn blares. I jump.

'Those are solid oak! The dummy – did you see how she looked at me?' Her excitement is unnerving. Mom leans over and rubs my head. 'Must have been you, kiddo. Nice work distracting her. You're my new lucky charm!'

I wonder, who is her old lucky charm?

Mom buzzes beside me. She puts her foot on the gas as we approach the curve. The road doubles back on itself, and the tyres squeal around the next curve. In the back of the truck, the two nightstands, peeling and smelling of damp, shift as we veer around the lake. The wheel on the ten-speed spins. The frame lifts as we pass over a river enclosed by a stone wall; the stands fall over as we head into the next series of bends. I'm thinking of the seatbelt long wedged under the seat, and probe into the crack in case I can feel it.

I check again to make sure the ten-speed has not bounced out of the truck, and when I turn back, we are spinning. My hand closes over the door-handle as though it is the only thing holding us to the road, the one thing keeping the possible impossible.

Mom somehow steers us through the next bend, but as we come out, she loses all control.

Even as the wheels squeal, even as the truck spins, even as a cursed prayer leaves Mom's lips as we crash into the marsh, as the cattails rush to meet the windscreen – there it is again: that unnamed thing, a calm. The knowing takes over as I fly, arms outstretched, headlong toward the windscreen.

16

WHEN I FIND THE border between surface and air, the water has become an impenetrable layer, as though it is made of unbreakable ice. I hit at it and kick, but there is no breaking through. I can see it, but I cannot reach the bulging concave of blue sky on the other side. Figures come and go, and I do not know if I am dreaming or awake.

I am on the couch in the dark of night, a sheet covering my legs, a pillow under my head. A weight slides off the pillow. I lift it and find a bag of frozen peas wrapped in a dishtowel, now room temperature. My head hurts, and there is ringing in my ears. I think I hear Mom humming and then speaking softly in my ear.

I open my eyes, but no one is there. My lips stick to one another. I am so thirsty that I can barely swallow.

'I'm here,' a voice tells me.

'Water,' I whisper.

I feel a hand on my neck, supporting my head – wet on my lips. I know then that I am awake.

It hurts to sit up. The ache in my head splits my thoughts. I put my hand to my forehead. There is a lump the size of a baseball. The glass is put to my lips again and I drink. The room spins, and when I lie back, I fall into a fitful dream.

When I wake next, Lucinda sits at the end of the sofa smoking a cigarette. There is something cold at my head.

'Frozen French fries,' she says. 'You're out of peas. Does it hurt?' She is staring at my forehead.

I nod.

'You could have died. I know someone who went through the windscreen – straight through. He was decapitated.'

I hold up my hand – I need her to stop talking. The littlest sound crashes through my skull.

'You can't smoke in here,' I whisper.

She stares at her hand, watching the smoke trail up her finger. 'I don't know what's wrong with me,' she says. 'I don't know why I did that to you, told those girls the things I did. I guess I got scared, you know, all of that. I'm bad.' She stares at the glow of the ember. 'I'm bad, like my father.'

It's not that I don't want to work it out with Lucinda, but I can't, not right now. Even her softly spoken words split my head. I close my eyes, and when I open them again, Lucinda has placed the ember of her cigarette against her skin, below the line where her elbow bends. A shudder passes through her shoulders, moves down her spine. She puts her head back on the couch and breathes.

'Stop.' I think I am yelling, but it barely comes out as a hoarse whisper. I can't reach her. It is as though my nerves are cauterised. 'No, No, No . . .' I kick at her hand holding the cigarette, and the red glow bursts into sparks and falls onto the couch, then onto the floor. I manage to raise myself up and pat out the embers, stomping out the ash. It cuts at the ball of my foot like icy water, like glass.

Lucinda stretches her burned arm in front of her body, cradles her elbow in her other hand. A clean hole flares red. She closes her eyes; her face twists in a pinch. She breathes so deeply through her nostrils that the air seems to cleanse, to soothe something deep inside. It seems to lift her straight up into the night.

I hunch in next to her and pull her to me. She leans in, rests on my shoulder. 'Don't do that,' I whisper. 'Don't do that to yourself.'

*

When I wake, the room glows orange from the late morning sun streaming through the sliding door. My eyes open in slits.

Hare sits at the end of the sofa. Her forehead wrinkles with worry. 'You've been sleeping a long time,' she tells me.

Dad comes in through the door from the deck. Freddie follows. I cover my ears to stop the noise amplifying. They move as though they are attached to one another, trying to keep quiet. Dad's toe catches the wooden frame of the couch, and he curses.

I think they will sit down on us, but Hare calls to them before they reach us.

'You're drunk.'

Dad puts his arm around Freddie's shoulder to steady himself. They stare as though they are trying to see into the dark, even though it is broad daylight.

'Shit.' Dad laughs. 'Why's everyone still up?'

Hare is not impressed. 'Because it's morning.'

'You're in the doghouse.' Freddie sniggers.

Dad shushes him.

'What do you call this?' Hare asks. 'Have you been out all night?'

'What are you now, my mother?' Dad asks.

Freddie laughs even louder. 'Good night,' he snorts.

They change direction and walk out toward the kitchen, clinging to each other, stumbling together as though they are bound in a two-legged relay.

Dad's body, heavy with drink, sits down hard on a chair.

I cover my eyes from the sunlight and feel the bump on my forehead. It seems worse than it did last night.

Hare winces as though she feels my pain.

Freddie walks back through the room. 'Ladies.' He bows to us and stumbles out the door, singing 'Goodnight Irene'. The noise splits my head.

When Freddie is gone, I lie back onto the pillow – but then he is back, calling through the sliding door. 'What the hell happened to your truck?'

Dad is on his feet, moving toward the door. He staggers, mumbles under his breath, makes an about-turn and heads toward the stairs, gripping the railing with effort. His words slur together. 'I'm going to lie down for a minute, girls. Call me in ten . . .'

Mom pushes past him on the stairs. 'You're a disgrace,' she tells him.

'You need help,' he shoots back.

She leans over me, wearing the same dress she wore yesterday. The silk front is unbuttoned now, and the bottom has a little tear at the hem; it is smeared with grass and droplets of dried blood where her leg is cut. She takes my hand and kisses it, then kisses it twenty more times. I don't have the strength to pull away.

Sammy comes down the stairs and sits beside Hare at my feet. 'You look like a panda,' he says, staring at me.

'It's true,' Hare says. 'You've black rings around your eyes.'

I want to smile and assure Sammy that I am all right, but smiling hurts my face. I place my foot on his knee, and he holds it like he is holding my hand.

'Are we going to have to stay quiet all day?' he asks loudly.

'We're going to a party,' Mom says. 'It looks like they're still up over there, after all.'

'I hate be the one to tell you, but the party is over,' Hare says.

'Nothing is stopping us dropping by and congratulating your grandmother.'

'She'll love that,' Hare says dryly. 'Shouldn't you tell Dad about the accident?'

'Did you see the state of your father? We'll tell him about the truck when he sobers up.'

'I mean about Joanne. I don't think she looks so well.'

'I'll get you some aspirin.' Mom jumps up and goes to the kitchen. It sounds like she opens every cupboard and slams them all closed.

'Is Lucinda here?' I ask.

'She's gone to work,' Hare says. 'I told her to send Aunt Rita.'

'Why'd you do that?' My head is still hurting, but I can sit up by myself.

'You don't look so good,' Hare tells me.

Mom has brought back a bottle of aspirin and a fresh glass of water.

'I'm fine,' I tell her.

'Take them – they'll kick in before the party.'

Hare speaks sharply to Mom. 'There is no party, Mother.'

Mom raises an eyebrow at Hare. 'You're always so negative.'

Hare looks at me in disbelief.

Mom moves back into the kitchen with a frenzied energy, slamming dishes. She pulls a wooden spoon out of a drawer, then throws it back again, rooting around for a spatula.

There is a bottle of wine open on the counter. She pours some into a coffee mug and takes it upstairs.

When she comes back down, she has changed into a blue skirt with a white blouse over her tank top and a necklace with big round rings that I have never seen her wear before. She takes up her bottle of wine again, tipping the remains into the mug, filling it to the brim.

She slices pineapple on the chopping board; the knife dragging across glass sends a fresh wave of nausea through me. I should stand, I think, and run to the toilet. But I don't feel like my feet will hold me.

Aunt Rita comes through the sliding door. Albert and Gabe stand either side of her.

'Your truck,' she states. 'The front end is buckled like an accordion.'

Mom calls to her from the kitchen. 'It was only the ditch. I didn't hit anyone.'

'Did you call the police?'

'I backed it out and drove away. It's fine.' She comes to the kitchen door holding a tin of fruit cocktail, emptying it into the bowl full of Jell-O that she holds in her other hand.

Every sound is magnified and connected to the nausea rising in my head, flagging my stomach for readiness: the movement of Gabe shifting his feet; the creak of Sammy rising off the couch; Mom returning to the kitchen, ripping the lid off a packet of frozen whipped cream; the beaters whirring into motion. I raise my hand, try to make it stop – I can see her hitting at the solid mass of white, breaking it into small chunks, droplets flying onto the backsplash, pineapple shredding in the whirl.

'You can't leave the scene of an accident without calling the police,' Aunt Rita calls over the beaters.

'No one was hurt.'

'What the hell, Mom? Joanne is hurt,' Hare yells.

Aunt Rita turns to look at me. She gasps. 'Jesus, Mary and Joseph!'

I try to stand, but I am too weak. I lean over and am sick right there, all over the floor.

Sammy runs away; the boys follow him out the door, shrieking.

Aunt Rita is at my side, sending Hare for towels, covering the vomit. She won't let me close my eyes. I want to put my head down right there and sleep. I want to cry with tiredness.

'Was there any blood?' she asks.

'None,' Hare says.

Aunt Rita probes my head, running her fingers all along my skull. She checks my arms and neck and squeezes my shoulders. She comes back to my forehead and touches it. Her doomsday voice is absent. She speaks calmly, softly but her lips are tight and drawn.

'There's no break, but you are black and blue. This is possibly a closed-head injury. Has she seen a doctor?' Aunt Rita calls to Mom.

'No, she's fine,' Mom calls.

'Don't fall asleep, honey,' Aunt Rita insists. 'Joanne, stay awake, you hear?'

'She's already been sleeping – don't make a fuss,' Mom calls from the kitchen. 'She just needs to sleep it off.'

'She's been sleeping since they arrived home yesterday afternoon,' Hare tells her.

'Yesterday?' The alarm in Aunt Rita's voice frightens me. 'Go get your father.'

'He's sleeping – I don't think he should drive.'

'I'll drive. Get him now. Tell him it's an emergency.'

'Always ready for a crisis,' Mom says flippantly, coming out of the kitchen; she has slipped into her shoes and is holding an egg-blue bowl with speckles in one hand and the mug in the other.

'Ready,' she tells us.

'Ready?' Aunt Rita asks.

'It's the sesquicentennial!' Mom says. Her eyes are wild. 'You coming?'

'Christ, Rosemary, this child could have a fracture – her brain could be swelling. What are you thinking?' The only place we're going is to the hospital,' Aunt Rita says.

Mom takes a swig from the mug. 'You like to ruin the fun.'

'Look at your child,' Aunt Rita says sharply.

Mom peers down at me, as though seeing my two black eyes, the lump and bruises in the middle of my forehead for the first time. Her body sways. Aunt Rita takes the bowl and mug out of her hands. Mom's hand comes to her mouth, and she sits down next to me.

'Joanne.' Mom touches my forehead. 'Oh, Joanne.'

Aunt Rita presses her lips together. She calls to me again. 'Stay awake, honey. You must keep your eyes open from now, until a doctor sees you.'

Dad comes down the stairs, following Hare. He looks rough.

'Joanne . . .' Hare is calling me; it sounds like she is getting farther away.

I try – I really do. Aunt Rita sounds so urgent. I know I should keep my eyes open, but they close, only for a moment.

'Stand up, Joanne. I need you to stand up.'

'OK,' I tell her.

In a moment, I will get up. I have no more strength to speak. The lids of my eyes sink down into darkness. It feels so good to rest them, only for a moment. And then I will get up.

17

THE HOSPITAL IS A blur. I want only to sleep, but the nurses and doctors have other ideas. They wake me every hour, shine lights into my eyes, prick my arms for blood, poke thermometers, order me to swallow chalky pills that catch in my throat, send me for scans and X-rays inside loud rooms filled with fluorescent lights that hurt my eyes and buzzing sounds that hurt my head.

At the end of all this, which has felt like weeks but has, in fact, only been forty-eight hours, they tell us I have a hairline fracture on my skull. The doctor tells me to rest for the remainder of the summer. No climbing trees, no contact sports. Nothing that will put stress on the fracture.

I have one question for her. 'Can I swim?'

'Pool or lake?'

'Lake.'

She shakes her head. 'Too unpredictable. Is there a pool nearby?'

This hasn't occurred to me until now.

'I could try our school's.'

'No high dives?' she asks.

I shake my head. 'No high dives.'

'You have no open injuries. Give it a week or two, let things settle, and then laps should be fine. You're making a good recovery.'

She looks at Dad, who is waiting to take me home. 'Lots of rest and no stress,' she tells him.

At home, the ten-speed is propped against the rails outside the door. At some stage over the past two days, Mom has recovered it from the marsh. The sofa bed is made up for me. She has piled it full of pillows and cushions and blankets, even though it is the middle of summer. I can't climb the stairs without her following behind, watching me in case I fall. I walk out into the yard, down the road and to the fence that separates Grandma's farm from our property. Mom doesn't follow me here. I poke around the barn and find a box of *Reader's Digest* condensed series she had dragged home from a garage sale one summer. I read through them one by one.

At the end of the first week, I hear her footsteps in the middle of the night. Mom wears a white nightdress, her hair hanging loose all around her face. I think I am dreaming until she crawls in beside me and we lie face to face. Here she is again, the stranger from my youth. She strokes my cheek and then my forehead where I hit the windscreen. The egg has reduced in size, and now it is black and yellow. Sammy says I am the colour of a bumblebee. It still hurts a little to smile.

'You asked about Billy,' she says.

This startles me. I didn't ask about Billy, not that I remember.

'You were in and out of consciousness on the way home after the accident.'

I have no recollection of this. It is strange, to lose a piece of time – and even more so to know that I met this stranger, my mother, on a different plane; when the borders of my body were shutting down, something else opened.

'Billy was my brother.' It seems to hurt her to speak his name. 'I let him down.'

I take her hand.

'And now, look how I've hurt you.'

'I'm OK, Mom,' I reassure her.

'I've made such a mess of things. I wish it were different.'

'You didn't mean it.'

She pulls her knees up to her chest, and it feels as though I am lying here with a sister – not Hare, but someone younger and more vulnerable. The house is quiet; the *whish* of the ceiling fan above us circulates a current of air, her hair wisping over her face. I brush it back behind her ears.

'My father brought home a little boat.' Her voice is sad. 'Sammy took it out all by himself. Wasn't that brave?' Her words send a shiver through my spine.

'Billy,' I correct.

She doesn't recognise her mistake, as though they've become one and the same in her world. 'Billy was laughing all the way out, and I'm waving at him, running along the shore, wading out into the water, calling to him to come back, asking him to wait for me. He was already so far out

by the time Rita started screaming and Dad started swimming out. The sun is setting. And Billy is rowing – rowing
and rowing. It could have been a bad dream – that's what
I kept saying. But it wasn't. He was rowing for Italy.' She
smiles. 'That's where I told him I would take him.' Her
breath catches as though it is all too overwhelming.

I squeeze her hand.

'And I stood there, surprised by how hard he could row.
I couldn't wait to tell everyone how good he was.' She
rakes her fingers through my hair. 'But the thing was – he
wasn't rowing. He didn't know how. And he was too small.
He could have never fought the currents back to shore.'
Her eyes look lost. 'I tried to follow him out.' She smiles
sadly. 'I waded as far as I could, but I couldn't reach him,
and Rita grabbed me back. I wish she had let me go. I
wish it had been me instead of Billy.'

'Mom,' I whisper into the dark.

She turns and stares up into the rafters.

'You don't have to talk about this, Mom. Everything is
all right. I'm all right.'

She turns to me and touches my face. 'Does it hurt?'
she asks.

I nod.

'Some things never stop hurting.'

*

In the morning, she is up and moving around the kitchen.
She stands in the doorway, watches me on the sofa, where
I am finishing the last book in the box.

'Are you sore, do you want a pill?'

I don't.

This last book is beyond my comprehension, but I read it anyway, just to keep someone else's words flowing through my head, to prevent my own thoughts settling. I don't understand much of *The Day of the Jackal*, apart from the fact that there is an assassin moving through a world that fails to understand the danger he poses, the terrible secrets he holds. When I close the last page, I am ready to get up from the sofa; ready for a new day.

18

DAD DROPS ME OFF at the high school on his way to work. I enter the pool through the showers, carrying a towel through the narrow, chlorine-filled corridor, out to the pool deck. The swimmers are in their lanes; there is no longer a leisurely feel to their movements as there is when they swim at the beach. They are focused now, a team with a mission.

Coach watches the swimmers from the side of the pool in deep concentration. He doesn't see me cross the deck toward him, holding my arms across my chest, feeling exposed. Aunt Rita says I am growing like a weed, but the material across the bust hasn't filled out yet, even though it has grown tauter. I am considering walking back toward the showers when Coach senses me and turns around, surprised by me standing there – and even more surprised when I tell him why I am here. He blows his whistle, directing the swimmers to take their marks for the relays. Once they take their places on the blocks, he blows the whistle twice and the swimmers dive into the water. He turns his full attention to me.

'Sorry,' he says, eyeing my goldenrod swimsuit. 'Try-outs were at the beginning of the summer.'

I don't know why it feels like so much depends on Coach saying yes. 'Please,' I plead. 'The doctor says I can't swim in the lake, it has to be a pool. Give me a chance?'

He is shorter than I am; he looks up into my face, which is burning with shame. I slouch now, apologetic for my height, for the fact I came all the way down here thinking I could just join the team. He eyes my broad shoulders, my yellow swimsuit; he looks doubtful.

'Can you swim?'

I nod.

He points to an unused lane at the far end of the pool. 'Warm up.'

I breathe again and thank him.

I stand taller as I walk toward the lane. I heed the doctor's warning and ease into the pool at the side. The water brings a cooling relief, dissolving my shame. I swim the first length, feeling inhibited, knowing he is watching. I start with my strongest stroke, the front crawl. I swim to the end of the lane and flip, turning off the wall. I swim the breaststroke back. By the second length, I have forgotten that I am on trial; I could be in the kettle lake swimming for the birch branch or out at the hook beyond the bay house. Everything else disappears. A whistle blows above my head.

At the edge of the pool, Moose and the rest of the team climb out and towel-dry, watching me. I swim to the edge.

'You have stamina,' Coach says, 'and speed. Swim meets are all over the county. We meet three mornings a week for the rest of the summer, and two afternoons at the beach. If you have a doctor's note, you can refrain from the lake swim, but you'll have to row a boat, be an extra pair of eyes. Agreed?'

I nod.

'And when school starts back in a few weeks we'll practise most mornings before classes begin, plus forty lengths at lunchtime. It's gruelling, not for sloths.'

I agree.

He lowers his voice. 'The truth is: everyone who tries out makes the team. We could use more competitors. What's your name?'

'Joanne Kennedy.'

'Right, Kennedy. You'll need a new suit. And a swim-cap.'

By the time I climb out of the pool, I have a place on the team.

I call Aunt Rita that night to ask her to take me to the city to buy the swimsuit. She says she'd be happy to, if I keep my promise to work a day or two a week in the Bait & Tackle. I don't recall making this promise. It was Lucinda who was interested in the job. But I guess we have a deal.

19

THE NEXT MORNING, I walk across the back of Grandma's field, climbing over a fence, walking along the Wildlife Refuge until I meet the marina road, keeping some promise Aunt Rita thinks I made.

When I come to the dirt track running between the shop and the marina, I stand gazing to the right, down the road, to where the dock juts out into the Great Lake. Sammy runs through the marsh with Albert and Gabe, catching bugs and snakes; they are covered from head to toe in muck. Sammy shouts out to me and I wave, envying his freedom.

On a day like this, the grey sky releases a steady drizzle over the Refuge. The days are still charged with heat, but there is an occasional break now, a reminder that fall isn't far away. The fishermen come to the slips early and leave late, respecting the solitude of the lake. In less than four weeks, the slips will be full of motorboats arriving for the open season on waterfowl. They will disembark and stay all day behind their duck blinds at the water's edge, even when the chill of autumn is here to stay. But now it is mostly deserted, except for a clinker-built trawler moored on a slip, the motor running. The wheelhouse is empty.

The pilot works on the deck, stooping over the stern, arranging his lines.

Inside the shop, Lucinda is in the middle of a stocktake. She ignores me until Aunt Rita instructs her to train me in the areas she has already shown her. Lucinda looks up from her clipboard and stares at my forehead.

'You OK?' she asks. I nod.

She reaches to straighten a shelf; her long-sleeved top lifts. I try not to notice the pale, pus-green crust growing over the crater where the cigarette left its mark.

We move around each other, uncertain, as though we are strangers. She shows me the wooden boxes holding assorted lures, hooks, spools of braided fishing-line. I shadow her as she deals with customers. She knows which weight the fishermen are looking for, which size sinker they need for bass, perch, pike. All this knowledge, when she has never been fishing once in her life.

When customers are slow, she shows me the dusters. We straighten the inside of the drawers of the old dressers Mom refinished. An assortment of ceramic knobs are attached to each drawer to identify what is within. She shows me the system, telling me to ask for something, like a sputterbug, for instance, or the hollow-body frogs. I say the name, and Lucinda replies with the correlating knob: 'China blue' or 'bevelled clear'. There are systems upon systems like this in Aunt Rita's shop, and it doesn't take long to figure them out, though it seems to leave the fishermen perplexed.

After Lucinda has shown me around, Aunt Rita puts us to work touching up the front of the shop. She seems to sense the change between us. She hands me a can of off-white paint and tells me to cover over the cerulean on the flower-boxes. 'Mom won't be happy,' I tell her.

'I'm not going all the way into the city to buy a blue can of paint. Maybe she'll get out of bed when she hears you're assaulting her flower-boxes.' Aunt Rita chuckles. 'And while you're at it, tell her the geraniums are dead.'

She sets Lucinda to touching up the fish above the door. Lucinda is a good worker, it seems, and this alone is enough to redeem her in Aunt Rita's eyes. 'You stay off that ladder,' she warns me, before going back inside. 'One fall and you'll crack your head like an egg.'

'Get to work, Humpty Dumpty.' Lucinda smirks.

My lips want to curl, but I force a straight face and focus on prying open the lid on the can. We work in silence for the rest of the morning.

When we finish, Lucinda tells Aunt Rita that we have decided to go for a swim. Aunt Rita gives her a look and tells her to go boil the kettle.

'We're hot, we don't want tea – we want to swim,' Lucinda says.

I search the storage room for the toaster. I don't want her to think that Lucinda and I want the same things.

'It's all relative,' Aunt Rita is telling her when I return. 'A hot drink tricks you into thinking you're cold.'

'We're dying of heat, aren't we?' Lucinda turns to me for support.

I shrug, maintaining my distance, placing bread into the toaster. Aunt Rita takes three plates out from under the counter, overspill from a mismatched china collection Mom bought at an estate sale. There had been crates of the stuff. Aunt Rita protested when Mom pushed some onto her, but she took them anyway, and it turns out they are useful for displaying fly-hooks, herring rigs, feathers, weights – anything small and plentiful enough to pile onto the dishes. Once, when I was in the shop with Sammy, buying bait, I heard a local man comment, chuckling, 'China in a bait shop.'

Now, Aunt Rita brings out a jar of yellow mustard and some canned northern pike that a regular fisherman caught, pickled and bottled especially for Aunt Rita.

Lucinda wrinkles her nose.

'Try it,' Aunt Rita insists, shovelling in a mouthful. 'You'll love it.'

The bells ring on the front-door. Aunt Rita sends me out to serve the customer. My heart bounces when I see Martin. He is smaller than I remember, standing there in the shop. His cheeks are gaunt, but he isn't wasted drunk, the way I have seen him the last three times. He stands straighter, somehow. Still, he catches me off guard, and I back toward the door, toward the counter where Aunt Rita is pushing toast into her mouth. She shoves the rest in and takes a gulp of tea, brushing her hands on her trousers, She pushes past me.

'What can I do for you, sir?' she asks, overcompensating for my rudeness.

'What?' Lucinda mouths.

I shake my head. She peers around the doorframe. I motion for her to stop.

'Fuck.' Her eyes grow wide when she sees him. 'Do you think he's here to tell on us?'

She peeks her head around the doorframe.

'Stop it,' I hiss.

'I need some fuel,' he tells Aunt Rita.

'Petrol or diesel?'

'Oh, I think maybe diesel. It's my first time filling up.' His voice is shaky. 'I'm sorry, I'm not exactly certain. I'm borrowing the boat. For a while.'

'Don't worry,' Aunt Rita tells him. 'We'll figure it out.'

'I could call the owner.'

'Go on, use my phone.' She points to the maroon phone on the wall, hanging from the wood panels behind the counter.

'I have his number somewhere.' He searches through a tatty leather billfold. 'Everett Reed is the man. He's got that land back there. He's back at the university now for a while, but he's helping me out some.'

'Oh, Everett. I know Everett. I'll just call him.'

She picks up the receiver and dials the professor's number by heart.

'It's long distance. I'll pay the charge.'

Aunt Rita waves Martin's offer away. She waits for the person on the other end to answer. When the professor picks up, Aunt Rita talks like they are old friends.

When she hangs up, she calls me to her, hands me the keys to the diesel pump. 'Joanne will head down with you now to the dock.'

When he sees me, he recognises me. He takes a step back. 'That's OK, ma'am. I can look after myself.'

'Well, you aren't going to get far with the lock on the pump.'

I think I will faint. I shoot a glance toward Lucinda, and she takes my hint.

She stands up now, off her stool. 'I'll come, too.'

Martin, when he sees Lucinda, also looks like he will faint. I feel a small warmth of gratitude toward her.

'Don't you girls go near that water,' Aunt Rita says.

Martin puts a twenty-dollar bill on the counter. 'Mighty thankful.'

'Anything else?'

He wants to look at the fifty-pound braided fishing-line. He intends to catch some mighty big fish, I think. I use the moment to run out the door and get a head start to the marina, so that I won't have to walk with him. Lucinda follows.

The trawler is parked in front of the pumps. I uncap his fuel tank and fill it up while Lucinda waits on shore, staring Martin down. As he makes his way back to the trawler, she throws him dirty looks. He shifts uncomfort-ably at the side of the dock, and when I finish, he nods his thanks. He hesitates, as though he wants to say some-thing to me, then he boards the vessel.

When we come back up from the docks, Aunt Rita waits at the door. I think she will give us another job, but instead she folds her arms and won't let us pass.

'We don't judge people,' she tells us. 'We treat everyone with dignity in this shop. You have no idea what that man has been through, and neither do I, but we start with dignity.'

'You wouldn't say that if you knew what he did to Joanne,' Lucinda tells her.

I stare at her, warning her with a look. I wonder, has she forgotten that it was her in the van, undressed, John poised to start the business on *her*?

Aunt Rita looks at me, stunned.

I close my eyes and shake my head.

Aunt Rita maintains her sternness. 'Joanne knows she can tell me if there is anything I need to know. In the meantime, this town is full of people who judge on appearances and proliferate unfounded gossip – but it won't happen in my shop.'

'Fine,' Lucinda says and pushes past her.

Aunt Rita looks at me, and her sternness changes to a question. I shake my head. I wish she'd suggest I go home early. My head is beginning to pound.

I walk into the shop and pick up the dust-cloth, wiping a shelf that I have already dusted.

When Mr McCarthy picks Lucinda up at the end of her shift and it is just Aunt Rita and me, she corners me, wanting to know what happened with Martin.

I shrug and tell her it was nothing.

'Nothing,' she repeats, shaking her head. 'Always the secrets.'

20

I HAVE SPEED, COACH tells me. And I have strength. But I can't swim.

'You're built like an Olympic swimmer,' he tells me after my first Monday practice. 'But you don't know how to use your machine. You've got to make all the parts work together.'

I agree, nodding, though I have no idea what he means.

'There are three things you need to do.' He crouches down, hands on knees. I crouch, too; he places his hand on my shoulder. We huddle as though he is telling me a secret. 'Number one: get in the water. Number two: move forward. Number three: breathe. Watch.' He claps his hands. 'Hansen!'

Moose comes toward us.

'Meet your new partner. Kennedy, watch how it's done.'

Moose climbs up on the starting block.

'50 yards, Hansen.'

He blows his whistle, and she dives, swims the length of the pool and back. Her strokes are flawless.

Coach instructs me to do the same.

I do front crawl all the way to the end of the pool. I know my arms; my hands are placed exactly in the position they need to be. My body speeds forward. I flip at the end of the pool and come back, bobbing expectantly in front of him. That felt good, and I did my best.

'Don't *act* like you're swimming,' he shouts. '*Swim.*'

My face burns. I don't know what more I can do. I begin to feel that he is sorry, that he will tell me he has made a mistake.

'Do it again.'

I swim the lane. He isn't any happier on my return.

'You swim like you learned from the back of a Cracker Jack box. You've got to *propel* yourself forward. Come on.' He waves his hand, directing me to climb out of the pool, but then he walks away, clasping his hands together, pacing with nervous fervour.

I bite my lip and look to Moose for direction.

'Go,' she tells me, a deep dimple appearing at the side of her mouth. 'He's going to tell you about bicycles.'

I climb out of the pool.

'Don't worry,' she tells me. 'He does this to everybody.'

'Dive, pull, kick, breathe.' He claps his hands to emphasise each word. 'Your kicks are fine. Your strokes and breath need work. We'll deal with the rest later.'

He circles me like a raptor deciding where to land. 'Dive,' he mimes. 'Pull.' He taps the bones in my back, the ones that jut out like the triangles of chickens' wings.

'See here, your scapula propels your arm. Your arm doesn't propel your scapula.'

201

'Scapula?'

'Shoulder blades. You've got to move *forward*. What you're doing is moving them wide, like you're sweeping out to catch a ball.'

I am sure I am not going as wide as he demonstrates. Everyone on the team stops to watch.

'This isn't basketball. This is swimming. You've got to think of a crank.'

If it was any other teacher, I think I would have burst into tears, but something in his manner – his intensity mixed with kindness – and the others giving me supportive looks and sympathetic nods, makes me catch a fit of the giggles. Moose smiles wide, too.

'Crank. You got me?' He tries again. 'Crank! Pay attention.'

'Crank?'

'A crank, a crank – a bicycle crank,' he hollers as though the volume of his words will force an understanding. 'The thing that turns when you put your feet to the pedals. Am I going to have to bring my bicycle down here to show you how to swim?'

The rest of the team laughs. I smile, clutching my cheekbones so that he won't see.

'Give me 250 kicks,' he shouts, without looking back at the team. They groan and splash back into the water.

'Never mind them,' he says. 'They'd rather be at the zoo. But you, you're a swimmer, I can tell. Come on.'

He comes in close and taps my back again. His intention is unmistakable. There is nothing more important to him in the world in this moment than to reach me, to make me understand. I focus on his words; I really want to get him, too.

'This here is the crank. And here' – he pounds his own chest – 'here is the pulley. You are not a girl. You are a simple machine! You get these parts to move like you're turning a bicycle – move them in a circle. Your arms will come into it later – forget them for now. You're not reaching outwards, not swooping. Move forward! Propel yourself from here. Feel the power in these shoulders.' His face is red. He thrusts his palm on my muscle. He comes in really close then, as though he has a secret. 'You get this right, and you're going to kill anyone you swim against. Even Hansen. Got me? Go home, ride your bicycle, and see how it feels to turn that wheel. That's how I want you to move tomorrow. Got me?'

21

After practice, Aunt Rita takes me to the city for my team swimsuit. The red bus smells of earth. She is transporting worms to the city, making double use of the trip.

'How's the swimming going?' she asks.

'Fine.'

I usually don't mind the hour drive to the city, but today it feels long. She reaches the crossroads and waits for the traffic to pass in both directions, then turns onto the main road. I watch the cornfields pass.

'You're not yourself these days,' she says after a while. I wonder if her motive for agreeing to this trip is to have this conversation. 'And I don't think it's that bump on your head. Have you and Lucinda had a falling out?'

I shake my head, not sure why she thinks Lucinda could be my only problem when everything at home is in upheaval. Every time I walk back through the sliding door, I feel sick with relief that Mom is still here, that she hasn't run off to the city or to Italy with Everett, the *love* professor now in the habit of lending boats to frightening, frightened homeless men – and relieved when I hear Sammy is at Aunt Rita's and not at home. And once this relief has passed, I feel angry and then guilty almost at once, knowing how sad Mom is all the time. It is exhausting being trapped in this cycle, waiting for your mother to abandon you, waiting for some unknown catastrophe to befall you.

'I'm afraid,' I blurt out. 'I'm afraid Mom is leaving us.'

Aunt Rita considers her answer. 'She hasn't gone anywhere yet, honey. Mothers only leave for a good reason, and the reason is never because of her children. She loves you dearly; she is trying to stay.'

I try hard to squeeze my lids, to swallow the tears, keep them from spilling.

'Your poor mom – she hasn't had an easy life.'

And then it is out. It breaks, like a dam, before I can contain it. 'I know about Billy . . .'

'Oh, Billy.' Her voice aches. 'So, your Mom spoke about him, finally?'

'Sort of.'

She tilts her head.

'Mom told me bits, but I already read about it, in the library archives.'

She tilts her head to the other side, like I am an odd bird she wants to identify. 'The archives?'

'Miss Hughes showed me a scrap-book about the accident.'

Aunt Rita looks at me like she can't believe what she is hearing. 'This town,' she says, then she shakes her head as though shaking it off. 'Honey, all you have to do is ask. *I'm* not secretive.' She shifts the bus into a higher gear. 'It was our father's idea to come here from the city. He had this dream about getting back to a life he remembered as a boy.'

205

She tells me her own childhood, growing up in Detroit. A female doctor – unusual in those days – delivered Mom, Aunt Rita's new baby sister. The doctor wanted to adopt her. She remembers this most of all.

'That woman delivered babies into poor families every day. I'm sure she didn't offer to take every neglected child home.' Aunt Rita speaks quietly, one arm on the steering wheel, the other stroking the side of her neck. I am listening. 'She saw something in your mother. I don't know what it was. A vulnerability. She could see that in your mother, even as a baby.

'Our father and mother came out to Kettle Lake one weekend on a whim. When he saw the bay house at Mulberry Point, he remembered it as being something grand and couldn't believe his luck that they could rent the place so cheap. But it wasn't grand. It was damp and cold, and I can still feel the chill all the way through to my capillaries.' She shudders. 'The town wasn't impressed with us – for the fact our father claimed to have roots in this area when he was so clearly an outsider. That, and we were poor. To some people, that is an unforgivable character flaw.'

The corn outside my window rushes by at a dizzying pace.

'Our father figured life would work out the way it was working out in his head. He was a dreamer and could never get those dreams to function. That's where your mother gets it from.' She glances at me. 'They were both big drinkers. Our parents took good care of us when they were sober, but when they started drinking, that was another story. Our mother would get lonely – she wanted

206

to leave for the city, and our father would take her. They'd forget we existed. It's hard to imagine that kind of neglect, I know.' She clicks her tongue. 'But that's how it was in those days. They left us for days out here on the Point, sometimes a week at a time. I had to go to the neighbours and ask for food.' Her hands tighten on the steering wheel; her knuckles come up white.

'The Kennedys,' I say.

'That woman – I know she's your grandmother – it is hard to believe people can be so unkind and unforgiving, especially to children.'

'They didn't feed you?' I ask.

'They did, of course. They did what they thought was their duty. But that woman let us know nothing was free. That daughter of hers is still letting us know.'

I watch her now, her lips pressed together. You don't need tears to feel sorrow; it is etched all over her face.

'Instead of giving us food and tutting at us as we went off, they should have done us the favour of calling social services. Billy might still be alive.'

'You miss him.'

'He was eight years old. I think of him all the time. Every time I see Sammy – he looks just like him, you know. Your mother was thirteen when Billy died. We all loved him, our Billy, but Rosemary and he were especially close. She hated to see him cold, or hungry, suffering in any way. She told him stories about the ships passing across the lake. She brought him out to the hook, and they'd watch the freighters slip by on the horizon.'

Shivers run up my back.

'They used our father's binoculars, took note of every ship that passed, wrote each name they could read in a little book. I still have that book. I kept it. The *Edmund Fitzgerald* passed once – can you believe it? Bringing iron ore into the city. What an exciting day that was.' She smiles, but her smile quickly fades. 'It was probably a premonition, too.'

There is a long pause.

'They didn't always do the right thing by us, but Dad always managed to remember to bring home a Christmas tree or an old car. And then he brought home the rowboat.'

She sighs. 'Your father found Billy. He had been out every day looking for him. Danny was only a young teenager, but he had the presence of mind to recover him from the water, alert the police. He came to our door to tell us. He wouldn't let us go down, knowing what we would find. I don't know where that family got him.' She sniffs, and I see the girl she once was. 'Your mother would kill me if she knew I was telling you this.'

I want to touch her shoulder. She wipes her cheek with the back of her hand.

We come to a stop sign at the edge of the city. A yellow warbler alights on the sign. The notes come through the open window. We watch him together, and when he flies away, Aunt Rita turns right.

I imagine Dad finding the child. I can't bear it for him. It strikes me that maybe this is what Mom and Dad thought they had in common, a shared grief that bound them for a time. There seems to be nothing shared now.

'After Billy and our father drowned, our father's sisters came,' she tells me. 'They sat around hating Mom, and then they went home. No one helped our mother. No one helped us. She died shortly after they took us away.'

In the quiet that follows I think of the rumours, remember what Hare said to Mom the day of my haircut.

'Did you actually see Billy in the boat?' I ask.

'The boat was too far out when my father and I arrived on the scene. Rosemary had waded so far into the water, I followed her while my father tried to reach—' She stopped suddenly, guessing what I am getting at. 'What do you want to know?' she asks, sternly.

'Do you believe Mom . . . that she . . .' I already know the answer.

'Intentionally drowned our brother and set him off in the boat to cover it up?' She sounds cross. 'No, I do not. And your father does not believe this either. Nor do the authorities. I know what people have said for years. I don't even think they believe your mother could hurt a child – but that is some people for you: vicious.'

My throat is heavy.

We don't speak for a while, but it feels easy sitting beside her.

'Aunt Martha – Mrs McCarthy's mother, God rest her soul – she saved us from the orphanages. For a thousand Grandmother Kennedys, you can find one Aunt Martha. She didn't have to help us. But sometimes I wonder if it would have been better for your mother if she had left Kettle Lake.'

So much sadness. 'Why didn't your father's family help?'

Aunt Rita shakes her head. 'I don't know. It was different in those days. Everyone had so little. But I do know that

I can't turn my back on anyone in need. And I know I'm not alone on that one. Look at that man you met the other day, Martin, in the shop, the one you girls were saying horrible things about—'

'I wasn't saying horrible things—'

'I heard what Lucinda said. If something happened – you need to tell me.' She looks concerned.

'It wasn't like that,' I say. I tell her the truth. How Lucinda went willingly into John's van, how Martin made a pass at me while we were waiting for them to return. How distressed he was when he learned we were still in high school and that Lucinda was the McCarthys' foster child.

She slows the bus down until I think she will stop in the middle of the road.

'Did he touch you, honey?'

'No!' I insist. 'Well, yes, but not the way you're thinking. We didn't *do* anything. He apologised once he knew.'

'Men.' Aunt Rita is furious and disgusted. She puts her foot to the pedal and the van speeds forward. 'Don't make excuses for either of those adults. None of it is right, even if he apologised.'

I nod.

'But saying that, it also isn't right Lucinda insinuated something happened against your will if it did not. That's how lives get ruined,' Aunt Rita says. 'And how people who need to be believed don't end up getting believed. Let your word be your word, then stand by your truth,' she tells me, and I know she is right.

I think about what my truth might be.

Aunt Rita pulls into a space in the shopping mall. She rummages around in her bag and pulls out a packet of tissues. We both blow our noses and wipe our eyes. She takes my hand and squeezes it. 'Come on, let's get your suit.'

We walk through the centre of the mall, looking for the sports store Coach has sent me to find. I watch shoppers glancing at Aunt Rita, eyeing up her gabardine pants. I am glad she has taken off her rubber boots and put on a pair of white canvas shoes.

'Not everyone thrives, you know.' She lets the weight of this sink in. 'It's our hope, but not our birthright.'

I think of the tundra swans. Now that summer is drawing to a close, those who can fly will be gathering strength. In late fall, they will return in great flocks, and for a few days, the Wildlife Refuge will ring with their chorus once again, a plea: pick me, pick me, pick me. They will come in a collective force with only the strong, the weakened young abandoned days ago amid the wind and whistling of disappearing wings: the last sound on the Alaskan tundra, the weak now lost amongst the cotton-sedge.

'Everyone is doing what they can for your mother – we are all trying,' Rita tells me.

'Not Dad,' I blurt, feeling the rage of this truth. 'Not Maureen.'

'OK, maybe Maureen's not trying. But your father, honey, he is a good man. I don't know where he came from in a family like that. But he loves your mother. You know that. He just doesn't know how to help. None of us do.'

'You went through a hard time, and you're all right.'

'Oh, I had my share of difficult periods.'

We stop at an ice-cream counter, and she orders two chocolate cones. We take napkins and sit on a bench by the fountain.

'I always knew something your mother didn't: you must look after yourself. If you get into trouble, it's your own fault. Either you are helpless, or you take responsibility. But you don't have to take on another person's trauma. You either pick it up and carry it, or you put it down. There was a time I was lost, and I came to the edge and said, "Rita, you have to lay this down or it will bring you right over the edge. Go under or survive." And I chose to survive.'

Mom didn't choose her lack of strength, I tell her. Like the weaker tundra swans who get left behind, she didn't choose this fate. 'I don't think you're being fair,' I say.

She almost smiles, considering my point. Something shifts between us in this moment. 'There is something in that. My own mother used to get indignant when she told us that story about that doctor at your mother's birth. "I kicked her right out of the house," she'd say, and you could hear the pride in her voice. But that was a good offer for your mother. She would have thrived in another place, in another time. It's a mystery. It's the nature versus nurture conversation, again and again. What makes us fragile? What makes us strong?'

I don't have an answer.

'Finish your ice cream,' Aunt Rita tells me, licking the drips from her own. 'Let's get that swimsuit. I must get

212

home to my boys. And you have swim practice in the morning.'

I wiggle my tongue into the point of the cone, fishing out the last lick, then stick the rest of it in my mouth.

'You know,' Rita says as though something has only just occurred to her. 'What we see as your mother's weakness might actually be her strength. Your mother needs beauty. She doesn't function in its absence. Yes, I mean her antiques and the way she has the eye to arrange a pile of junk into a design masterpiece – but also, she needs beauty in her environment. She always has. She needs to belong. She doesn't seem to have that self-protection screen that Maureen and I have. We are selfish creatures, Maureen and I. Your mother, on the other hand – she assumes the good, the beauty, in everyone. Your mother loved Danny. She loved his family. She thought he could absorb her into them, absorb her pain, that she could belong because he belonged. That is all she has ever wanted. Just to absorb into the beauty of the Point, into the beauty of the farm, into the beauty all around her. It broke my heart to see. I warned her – I knew what was coming. Exclusion hurts. Your father can't fathom her pain because he doesn't experience it. He belongs. He still has everything he has ever had.

'But Maureen and her mother – forgive me – it seems like the whole purpose of their existence is to find people to feel above, to feel better than. They are the kind of people who need vulnerable people like your mother. They need somebody . . . if not to hate, to exclude. They thought they were better than your mother because of our family's poverty, our tragedy. They couldn't get over Danny's association with her; it tarnished their family. I told her from the start that it wasn't a good idea.'

Aunt Rita has a lot of opinions, not all of which I agree with, but I know she is right about this one.

We find the store and she buys my bathing-suit and swim-cap. On the road home, we pass the Bait & Tackle; the lights are on in Rita's house. 'Who's with the boys?' I ask.

'Marylou,' she says and smiles.

We ride along in silence for a while.

'You asked how I survived. Well, Marylou is one way. I hope you find a friend like Marylou.'

There is a faint trace of pink in the outline of the sky. A family of sandhill cranes lift off the marsh, their silhouettes edged in gold under the setting sun. Aunt Rita flips on the headlights.

'What can I do?' I ask as she turns past Maureen's farm and turns onto our lane.

'Keep doing what you're doing. Love your mom. But mostly, you must make a choice, too, you know? Are you going to pick it up – her trauma? Or are you going to lay it down?'

'How?' I ask.

She thinks about this. 'You talk. Don't keep your secrets inside. And then you find something. Find something bigger than yourself, bigger than your surroundings, bigger than the damaged people around you – something you can put yourself into. For me, it was my boys and the shop – the shop, at first, because it was food for Albert and Gabe, but later it became something worth more than itself. For you, who knows? Find what you love.'

I think about what I love. The woods. Swimming. Is it enough?

'You'll find it,' she tells me. 'And sometimes it will find you. In time.'

There is nothing to do but believe her.

22

ONCE AUNT RITA PULLS away, I wheel my ten-speed out into the yard in the growing darkness, studying its workings. I turn it upside down and sit there looking at the chain ring, moving a pedal forward with one hand, watching the crank churn the gears. I remember sitting with Hare in the yard when we were small: how we turned our bicycles upside down, turned the pedals with our hands as though they were spinning wheels. We dropped mown grass into the chain-wheel like a miller's daughter turning straw into gold. We did this for hours, it seemed, under the warm summer sun.

Now, I let go of the pedal and move my shoulder blades like the crank. My arms move into place. Hare comes out from where she has been watching me from the sliding door, arms crossed; she shakes her head, then returns inside.

There is a sullen quiet hanging over the house. Mom either sleeps or stares at the walls. I wish she would go back to fussing like after the accident; for that first week she was full of life. Now, she doesn't even bother pulling up the blinds in her bedroom. She is still in her pyjamas when I come in. I think of a badger, slow and lethargic, tucking into its sett deep under the roots of a tree. When

Sammy isn't with Aunt Rita, he crawls right under the covers and snuggles in the blankets with her. He is here now; the lights from the television flicker on the wall.

I want to climb in with them, too, under the covers: feel her warmth, hug her until her sadness leaves. Instead, I pick up a book from her bedside and try to make out the pictures in the dim light: an Italian landscape, scenes from another world. As I turn the pages, I disappear from this house, this terrible emptiness growing inside like a fallen tree giving way to the hollowing rot of dead wood.

A letter falls out. I am certain I have come across something I am not meant to see. I wish I'd told Aunt Rita about the professor while I had the chance. I will tear this letter to pieces, flush it down the toilet.

I slip it under my T-shirt and bring it down the hall, into the bathroom, locking the door. I am surprised to see familiar, neat handwriting across the front: *Rosemary* is written in Maureen's tiny scrawl.

Dear Rosemary,

I know you haven't been well, and I should probably call the house and find out how you are. But it really annoys me that you once again ruined something special for our family. The sesquicentennial celebration was a time for my people to come together and celebrate who we are. It was also a 'welcome home' event of sorts. I cannot fathom what a spiteful person you are to both sabotage the Kennedy family once again and bring your own daughter to harm. Even if you didn't drive off the road in an act of attention-seeking, I suspect it might have been an unconscious act of sabotage. You had it in your mind from the very beginning that you would get our farm; we know this is why you married our brother. I want to assure you, if it hadn't been for you, this would be Danny's life; the farm is his inheritance, but how can we trust one hundred and fifty years of history to you when you can't manage a single day?

He has made his bed.

I'm sorry if you 'haven't had a great life' but honestly, wasn't that a long time ago? Get over yourself and get on with life. Count yourself lucky to have what you have.

Just a warning about your 'extracurricular' affairs. As though your antics at the balloon festival weren't humiliating enough, you were spotted, and you know what I mean. Don't drag Danny and your children through your misery endlessly. If you're going, leave.

I hope, saying all this, that you're doing better than Danny says you are.

Maureen

My hands shake. I walk down the stairs into the living room, scrunching up the letter and the envelope. I place them into the cold firebox, light a match. The ends curl slowly; flames spread across the paper. I watch until the hateful words disappear, and the flames burn out in the cold grate.

I return to Mom now. A vase beside her bed holds the wildflowers she picked the day I saw her coming from the professor's cabin. A dust of dried Queen Anne's lace settles on the top of the nightstand; the water smells like a stagnant pond in hot summer. I take the vase from the room and pour the water out. I wash the glass.

She stares at the wall when I return; the covers are pulled up to her neck even though the evening is warm. Sammy stares at the television. He grasps her toe as though it is a hand. I feel a downrush of ache off Mom, fractals of pain. I pick up the picture book from her bedside and open it to a page depicting an Italian city, blue hills in the background, a dusty orange sunset. I want the professor to transport her to this place, to rescue her from the awful hatred of Maureen, of this town, deliver her from Kettle Lake and all its limitations; he can have her, if it means he will give her this cathedral, this street, this dome bulging out of the cityscape like a hot-air balloon rising majestically into the sky.

I close the book and climb in beside her and put my arms around her. She lifts slightly in the bed and lets me fold into her. I can feel her tremble.

The other day in the woods, sitting under a tree by the lake, a lacewing landed, unaware, on the landscape of my knee. Did it feel the warmth of my skin? Did it know my hand hovered, ready to crush its filmy wings? How beautiful and frail – how unfair this world is.

I hold Mom close and let my warmth pass through her cold hands, forget what Aunt Rita said about laying it down. Mom's sadness permeates like water through mesh. The marsh holds water from melted snow until it finds its course. *I will hold this,* I think again and again and again inside my head. *I will hold this for you.*

When Dad comes through the door later in the evening, the rage I felt at Maureen earlier transfers to him. I want to scream, yell, lash out, tell him he is failing – that he deserves to lose her. But he looks so tired warming up his dinner that my anger diffuses before he even sits down at the table. It feels like forever until I can leave this unhappy house, this unhappy town.

Lying in bed, I think about Lucinda – Lucinda at the McCarthys' farm. I'm sure Mrs McCarthy gives her what she needs to survive: food, warmth, clothing. But beyond this, I wonder; is she loved? By anyone in this world? Which emollient has she for the pain of losing everything? And still, she brought me a cold bag of peas for my head. There is something alive in her, like Mom, wanting to thrive.

But hurt doesn't lessen. Its rot spreads and grows, hidden, but not dormant: woodworm tunnelling through the timber, eating out the joists. By the time it is noticed, it is too late. The pain is already bringing down the house.

23

THE MOMENT I TOUCH water, the *knowing* returns. I coil and lunge, push against the wall, turn the blades, propel forward. I am fast, now faster – now faster again. Coach chases me down the pool; swimmers stop in their lanes. I lead with a catch, turning outstretched hands through water, now air, spinning straw into gold. All else disappears. There is no Mom, no Lucinda, no Hare, no Cathy – only my shoulders flowing, freeing my form, pulling through water like sculpture: *The Winged Victory of Samothrace*, Nike rising from stone.

Swimming solves some things. But it doesn't solve everything. Out of the water, the weight, the worry return.

Mom works in the basement; she is revived as though a defibrillator has brought her back to life. She doesn't stop moving. At first, she varnishes and sands. Then she downs the tools and picks up paintbrushes. She doesn't sleep. I hear her all night, rummaging through drawers; she seems intent on a mission, though she hardly knows what she aims to achieve. Her antiques lie where she left off, like the remains of an abandoned life, ash-covered artefacts of Pompeii. She takes up painting now; her workshop fills with canvases. At first, she paints empty streets.

And then a boy begins to appear. Mostly on his own, but later, a girl has taken his hand, and sometimes they run together through the streets of Italy. It is hard to see from their backs, but I swear, the two of them could be Sammy and me.

One night, she brings me a pair of scissors and sends me out under the dimming sky to collect cattails by the handful. The tips of their grasses are beginning to bronze, but the seed holds fast to the stalk. I walk through the dry marsh and stand at the edge of the lake. An oriole sits on the dead birch in the middle. It flies off in a streak of orange to a higher branch in the pines, scolding into the dead wood: *sweet, sweet, sweet!*

The cabin stands empty on the hill. The professor has not returned. The shutters are down and nailed closed for the coming season. It seems to me, with his leaving, that he has carried some threat away from Kettle Lake. Mom is busy or happy – or both. It may be the same thing to her.

Sometimes, I hear her moving in the kitchen late at night. She arranges the breakfast bowls for morning, and then she moves down to the workshop. There are no sounds of painting or filling of jars, so I imagine she sits and stares and thinks, perhaps about stepping into one of her paintings – stepping out of her life and onto the warm cobbles of a narrow street in Italy. Perhaps, she is finding the beauty Aunt Rita thinks important to her life. I hope this will be enough.

I gather an armful of cattails and return to the house.

The clink of wood against glass rises up from the basement. Mom preps a canvas. Her workshop smells of damp and mothballs. New paintings lie drying, scattered across the tops of half-finished cabinets, a hallway table, a new Kalamazoo range: projects she abandoned at the margins of her workshop in the cause of her latest pursuit.

Mom sits in front of an easel, on one of the wooden high stools she restored: one foot on the rung, the other balancing on the cement-poured floor. There is a quietness to how she perches, studying the mottle of blue and green oils prepped on the canvas.

She nods to the workbench when she sees my armful of cattails. Her chisels and sandpaper, bottles of spirits and turpentine, are removed, tossed into a tool-kit underneath the bench. Now, jars of clouded water and paintbrushes are scattered like an array of hair sticks, tubes of pigment dinted and rolled at the ends like toothpaste; all of this has replaced the usual mess. I push a pile of rags to one side and pull a glass vase from the back of the worktop to arrange them – but she turns me around.

'You're so tall,' she says, as though she has only noticed, the way a distant relative might after too many summers pass. She tucks a wisp of hair behind my ears. 'You take my breath away,' she tells me. 'Do you know you are beautiful?'

She asks this as though she wonders if I know my own shoe size. I study her face and look for clues to the reason why she sees me here, right now, in this moment.

'It's important you know this,' she continues. 'It's important you know what you can have in this life.'

I look into her face when she parts my bangs. A most peaceful expression rests there, distant and soft. We reach one another in this moment: Venus, brighter than any star, illuminous and remote, broadcasting its mere point of light. I want to confide in her, tell her the things I know, connect the way I connected with Aunt Rita.

But then Mom looks at me from different angles, as though sizing me up to fit a dress. She leads me to a small stool in front of her easel, positions me sideways, arranges the cattails so that I am cradling them, an array spilling from my arms. I stroke the soft velvet brown of a stalk, pinch at the seed. It comes away like stuffing from a sofa cushion. She takes up her paintbrush and stands in front of her easel. I will not disturb this moment.

'Look over there.' She points to the wall. 'Pretend you are gazing off into the distance.'

I imagine I am looking out over the lake.

She takes a piece of charcoal and moves it around the page with brisk, energetic strokes.

When she comes to the finer detail, she draws the easel close, resting her brush, and looks at me; she sweeps her finger over my cheek, touches my forehead as though remembering. The bruising has faded. The accident has left no mark.

'I'm sorry I hurt you,' she whispers.

'You didn't. I'm OK.'

'Your hair is growing out.'

I touch it. It is still short but it is beginning to take on a shaggy appearance.

'Have you been to Italy?' she asks.

I want to think she is getting better. But I know she is not.

'No, of course you haven't.' She laughs. 'You'll love it, though – I hope you'll visit.'

This should be my sign. After everything Aunt Rita has said about Billy, after what Mom said about rowing to Italy. But Mom is talking now about the colours of Tuscany, how it feels to walk on the warm cobbles without shoes. The longing in her words should alarm me. Instead, they console, make me believe – believe that she will walk those streets, believe her dream.

She returns to the painting. I watch her out of the corner of my eye. This is a different woman to the one I know.

And then I realise, I don't truly know her at all. I never really did.

24

WITH SUMMER ENDING AND both waterfowl and hunting season opening in rapid succession, the Friday of Labor Day weekend is the busiest time of year. In between stock-ordering and rotation, Aunt Rita has slipped down to the water's edge, upending boats, setting them on sawhorses for her boys and Sammy to prime. She goes back up to check in a group of youths at the boat rental. She is antsy about leaving the boys down near the docks, but they know well enough not to go into the water. She instructs Lucinda to go down and help them, but then a delivery arrives from the city, and she diverts both of us to unload the truck.

'I'll be so happy when those boys are back in school.' She sighs, handing me a box off the dolly. 'I know they'd never go into that water, but my nerves are just about shot this summer, keeping all of you alive. I can't turn my back without thinking those boys are going to fall down a hole.'

Behind her, the oddity of the statement takes Lucinda off guard. She raises her shoulders and hides her mouth behind the box she holds, but her sniggers escape anyway.

Both Aunt Rita's foreboding and Lucinda's giggles are making me jittery. When Aunt Rita bends down to slide a stack of newly arrived galvanised buckets across the floor, we turn to each other and crack up laughing.

'I'm not paying you girls to sit around acting like fools.'

This makes us laugh even harder.

She sends us outside to stack forty-pound bags of birdseed the driver has dumped. We each take the sides of a bag, the way you might take the hands and feet of a small child, carry them across to the lean-to and swing them up onto a tall stack. The weight of the bags sobers us, but then Lucinda's shoulders start to shake again. I echo her trembles like aftershocks.

We struggle to put the last bags on top of the stack, which is reaching near the roof of the lean-to. The final bag tumbles and splits, spilling all over the pavement.

Aunt Rita sticks her head out the door. 'Lord Almighty – have some sense, girls,' she tells us. 'That stack will kill a small child if it comes down. Make two piles.' She closes the door a little too hard.

We begin to pull down the top bags, rearranging the tower into two piles. Sweat collects on my upper lip and across my forehead, even here in the shade.

'On second thoughts' – Aunt Rita pops back out – 'you shouldn't be doing that heavy lifting. One of those bags will split your head like a pumpkin.'

Lucinda's laugh has a sinister edge.

I am glad when Aunt Rita turns to me, sends me on an errand.

'Ride on out to Marylou's – she'll be waiting for you to collect some brass hooks. Your mother has another hare-brained idea for a display,' she says. 'It's not terribly urgent, but I suspect it will give your mother something to do when you kids go back to school.'

It seems like a ploy to keep me and Lucinda apart, a punishment for our giddiness – or maybe Rita senses some change in the barometer with Lucinda, too. Either way, I am glad to go.

'Marylou's?'

'Yes, you know where she lives? Out the road toward the lake?'

'With the tree growing out her porch?' I try not to sound too eager.

Lucinda looks at me with envy. I can't get to the ten-speed quick enough, in case Aunt Rita changes her mind, in case Lucinda convinces her to let her ride along. Aunt Rita turns to her while I am leaving.

'Go down to the marina and help those boys finish the boats. No one is to touch that water, you hear me?'

Lucinda narrows her eyes. I lift one hand off the handlebar as if to say *what can I do*? She turns and heads down toward the water.

'You know where you're going now? Be careful,' Aunt Rita calls after me. 'Ride on the shoulder. She's expecting you.'

Once on the main road, the asphalt bakes under the sun. Oily puddles appear, stretching across the paving in the distance. I chase them with all the speed I can muster, trying to catch one, only to find the road dry and the heat mirage relocated to a new vanishing point farther up the road. The freedom of the open space amplifies the fact that these are the final days of summer. The sky is the bluest shade possible; thin, wispy veils of cirrus clouds stream high up in the sky.

It takes forty minutes to cycle along the road, and I think of Marylou all the way, the tree growing out of her house, her horsey smile. I pass the bends in the road where Mom drove us into the marsh. I stop on the shoulder, expecting to see a sign marking that day – skid marks on the road or a crush in the undergrowth. But there is nothing, only the buzz of cicadas and the occasional rattle of a dragonfly. I pick up speed now, until I see the edge of Marylou's lawn ahead.

Her heavy front-door stands open. I knock and wait on the steps, peering through the screen door. Notes from a classical piece of music drift through the open rooms from somewhere at the back of the house. Nothing stirs. I bang a little louder – and then harder, until the side of my hand turns red and aches from the effort.

I walk across the yard to the side, down under the willow tree where I first saw Marylou sitting that day. This is the best view of the top of the tree; the leaves on the crown are already beginning to change. A gate opens at the side of the house, nearest the glass room, and Marylou comes out, pushing a wheelbarrow. She wears the same straw hat and gardening gloves. She holds a pair of pruning shears under her arm.

'Oh, hello, Joanne,' she calls to me, like we are old friends. She parks the wheelbarrow and wipes sweat off her fore-head. 'I'm ready for my lunch – you hungry?' she asks.

I follow her back through the garden gate. In the kitchen, she makes me a grilled cheese sandwich and a plate full of sliced green apples. She drizzles honey inside the arrangement in the shape of a flower. She talks all the while. I listen and try to peer around the doors, hoping to glimpse the inside of the screened porch where the tree trunk grows up out of the ground.

When the sandwiches are golden and the cheese melts down the sides, she loads a tray with the plates and a jug of sweet iced tea, slices of lemon floating amongst the ice. We sit in the garden on wrought-iron chairs like the ones Mom has refinished. Everything in and outside Marylou's house is beautiful: her furniture, her antiques, her tree, her roses, Marylou herself.

'Your Aunt Rita is some woman,' she tells me. 'I quite admire her.'

I nod, wiping a string of cheese from my chin.

'I've known her now a long time. She was very young when she came to the city, before we both became businesswomen.'

'How did you meet her?' I ask.

'She lived with me for a short time, rented a room in my apartment in the city. That was before I opened the shop and moved out here. That's a long time ago. I never would have ended up out here in Kettle Lake if it weren't for her.'

'Do you sell worms, too?' I ask.

She chuckles, but not in an unkind way. 'Rita sells more than worms. She has a great sense for both business and nature, don't you think?'

I agree. 'What do you sell?' I ask.

'Old things. I have a shop in the city, The Treasure Chest. Do you know it?'

I do. We often walk by the window with Mom. Sometimes we go inside and walk through the many rooms, watching Mom run her fingers over the wood, coveting the collection of bedsteads, dressers, lampshades.

'Antiques, paintings, anything vintage and previously owned by people who are now, well, rather dead.'

I drink my tea slowly, afraid she will send me away once I finish. I tell her about Mom, reminding her that we stopped at her yard sale that day, how Mom bought a pair of nightstands and that she gave me the ten-speed, though I leave out the part about the accident on the way home.

'Of course, I remember.' She smiles. 'I feel I know your mother very well. Rita tells me all about Rosemary. Your mother is a connoisseur of fine things, I believe. I don't have room for everything that comes into my shop, and I have a lot of junk in this big old house. So, I have yard sales from time to time. Your mother, she has a good eye. She went straight to the finest things in that pile. I don't think she knew me, or somehow, I don't think she wanted to be recognised. Sometimes that happens to people, you know – sometimes they must move to another world for a little while, to forget the one they live in.' She winks at me then, and her smile turns mischievous. 'I know you saw the top of my tree, but do you want to see my tree room?'

We walk through the house and through a pair of French doors. Here, the trunk grows straight up through the room, breaking out of the tongue-and-groove roof. The floorboards curve in a three-foot diameter, circulating the base where the earth packs around the roots. Little blue flowers grow in clumps around small evergreen shrubs planted along the perimeter. Old tin signs hang from nails pounded into the bark: an advertisement for DAD'S OLD-FASHIONED ROOT BEER, another depicting a rooster crowing WAKE THE HELL UP.

'How often do you water it?' I ask, when she brings us two glass bottles of cola. We sit on the little sofa under the tree.

'Oh, I bring the hose in most days and give it a good wetting. That's mostly for the shrubs and flowers, though. The roots know how to find what they need. They go out two, three times longer than the tree is tall.'

I look down her lawn to imagine how far they spread, how far they sink down under the house. We sip our colas.

'It's nice having your company,' she tells me. 'Thanks for coming. It gets awful lonely around here since my boys went away.'

'Does your husband work in the city?' I ask.

She chuckles. 'I haven't had a husband since the boys were very small.'

I feel my face flush. 'Sorry'.

'Don't say sorry,' she says. 'We didn't make each other happy. Besides, I like being on my own, most of the time.' There is something about Marylou – complete and bountiful, she offers herself like the habitat of a marsh, a refuge for the returned. I know I can tell her anything. So, when her face tilts sideways with concern and she asks, 'Everything OK, kiddo?' I confide in her, talk to her about something that has been on my mind.

It's not about Mom or Lucinda – but about Cathy, how, I wonder, was there something I should have done? Might I have spared her family's grief if I had recognised the signs, recognised that she was drowning?

'You bring a lot on yourself. Sounds to me like you didn't see a girl drowning – you saw a girl floating. If you had realised she was in trouble, you would have told your aunt, you would have called for help. You know that, right?'

I nod. I do know this, for certain.

'There are so many reasons why you are not responsible, and you are certainly not responsible for her family's grief. But your intuition is telling you something now – maybe it's time to find a way to let it go, forgive yourself.'

I tell her about the vigil that I overheard one of the old-timers mention to Aunt Rita at the Bait & Tackle. Cathy's classmates will hold a memorial on the beach once school is in session.

'Should I attend?' I ask. 'Maybe tell the parents what I saw?'

She considers this, then shakes her head. 'You could certainly attend, if you want to. There would be no harm observing a moment of silence, if it could help you move on in your own self. But no, it's not the place to speak with her parents. Grief is a very raw thing.' She says this as though she knows from experience. 'Have you told your father or Rita what you saw?'

I shake my head. I tell her how I confided in Lucinda, how her reaction turned the very next day.

'Sounds like she is not a very nice friend. It's important to have people in your life who you can be close to. I have lots of friends, though some say that I'm too *close* to one of them.' She raises an eyebrow and smiles, and I think I understand.

She listens while I tell her how Lucinda has this hold over me; how she seems to like me one minute and hate me the next. I tell her how we kissed and then did other things; how she hurt me at the beach, made up lies about me and spread rumours; how she went off into a stranger's van.

'And then there are the burns,' I say.

'Tell me about the burns.'

I tell her how Lucinda harms herself. I slip and tell her how she confessed that she was seeing her ex-foster father, the way he spoke harshly over the payphone at the beach.

Marylou touches my arm and sits very still for some time; even the birds are quiet in the afternoon heat. Everything inside me grows cold, even though my palms are sweaty. I wish at once I hadn't told her these things, and at the same time I know I had to tell somebody.

'Is Lucinda in trouble?' I ask.

She clears her throat. 'Yes, your friend is very much in trouble,' she says quietly. 'But not for the reasons you think.' She pats my knee. 'Lucinda is a child. She has been let down very badly by the adults in her life.' She looked at me for a long moment. 'You know, Mrs McCarthy told me some things about Lucinda's father. Do you know anything about this?'

I shrug.

'The level of trauma a child experiences when those who are meant to protect her let her down is unimaginable.

234

Your friend has dealt with too much in her short life. Lucinda's behaviour isn't her fault. She needs help.'

'What should I do?' I ask. 'How can I help?'

'You've already done the only thing you can by telling an adult. Try to put all this where it belongs. You are a child, my dear, a teenager. And you have so much to discover about yourself. And, by the way' – she clears her throat – 'not *all* these things you told me about are a problem.' She waits for me to look at her. When I meet her eyes, she is smiling again. 'I promise you, at least one of them will turn out all right. In my day, we didn't even have a vocabulary for the way we were. No one called us *lesbians*, but we found our way all the same. The one big thing – and this is where courage comes in – is to put aside any sense of wrongdoing. You'll find a way to go with what is right for you and find a voice to speak to those who might not want to hear who you are. I find that hard to this day. But I think you and your generation will find it easier than mine, anyway.'

When it is time to ride back, I am reluctant to leave. Halfway down the driveway, I remember the hooks. When I call to her through the screen door, remind her of the reason for my errand, she puts her hand over her mouth and gives a devilish laugh. She returns inside and comes back with a brown packet small enough to fit inside my pocket.

'Come by any time,' she calls. 'I love a good visit. You made my day.'

I believe her. And I promise I will return.

25

THE GOLDEN BUZZ OFF the marshlands merges with the rosy warmth inside my chest as I swerve in and out of the middle of the road, back toward Aunt Rita's, reckless on the straight ways, crossing back onto the shoulder around the bends. I stop once to rescue a turtle parked in a patch of sun in the middle of the road.

A wind pushes at my back, propelling me forward as though I am a sail. I round the last bend. From this point in the road, Aunt Rita's roof rises out of the marsh, and far away in the distance comes the sound of the siren blasting on the firehouse all the way back in town. It reaches my ear, dampened by the marsh, but still unmistakable, warning of impending weather: a violent thunderstorm, straight-line winds, possibly a tornado. The wispy cirrus clouds from earlier have given way to patterns of fish-scaled cirrocumulus clouds, properly ordered folklore signalling troubled weather: *Mackerel scales and mares' tails make lofty ships carry low sails.* But out here, as the road runs alongside the buzzing marsh, the sky is so blue, the day so perfect, that it must be a drill. But it isn't the first Saturday of the month. It isn't even Saturday.

Up ahead, Aunt Rita's bus is on the driveway, readying to pull out onto the main road. A fire truck speeds toward her from the opposite direction, coming from town. The truck passes, sweeping past me, its gust blowing me sideways, farther toward the edge of the road. Aunt Rita sees me now and stops halfway through her turn; she backs off the road, reverses into the drive.

'Hurry, hurry,' she shouts. 'The boys are down at the lake.'

I am already calling to her, telling her it is only a drill. That's when I see the black line marking the cold front on the horizon – a shelf cloud ploughing across the bay. The wind kicks in from behind; the first rumble of thunder pulses the air and vibrates through every blade of grass, every cell under my skin.

'I was coming for you,' Aunt Rita hollers above the wind. 'Marylou was frightened you'd be caught in the storm. Get off the bike.'

I jump off the ten-speed and open the sliding door to lift it in.

She yells at me to toss it into the ditch. 'Come back for it later – there's no time now.'

I jump through the back-door. She turns the bus and grinds the gears, placing the gas pedal all the way to the floor. We bump down the dirt track toward the marina. We haven't gone far when Albert and Gabe come running up the road toward the bus. They are followed by Lucinda. She isn't in as much of a hurry.

Aunt Rita breathes a sigh of relief as she pulls up beside the boys. 'Get in.' She honks the horn, calling for Lucinda to pick up her pace. 'What is that girl doing?'

The boys climb in, their hands and legs spackled with paint.

'Where's Sammy?' I ask, panic rising in my voice.

Aunt Rita turns back to us then, and moves her mouth, counting. She lets out a sharp note.

'Where?' I scream. 'Where is he?'

The boys look more frightened of me than they do of the storm. I jump out of the bus. Heavy drops of rain begin to fall; the storm is already on top of us.

Lucinda saunters up to the bus. I want to shake the lethargy out of her, make her tell me where my brother is.

'Where is the child?' Aunt Rita demands.

'Don't worry.' Lucinda looks at me coolly. 'He's with your mom.' She looks at Aunt Rita as though she requires a translation. 'He's followed Rosemary out on the boat.'

'Rosemary took him out on a boat?'

'No. Rosemary took a boat. Sammy swam out after her.'

'Oh, for the grace of God,' Aunt Rita gasps, 'not again.'

'Oh, yeah, I forgot,' Lucinda says dryly. 'Rosemary's not supposed to be alone with her own child.'

Little barbs like wire prickle all along my spine and down into my fingertips.

Aunt Rita has taken Lucinda by the shoulders. 'This is not a joke. Did Rosemary know that the child was following her?'

Lucinda is looking at her with disdain. 'How am I supposed to know?'

'Did she turn around and see him at all?'

'He's fine. He reached her, and I saw him climbing on board.'

Aunt Rita lets out a sigh of relief.

'Plus, he had a life jacket with him.'

'With him or on him?' Aunt Rita asks through gritted teeth.

'With him, like a float.'

'Lord help us.' Aunt Rita is stricken. 'Why didn't you get me?'

'He was screaming like a brat.' Lucinda narrows her eyes at Aunt Rita. 'She's his mother – if she is fine with him following her out, who am I to say he can't go?'

'Oh, dear God,' Aunt Rita says.

And like a prophecy the wind hits the bus, rocking it back and forth. The long grasses on the marsh sway and lift toward the clouds. A pair of bitterns rise out of the tall grass in alarm.

'Get in,' Aunt Rita tells us.

Lucinda climbs into the bus.

'They could be anywhere out there. Get in, Joanne. We have to call the coastguard.'

'There isn't time,' I shout.

'Calling the coastguard is the only thing we can do right now. Get in – you're wasting time,' Aunt Rita screams at me from her open window. 'It will be all right—'

I can't believe her. I can't believe this is going to be all right. I turn and run all the way down the dirt track toward the marina. I hear her calling after me, but soon her voice disappears on the wind. She has turned the bus around, back toward safety for her boys, back toward a phone.

The rain slaps at my face. It wraps itself around the marsh, blowing sideways. Hailstones leap like tiny frogs in spring off the road and grass and dock. I pass the boats still up on the sawhorses, the tins of opened paint catching raindrops and icy balls of hail. A crumpled towel lies on the beach; Mom's bag and a pair of sandals lie beside it. Sammy's flip-flops are strewn down the beach as though kicked off while running. I follow the dock out to the very last slip.

The lake turns over and over on itself; walls of water roll in and break over the dock, obscuring the vista of the lake. A single rowboat tied to a slip churns on the waves; the water lifts the vessel, shakes it violently, slams it into the dock where it rocks in a small reprieve, before it is lifted and tossed again by an incoming wave. There is no sign of Mom and Sammy returning to shore. Not far in the distance, lightning strikes the water and explodes at once in a burst of light and sound.

'Sammy!' I shout into the wind, frantically searching the skyline.

Down the shore, out beyond the breakwater, beyond the sandbar, where the lake bottom drops off, is the professor's fishing trawler. It has dropped anchor to ride out the storm. It swings with the wind, reeling in the waves.

It is easy to forget how quickly water turns from something as still as a frosty field at dawn to this turbulent, ferocious, living thing. Whether Sammy is out on the water in a rowboat or floating on a life jacket will make little difference. I kick off my sneakers and walk out into the water. The lake bites my calves with its coldness; it stings my thighs, my hands, my back; there is no order to the attack.

Waves lift me in their swell, then release their hold; the undertow pulls my legs out from underneath and another incoming wave lifts me once more. For every stroke I take toward the trawler, the waves push me back two and knock me sideways three.

The sky falls into the lake in ribbons of diamond-lit veins, splitting the air all around. I make it to the sandbar. Martin's face presses up against the window of the wheel-house in the fishing trawler. He comes out onto the deck and waves frantically in my direction, signalling for me to return to shore. I plunge forward then, trying to swim out the ten yards to his boat, hoping the current will bring me where I need to go. I progress only two yards before I realise that I can't get any closer. The waves churn and pull. They have me in their grip.

Martin wheels around, finds a life ring, throws it toward me. Water fills my mouth and stings my nose. I can't reach or breathe or get my head above the water. All at once a calm overtakes me. I stop struggling and lie on my back, floating. I surrender and let the power of the waves lift me in their swell. When the fulcrum of their force has passed, I press my arms outwards in a backstroke, making slow progress toward the ring. Martin reels it in and flings it out again; this time it lands within arm's reach. I grab it and cling to it, and he pulls me in. I climb the stairs and collapse onto the deck.

'What the hell are you thinking?' He grabs my arm, more to steady himself than reassure me.

'My mother is out here somewhere – you have to help.'

'We can't go anywhere until this passes. I'm moored here to keep from crashing on the shore. We'll go when it passes.'

'Please,' I beg, catching my breath. 'My mother is unwell. She's in a rowboat with my little brother.'

He shakes his head then, as though trying to convince himself of something. Finally, he nods vigorously. 'We'll find them.' He unties a life jacket from the roof and pulls it over my head; it rests on my shoulders. 'Tie that,' he commands. 'Don't take it off until we're back on land.'

My fingers fumble with the tapes across the chest, shaking. The boat rolls to one side and I fall against the rails. Martin grabs my arm and pulls me into the wheelhouse. He wraps the tapes around my waist and secures them. He lifts the lid off a box along the side of the cabin and takes out a woollen blanket, places it around my shoulders. My teeth chatter – and my knees, my elbows – my entire body shakes all over. I feel like I will be sick.

'I'm going to up anchor, and when I do, I want you to ease back on this throttle.' He shows me how to do it. 'Take it easy, count to three. Got it? When I signal like this – it's forward, and this – downwards, toward the floor.'

He slides open the door and walks out onto the deck, back toward the stern. He signals and I push the throttle backward. We move toward the anchor. The chain rises from the water and spills onto the deck.

I move the throttle until the boat floats above the anchor; he signals forward, then backward again, and finally it breaks free and lifts.

Martin returns to the wheelhouse, his shirt dripping; his hair sticks to his cheek. He takes the wheel, his hands red and calloused, pushing the throttle forward.

'Where were they headed?' he asks.

Looking out at the bay, the hook is to the right. Through the sheets of rain, it is impossible to see the bay house or the form of the dormer window sticking up out of the roof. 'Out to the right, then toward the horizon,' I tell him.

He increases the throttle, and my legs turn to liquid; the boat's floor may as well be molten. Martin steers the boat into a corrugated sea; we rise up one crest, crash into the trough of the next, before rising again.

'No one expected this squall,' he says.

I focus on the horizon and try not to think about how even this fishing trawler, built for travel on the Great Lakes, tosses us around like a kernel in a popcorn pan. How much worse will it be for Sammy and Mom? A lightning strike hits the surface ahead. I realise I am praying.

'Good news is this storm is quick-moving – it'll be over soon,' Martin tries to reassure me.

If Mom and Sammy made it out toward the freighters, the worst of the storm might have passed for them already by the look of the clouds. The water churns a steel grey, but it isn't as choppy the farther out we travel.

A sheet of wind and rain hit the boat and we list. I slam into the port-side window. When the boat corrects itself, it tosses me back to starboard; I brace my fall to protect my head.

We lurch and totter this way, in Martin's temporary home, over the waves. The farther we speed out, the farther away the horizon appears in its emptiness.

'It's a big lake,' he says. 'Could they have rowed in for shelter?' he asks.

I hope it is possible.

'What's that?' he asks. 'Give me the glasses.'

I hand him the binoculars. He looks out the front window, veering toward starboard, the direction the wind and waves are steering our course.

'Shit. Someone's in the lake.' He hands me the binoculars and increases the throttle. 'Hold on.'

He pushes the trawler full speed across the waves.

A lone figure clutches the side of the half-sunk rowboat. Martin churns the trawler to a halt. Sammy wears an adult-sized orange life jacket, the tapes untied; his head bobs out of its empty middle, a shaft leading deep, deep down into the many tons of water waiting beneath him.

Martin creeps the trawler forward now, careful not to upset the rowboat with our wake.

'Sammy!' I shriek.

His teeth chatter and his lips are blue. I can see him trying to call my name, but he doesn't have the strength.

'It's OK, Sammy. We're coming.'

'Mommy!' he cries.

I can see his little body shaking from cold and terror.

'I need you to stay here,' Martin tells me. 'Remember the signals.' He runs through them again, in case I have forgotten. 'Don't move, son,' he tells Sammy. 'I'm coming now. Hold tight.'

Sammy scoots himself farther up the rowboat, struggling for a better grip. The boat plunges a little lower in the water, and he cries out.

'Hold on, Sammy, one minute more,' I yell to him. *Hold on*, I plead quietly, watching his fingers slip a bit here, now, again.

Martin takes off his shoes and his shirt. A mark runs from his shoulder down his arm, across his chest – a smooth scar of melted skin. He hands me the tow-rope.

'Throw this out to me.' He climbs down the side of the boat, down the ladder, into the water. His face doesn't change – not a flinch from the cold. I lower the tow-rope down and he takes it and swims toward Sammy. The waves are calmer from the peak of the storm, but, still, they lift and churn against the hollow of the boat. The hull of the trawler rocks back and forth, displacing the water. The sky flashes in the distance, and Sammy leaps again, reaching for a grasp, pushing himself up out of the water, onto the sinking boat.

Martin reaches Sammy.

'Don't be afraid, son,' he tells him. 'I'm a soldier. You're going to come aboard my boat. Is that OK?'

Sammy nods. His lips shiver. His whole body shivers. Martin supports his weight; Sammy lowers himself; the boat sways as though it will flip on top of him. He scrambles back up.

'It's all right,' Martin says. 'I won't let you go under. I want you to take the rope, Sam, and I want you to hold it tight – and don't let go. Then, when you're ready, you lower yourself down, let go and I'll be here to catch you.'

'Mommy?' Sammy's voice quavers.

'I've got you; you can feel my hands.'

Sammy takes hold of the rope. Whimpering with each movement, he slowly lowers himself down into the water, into Martin's hands.

'Come on now, let's get you safe, then we'll find your mother,' Martin soothes, pulling him gently toward him.

I pull in the slack of rope. When Sammy reaches him, Martin takes him gently into his arms; he paddles the rest of the way, Sammy clinging to his neck.

They reach the bottom of the ladder, and I hold out my hands, grabbing Sammy to me when he reaches the deck.

There is no sign of Mom.

Martin is still in the water; he turns and swims back toward the rowboat. I think I see a waterfowl circle the boat, maybe a bittern; then it looks more like a turtle surfacing, surprising and unexpected. Then I realise it is a hand – and then a head, shoulders, a person, pushing off from the underside of the boat, out into the water.

Mom has been clinging to the back side of the rowboat all this time, hidden from the trawler. She was holding on to keep Sammy alive. Now that he is safe, she is letting go, swimming out beyond the rowboat.

I sense the volume of the lake spread out underneath her. The rowboat takes in more water; it sinks a little farther under the surface.

'Mom!' I holler.

Sammy startles and looks around.

'Get him below deck,' Martin commands. 'Get his wet clothes off and dry him. There are blankets down there.'

He swims off after Mom. I hurry Sammy down the hatch and into the cabin below deck. I open the hatches; there are dishes, food – and here is a pile of dry clothes, a winter hat, a towel. Both Sammy and I shake from the shock and the cold. I take Sammy's clothes off and dry him, dry his hair, fitting the hat onto his head and tugging it down over his ears. I work quickly, pulling a sweatshirt belonging to Martin over the top of his head. It falls to his knees. I remove the woollen blanket from the bed and wrap it snugly around his thin body, like a towel after his bath. I help him slip into the bottom bunk; he lowers himself onto the pillow, his teeth chattering wildly.

'Pull your knees up to your chest,' I instruct, remembering this from a first-aid manual from the library.

I search the cabinets in the space under the bed and find another blanket. I wrap this around him, too, cocooning him in wool.

'Will you stay here?' I ask. 'I'm going to help Mom. Then I'll come back with her, and we'll all go home. Can you be brave for a few more minutes?'

He nods. His lips are blue. They chatter when he speaks.

'Mom's going to I-i-i-taly.'

'No, Mom's coming home. Right now. I'll be back with her.'

'Tell her my name is Sammy,' he calls after me. 'Tell her I'm Sammy.'

When I emerge above deck, the orientation of the trawler has shifted. We are pointed toward land. The ominous clouds move off in the distance; shafts of rain empty in a downdraught from the rear flank of the storm.

The rowboat has sunk. Martin swims as far as he can go with the tow-rope; Mom treads water out beyond him. Her fingertips make circles in the black water. She makes no effort to move toward Martin. The lake clunks against the trawler; it sends a spray of water up onto the deck.

'Rosemary, come back here – take my hand,' Martin calls.

This is how I stand: holding the tow-line, watching her drift like an abandoned inflatable on the breeze.

Mom is silent. There is the sound of a motor in the distance.

'You know we've come all the way out here to get you? Come in now – your children are waiting for you.'

'Go back,' Mom tells him, her voice thin and sad. 'I've made up my mind.'

'Your kids are right there. You don't want to do this to them. What would I tell them?'

'Tell them I've gone to Italy.'

'Italy's a long way off – I reckon there are better ways to get there. And I'll tell you now, if you start heading to Italy, I'm going to have to come with you. Now, I've been twenty days off the drink – twenty days sober. I'd like to make it to thirty. So, if you don't mind, let's get you on the boat and get you home.'

'Let me disappear.' Mom sounds a note so deep it seems to roll out from under the water.

'Oh, I've felt like that plenty of times,' he tells her. 'I've been silly drunk for the past ten years, practically. Lost everything. There are days I want to swim out, too. But I say to myself, "Martin, stay one more day. See how you feel in the morning." And you know what? I'm still here.'

Mom turns toward the horizon. She paddles slowly off, sinks low, with her face turned away; only the top of her head is visible.

'At least wait until your kids aren't here to see,' Martin calls.

'They're better off without me . . .'

'No,' I cry.

Before I know it, I am in the water again, swimming toward her, slowly at first, the water a wall, pushing back, rippling and black. Mom's head drifts farther and farther out, away from the trawler, away from Martin.

The sound of the motors are nearer now, coming closer. They have spotted us.

The cold blackness of the lake encases my hips, swirls around my chest, my shoulders. I push myself out with a breaststroke and slowly move toward Mom, the life jacket restraining my movement. I steer toward her. A swell lift us in its curl and sets us back down. My stomach drops.

'Mom, please,' I call. 'Mom, we're here. We love you. Billy's gone, but we are here.'

An orange lifeboat bounces over the waves toward us, moving from the direction of the town. The driver and her crew are strapped tightly into orange life jackets with black tapes and helmets. The rescue swimmers pull their scuba masks down over their eyes as the boat approaches. A diver is kitting up with a tank, hoisting it onto his back, readying to enter the water. The boat slows a way before reaching us; it manoeuvres in a wide circle, calming the wake that lifts our heads. We bob in and out of the water.

The first rescue swimmer drops in and swims toward us, a tow-ring hitched to her side. She reaches me first and hands me the ring. I put an arm through the hole and let it take my weight.

'My brother is on board.' I point toward the trawler. 'Below deck.'

'He was in the water for some time,' Martin tells her. 'He may have hypothermia.'

She gives him a thumbs-up and motions to the rescue boat, sending a signal with her hands, and then turns back toward us.

The lifeboat manoeuvres closer, and one of the crew boards the trawler. They turn and steer back toward us, closing in. Two remaining swimmers enter the water.

'How many?'

'Just my mother.'

Mom floats on her back, looking up to the sky.

'She's thinking of going under,' Martin tells her.

'Got you,' the swimmer says. She turns, signals to the driver. The other rescue swimmer reaches me; his mask frames his bushy eyebrows. 'Let's get you on board.' He guides my ring toward the lifeboat, where a diver is pulling his mask over his mouth. He sits at the edge of the craft, an oxygen tank hanging off his back, watching the water, waiting to drop in if the call comes.

'I'm sorry, I'm sorry for all of this . . .' Mom calls.

And then she sinks under, and the water is a bed, swallowing her whole into the darkness. A circle emanates on the surface. The diver rolls backward into the water.

I pull away from the life ring and swim toward Mom.

The first rescue swimmer stays with me, warning me to stop. 'She'll pull you under. Wait for the diver.'

I swim to the place where Mom has gone under, feeling all around into the darkness. Something brushes my leg; I reach down and feel the top of her hair. I find an elbow and pull – then I lose my grip. She sinks. I try to reach her again, to follow her down the hole she has disappeared into, but my life jacket resists, propelling me back toward the surface.

'Help her,' I call.

The rescue swimmers sink under vertically, searching for Mom. They won't come closer without the diver; that is clear.

I dive down into the water, fighting against the buoyancy of my life jacket. I flail and push but grab only water. I rise again, wipe my eyes, tear at the tapes, trying to remove the life jacket – but my fingers are too stunned with cold to dislodge the knot. I put my face into the water and peer down into the darkness for movement. A figure slides past, and there is Martin, pushing his life jacket over his head, abandoning it to the surface. He makes an incision in the water and dives, disappearing down into the black.

I push my face under the surface and watch Martin disappear, propelling himself deeper toward Mom's sinking figure with the force of his kicks. He reaches her and grabs her under the arms, reorientates himself, and begins to propel her toward the surface, just as the diver reaches them. Together, they pull and wrench and grapple with Mom's flailing limbs; she fights to go under, while they struggle to return her to the top. She wrestles against them, flipping and twisting and floundering like a fish pulled on a line.

Then she stops struggling.

Martin and the diver guide her toward the surface.

The three of them push up out of the lake. Martin gasps for breath. Then Mom does. The lifeboat comes nearer, and the driver throws a buoyancy cylinder toward them. The diver grabs it and winches it in under Mom's arms. She doesn't resist.

'Let me go,' she cries.

A sound like a sob comes out of Martin's throat, and he reaches in from behind her, cradles her against his chest, holding her against the cylinder so she won't slip away.

'No, ma'am,' he tells her. 'Not today.'

His eyes reflect the sparse light.

I tread water beside her. Neither of us will leave her side. 'Mom.'

Mom turns toward my voice. I recognise the terror on her face, the familiar dead-of-night terror, waking to dark shadows, reaching for some uncertain conclusion.

'I'm not well,' she tells me, as though confessing a secret we have both known for some time. 'I'm sorry, Joanne – I'm not well.' And the way she says it, it sounds as though to her the worst thing she could have done is let me down.

Martin refuses to let the diver take over.

'I'll bring her in.' He paddles backward then, towing her toward the lifeboat.

My eyes stay fixed on Mom. I watch her all the way to the boat, watch the crew hoist her listless body up onto the side, watch them haul the weight of her into the boat, roll her torso and arms and head so they fall heavy over the edge. Martin and I are escorted back toward the trawler. Only then do I let the swimmer take my arms and place them through the ring.

'Hold on,' she tells me gently. 'Your brother's waiting for you.'

She tows me toward the trawler. I watch the lifeboat. The diver climbs aboard with Mom. The driver turns the lifeboat around then, speeding full throttle, shuddering and bouncing back toward the town. Out over the bay, the storm flank continues toward the city; it appears detached and benign, a cluster of white, shockingly bright, moving off into the distance.

26

THE APARTMENT ABOVE THE Treasure Chest is small but cheerful. Plenty of light streams in through the windows. There is a little balcony overlooking the backyard where Mom refinishes pieces for Marylou in exchange for living here. She has fixed up an old wood and gesso frame, golden gilt leaves woven around the outside. My throat tightens when I see that she has framed my portrait, the painting of the cattails; it hangs over her bed.

We feel for Dad every time Aunt Rita pulls up to collect us for our visits. Mom doesn't want to see him.

'She *can't* see him, honey.' Aunt Rita thinks this is explanation enough for Sammy. This is how it has to be.

Aunt Rita drops the three of us off at Mom's, and we climb the stairs and sit in the quiet light until Aunt Rita returns to take us home. Sammy looks ridiculously grown up with his long legs stretched out in front of him, leaning into Mom on the sofa. She kisses him over and over, and he lets her pet the top of his hair.

Sometimes Everett and James stop by and drop sandwiches and salads in with us. They never stay – they just hand the food in the door – and Mom puts out her mismatched assortment of china plates, and we spoon the salads out of the ceramic bowls. Mom doesn't say much during our visits, but she sips the tea I make, and she doesn't look so frightened or desolate anymore.

*

Mom has been gone from the farm for nearly a month, ever since they released her from the hospital.

After the rescue, the doctor kept Sammy and me in for observation for one night. Martin didn't stay overnight. A nurse brought him by our room after he was discharged. Dad shook his hand and told him he was beyond thankful. Martin dismissed his gratitude, saying that it was his duty. Dad offered him a ride back to Kettle Lake, and a place to stay, but Martin said he was going to stay in the city for a while, with friends.

'I hope your wife is better soon.'

'Appreciate that.'

Martin nodded to me; he stopped at the door and stood to attention, saluting Sammy. 'Take care, soldier,' he told him, and Sammy saluted him back.

'Where's Mommy?' Sammy asked when he was gone.

'She's seeing a special doctor for mommies,' Dad told him. 'We'll visit her soon.'

'Can't we see her for a few minutes?' I asked. 'Just peek into her room?'

'They have to stabilise her first.'

I didn't know what *stabilise* meant, but I imagined it wouldn't be long before we could bring her home, climb into bed beside her, moor her to us with our love.

I had X-rays of my head, even though I hadn't hit it this time, and the doctor told Dad the next morning, over the whir of the motorised bed – Sammy lifted and lowered it on repeat – that we were out of danger. The doctor said she was releasing us and gave Dad signs to watch out for, all the while reaching for the remote, pulling it from Sammy's hands, putting it high up on a shelf.

Everett and his friend from the night of the balloon race waited with Aunt Rita and Marylou in the lobby. I thought they were there to see us, but I quickly realised they had returned from Mom's bedside.

Aunt Rita looked strained; she had been crying. Dad was angry when she told him about Marylou's apartment, that they were preparing it so that Mom could move in on her release.

'Rosemary agreed – she is going to take up the offer,' Aunt Rita told Dad.

'This isn't right,' Dad told her.

'Danny.' Aunt Rita said his name lightly. 'Rosemary can't see you. Not for a while.'

It had all come down from her doctor. Mom needed a break from Kettle Lake. This was her first step toward getting better, Aunt Rita told Dad. She would bring us to the apartment when Mom was settled, once her medicine had time to work, when she was more ready for visitors.

He was stunned. A new ache started up again, around my chest. I ached for Dad.

'She has to save herself this time,' Aunt Rita told him.

Even with all I knew, I couldn't help feeling that there was nothing in Kettle Lake to save herself from, except for us.

Marylou put her arm around my shoulders; she gave me a squeeze. It was hard to believe not even twenty-four hours had passed since I sat in her garden; it felt like a lifetime ago.

Everett rose out of his chair and came to Dad's side.

'Rosemary and I have become good friends,' he told Dad. 'If there's anything we can do—'

Dad pressed his lips together.

Everett directed his hand behind him, exaggerated, so as to clear up any misunderstandings, '—my partner, James, and I are ready to help.'

James nodded from his seat.

Dad turned back to Everett and told him he appreciated that; he was beginning to say this, and not much else, more often.

On the drive home from the city, I stared out the window, watching the cornfields pass. The stalks had grown so high in some fields; others were stripped bare already. How absurd, I thought; how little it takes to convince ourselves of something with few or no facts. How quick we are to believe the worst of each other.

'Hippies,' Dad said suddenly. 'Gays and hippies. Can you believe that? The city is full of them.' He shook his head, half amused, half puzzled.

After that, Dad stayed quiet the rest of the drive home.

*

After we eat Everett's food, there isn't much to say or do. It feels as though it will be hours before Aunt Rita returns.

Mom watches the light dancing across the floor. Her smile is distant. Hare's impatience rises. She looks out the window, tapping her foot.

'Joanne won her swim races,' Sammy tells Mom.

'Yes, tell her about swimming,' Hare says, relieved.

Mom turns to me and smiles. 'How wonderful.'

It was a 'friendly' swim meet, though the tension was still high, and I placed in all my races. It isn't much of a big deal; it was only another farming community. It would have meant more if we competed in the city where the competition is tight. I tell Mom about my teammate, about swimming the relay with Moose and how we came first in that one, how Coach thinks we'll be good enough to place for the state championships once the real meets begin – if we put in the work.

'You're getting there, but you have to want it.' I don't tell Mom that this is what Coach said. He always wants more, then more – and after that, a little more. 'You should be first in every single heat, and your teammates should be following you out the door. You could go all the way. If you worked hard, you could do it.'

I am not sure what he means by 'all the way'. Maybe I am not as focused as Moose; I am content to swim, to get into the pool. The moment my feet touch water – the sadness, the ache, the worry, all of it disappears. That is enough.

Mom is happy for me. She smiles while I talk, and she loops her finger through my hair. When Aunt Rita sounds her horn below, Mom holds each of us to her. When it is my turn, she holds on long after I have let go.

27

CONTRAILS WEAVE PINK THROUGH the October sky, trailing the setting sun. The clocks have not yet gone back, but the evenings draw to a close earlier every day. The doctor has allowed me to lake-swim once again. The air is cool on the beach but Coach insists swimming in all seasons will acclimate us to the cold and improve our form. My teammates grumble and say Coach would have us out with the fishermen once winter sets in, drilling holes in the ice for a swim if he had his way. But I don't mind the cold as I once did, I have learned acceptance takes less of a toll than resistance.

We finish early and towel-dry, pulling our sweatshirts and pants over damp suits. Coach calls us into a huddle, telling us we are strong; we are ready for whatever the new season brings.

Our team dissipates while another circle forms down the beach, in front of the lifeguard tower. Teenagers arrive from the city. Their group is small and feels too intimate to join. The mourners link arms, clutch purple and white balloons – school colours. Someone draws a large heart in the sand, and the students light votive candles, embedding the glass holders into the perimeter of the heart. I lift my ten-speed from against a tree and wheel it toward the toilet block, stopping at the top of the hill. A chill moves in off the lake. I look across the stretch of shoreline and remember where Cathy sat with her friend – and out to the water, where I saw her swim.

'Kennedy,' Moose calls. 'You coming?' A dimple appears on her cheek.

Behind her, a woman passes, supported by a man on one side, a boy on the other. I know they are Cathy's family. They move slowly from the car park, downhill toward the candle-encircled heart, which has taken on its full shape in the soft glow. Cathy's mother and father tread carefully through the sand, watching their feet, as though, at such a pace, they will never arrive at the wretched conclusion below. I swallow back tears, but they come anyway.

I lean my bike against the block.

'Not yet,' I tell her.

'OK, see you Monday,' Moose says. It feels like a promise.

Down at the edge of the crowd, a girl smiles bleakly and hands me a laminated memorial card. The photo is not the yearbook thumbnail they printed in the newspaper. It is Cathy captured in a quiet moment of her life, cuddling a kitten to her chin.

Cathy's family take their places; Mrs Allen clutches a framed photo of her daughter, the same smiling picture on the memorial card. The pastor bows his head and begins a prayer.

A mosquito lights on my ankle – I slap it away. Someone joins me to my right, and now someone on the left. I turn to offer a sympathetic smile. Lucinda stands there, smirking. Heather and Jessica stand on the other side.

'I invite you,' the pastor is saying, 'to remember Catherine as she was, as you have described her to me these many painful days, weeks and months that you have now lived without her physical presence. But as you know, she is not gone, she is living, just beyond the veil that separates us . . .'

Lucinda steps closer; she links her arm in mine.

Cathy's classmates walk to the water. They throw stems onto the waves. The tide returns some to the shore; others float out, make their way past the milfoil, toward the buoys, floating on the current. The clusters of mourners begin to break out of their circles; they form a line, filing past the family. Lucinda is nudging me forward, toward the line waiting to give their sympathy to Cathy's family.

Her father smiles sadly at each mourner and thanks them for coming. He looks tired. The mother clutches the framed photo of her daughter and watches the sand. There is a choke in my throat. The line moves and it is our turn. The father nods for us to come forward. The brother stares at us with a belligerence as familiar as Hare's. Lucinda guides me forward, and we step toward them. I try to force words from my mouth, words that don't sound wooden, that sound genuine.

Lucinda cuts me off. 'I'm so sorry for your loss.'

The father nods; the brother stays stony-faced.

Lucinda doesn't step away. I try to move, but she holds my arm tightly in hers. The father and son exchange glances.

When Lucinda still doesn't move, the father enquires how Lucinda knew his daughter. 'Were you a classmate?'

'No, no. Nothing like that. I didn't know her at all.'

His expression is blank. A renewed interest registers on the brother's forehead.

'Joanne Kennedy was the last person to see your daughter alive,' Lucinda says.

I stop breathing now. Mrs Allen looks up sharply, straight into my face, searching for a missing answer. The lines on her mouth deepen into dark grey crevices.

Lucinda lets go of my arm then; she steps behind me. There is nothing between me and Cathy's family apart from a tunnel, blurring and rushing away. Lucinda pushes me from behind. I fall to my knees on the sand in front of the family; my hand touches Cathy's mother's shoe. She reaches down, helps me to stand, confusion and pain etched on her face. Lucinda runs away. I want to run away, too, leave the family standing here with no explanation – no context for Lucinda's cruelty. It is something Lucinda might do. But I cannot.

'I'm sorry,' I whisper.

Cathy's family watch me, waiting for an explanation. I am trying, but nothing will come out apart from a wail that is rising deep inside me.

A hand takes my elbow. I flinch and close my eyes, expecting cruelty, expecting that this will not end until everyone is hurting as deeply as Lucinda is hurting herself.

But it is not Lucinda; it is Moose. She places her arm around my shoulder, comforting me.

'What she is trying to say,' Moose explains in her strong, soothing accent, 'is that she was here that day on the beach. She noticed your daughter – Catherine stood out because she was beautiful. Because she was radiant and full of life.'

Cathy's mother reaches out and takes my hand. She squeezes it. I squeeze it back but am sobbing too hard to say anything.

'We wish you peace,' Moose says and leads me away from the parents.

We walk up the hill together like this.

'You're OK, Kennedy,' she soothes. 'Let it all out.'

We reach the toilet block and I drop to my hands and knees. I can't breathe anymore.

Moose touches my shoulder. 'Can you sit?' she asks and tries to lead me to a bench outside the bathrooms.

'I can't, I can't.' My heart is beating so fast I think it will burst. 'I've got to get out of here.'

'OK, OK. I'll help you. But you have to calm down first. You'll be OK.'

'No, no, I won't,' I tell her. 'I'm not OK, and I won't be OK.' And I swear my heart will burst in my chest with the cruelty of people, with the cruelty of Lucinda.

Moose breathes with me, long slow breaths, and when my heart begins to slow and beat at a normal pace, she leads me to the bench.

'Your friends left,' she tells me.

'They're not my friends.'

'No. Friends like that, who needs enemies?' she asks.

I smile, but a new sob rises in my throat.

Moose sits beside me on the bench in silence. She feels like a tree in the forest; tall and sturdy and present. My body shakes, and I sob in a way I have never sobbed before, as though every tension, every sorrow, every knowing, makes its way to the surface.

When I have calmed down, she brings me out a handful of tissue from the bathroom. I blow my nose and wipe my tears.

'My father will give you a ride home. We'll put your bicycle in the back.'

I look beyond her. A man stands at the edge of the parking lot, waiting for us.

'Are you sure he won't mind?' I ask.

'Of course he won't.'

'Thank you.' I sniff.

Her smile turns the corners of her mouth upwards; the deep dimple makes her look younger.

'Come when you're ready,' she tells me. 'I'll wait for you.' She turns to leave.

'Hansen . . .' I say, embarrassed. I am reaching, trying to recall her first name, trying to remember announcements at the medal ceremonies. But only Moose comes to mind. She understands.

'Freja,' she calls back, amused. 'My friends call me Freja.'

28

COACH RECOMMENDS ME FOR the lifeguard training
course. Freja and I sign up together. If we pass, we will
become lifeguards when the beach opens again in the
springtime. The training is held at the Kettle Lake State
Park the last week of October, right before the Day Use
facility closes for the season. We're allowed to leave
school an hour early on these days. I cycle to her house
after school, and we walk down to the beach together.

We guess that Tom, the lifeguard, is middle-aged. We
say this one afternoon at Freja's house over a quick
lunch before practice; her mother overhears us and
laughs.

'He isn't even thirty yet, girls. If he's middle-aged, you
must think I'm ancient.'

'Stone age,' Freja says.

I like her parents and her brother. They are funny and
make me laugh. And then I feel guilty for enjoying the
warmth of her family.

At the training we sit on towels on the sand, wearing
our jogging pants and sweatshirts, while Tom talks about
rip tides and the current; he demonstrates the use of
throw-lines and spinal boards.

He struts up and down the beach, full of his own self-importance. Freja and I giggle a lot, hiding behind our hands. But I take in every word he says.

'You might remember, a girl drowned here on this spot in the summer.' He points out to the buoys with two fingers. We can't see his eyes behind his darkly shaded aviator lenses.

'A trained lifeguard stood right here where I stand now, talking, shooting the breeze, while the victim went under, and no one noticed. This is the nature of drowning.'

A hush falls over us.

'What does drowning look like?' Tom asks. He calls volunteers out of the class and tells them to stand in front and demonstrate the actions of a victim. I don't raise my hand. Most of the trainees are too embarrassed to role-play drowning. He picks a girl to demonstrate, and she shrugs and pretends to wilt. We all laugh. One of the more arrogant boys, a senior I know from the swim team, comes forward and mimes splashing; he makes like he is bobbing under, gasping for air. The class laughs.

'No. Not at all.' Tom dismisses him. 'Take a seat.'

The boy sits down, cross-legged on the sand, smiling triumphantly at the rest of us.

'This is the problem,' Tom tells us, strutting back and forth in front of us, his calves still brown from last summer. 'No one waves when they're drowning. Drowning, in fact, looks nothing like drowning. As a lifeguard, you are not looking for splashing, floundering or spastic movements of any kind. Drowning, shall I say, is far more *polite* than this.'

Some of the others laugh nervously.

Tom grins at his own words. 'In fact,' he continues, 'your average person will miss the signs altogether.' He tells us about a father in a pool, an arm's reach away from his child. We are quiet now, listening attentively. 'The father is completely unaware something is wrong with his son,' Tom tells us, 'until a lifeguard jumps into the water, dragging his child to safety. The father thinks the lifeguard is playing. When he is told his child was drowning, he is stunned.

'Most of the time you won't know what you're looking at, unless you *know what to look for*. Know the signs! I tell parents all the time, by law of nature, children are not quiet in water.'

We laugh. But our smiles fade quickly.

'If they are,' he continues, 'you get out there, and you get out there quick.'

*

The world of Kettle Lake expands as my friendship with Freja grows. Freja and I are a pair around school. At our first meet, I took three firsts. So did Freja. We did as well in our second meet. We are on the way to qualifying for the state championships, Coach tells us.

He takes me aside and tells me that a competitive swim club from the city is interested in signing me up. They watched me at an earlier meet and are impressed with my times. They want me for their team.

'I'm already on a team,' I tell Coach, confused.

'Look, you and Hansen, you've got something. Hansen is going to go home eventually – she'll swim for Denmark. Don't you want to swim for America? This club is looking for someone they can send *all the way*.'

I don't say anything, and I can tell he is frustrated with my lack of enthusiasm.

'You could go to the nationals. Who knows – Olympic qualifiers! You have that potential. You and Hansen might swim against one another someday.'

That doesn't sound like a way to convince me.

'You need a club to reach those goals.'

'I don't have any goals,' I tell him. 'I just want to swim.'

'Exactly,' he shouts. 'That's what they want you to do, too.'

*

One weekend, after our visit to Mom, Aunt Rita asks me to come by the shop to help with a display. I take Sammy, and we walk across the marsh. I have that feeling; a sense of anticipation I usually feel this time of year, the sense that makes me watch an airplane trailing far up across the open sky, wondering where it might be going, wondering what it might feel like to be moving, so rapidly, away from a place.

Out over the marsh, migrating birds prepare for flight. We stop to marvel at the Canada geese, watching them lift off in formation, disappearing into the western sky. We stand at the edge of the Wildlife Refuge for a long time in stillness.

Sammy runs ahead when he hears Gabe and Albert. They are digging with sticks in the mud at the edge of the marina road. The shop is quiet. Aunt Rita sits at the counter inside the front-door. She has been watching us cross the marsh.

'Your coach has a lot of faith in you,' she tells me.

I shrug, understanding now the reason she asked me to come. Coach has stopped harassing me. I can see he is putting it in Aunt Rita's hands.

'I'd like to pay the fees,' she tells me. 'And Vic says he can help me and your father with rides in and out of the city, when it ties in with his schedule, if that's what you're worried about.'

'It's not that. I don't want to join a club.'

'Are you afraid?' she asks.

'Of what?'

'Where it might lead you? Don't be afraid,' she tells me. 'Don't be afraid of leaving.'

'It's not like the club is sending me away,' I say.

'You know what I mean,' she tells me. 'It would be one foot out the door.'

While I am talking to Aunt Rita, a motorcycle pulls into the driveway. I tell Aunt Rita I'll go see what they want. The driver takes off his helmet, and I see a middle-aged man with hair beginning to grey. Lucinda is riding on the back of his motorcycle.

Losing Lucinda the first time hurt – losing all I had placed in her, my trust, my friendship, letting her see all that I was before she disposed of our friendship.

I am surprised then, how much this second time hurts.

When Lucinda sees me standing at the door, she waves. She gets off the motorcycle and comes toward me with her arms wide open.

'I came to get my last cheque,' she tells me.

The man waves. I don't wave back.

I heard she was leaving Kettle Lake. I am surprised it is this soon.

'Are you running away from McCarthys'?' I ask.

'I'm not *running away*. I'm seventeen at Christmas. No one is going to give a shit where I am for the sake of a year.'

She looks behind her to see if her boyfriend can hear us talking. She lowers her voice to a whisper.

'You better not tell anyone, though, until we're across state lines.'

I think of trying to talk her out of it, convincing her she should at least confide in Aunt Rita. But none of this will make any difference to Lucinda. She has made up her mind.

'Where are you going?'

'Florida. Mikey wants to get there before the snow, while we can still take the motorcycle. He wants to buy a trailer near a beach.'

I feel a pinch in my throat. Florida is another world away.

I study the man while she is in talking to Aunt Rita. He has that look, like he was once handsome when he had more hair. I can see Lucinda poring through his high-school yearbooks, imagining she is with this man staring up at her from the glossy pages.

Aunt Rita walks her to the door. 'You take care, honey,' she calls.

'I will,' Lucinda says. I think I hear her voice break.

'Don't drive too fast,' Aunt Rita calls to the man on the motorcycle.

The man revs up but Lucinda makes him stop. She jumps off the motorcycle and runs back to me. She gives me a tight hug; she doesn't let go for a long time. The muscles in my throat are constricting by the time she pulls away.

As they are turning out of the driveway, toward the city, she lifts her middle finger. I raise my hand, holding up my two fingers. I wish her peace.

Losing people hurts. Mom to the city. Mom without Billy. Us without Mom. Dad without Mom. It all burns. And one day, I know that I will leave, too. I have to.

'Think about what Coach has on offer,' Aunt Rita says from the doorway. 'Think about it good and hard.'

29

ONE MORNING AT FIVE a.m., I hear someone moving around in the kitchen.

I creep down the stairs. Light slants into the living room from the pass-through of the kitchen. I hear Dad shuffling, gathering things.

He looks surprised when he spots me, and he points toward a new sculpture in his hands. He gives a little, wry laugh.

'It's for your mother.'

'It's nice,' I tell him. 'She'll like that.'

A pair of Hare's tennis shoes sit by the door. They are clean, newly bought, white. I stuff my feet into them and cross the deck and go down the driveway, through the marsh, following Dad into the woods. There is a light dusting of snow, the first of the year. It will melt by sunrise. We pass around the kettle lake, the cabin on the hill, walking out toward the hook at Mulberry Point.

A faint hint of light glows between the faded cattails and the mist rising off the lake. Somewhere high above in a pine, a bird opens its throat for the first note of the morning. It trills into the dark, startling and shrill, ending as abruptly as it started. The woods awaken now, wintering birds stirring.

Dad lays the sculpture in the long grass, waiting to be placed in position. Nuts, bolts, wires, scrap metal, all welded together: a migrating bird lifts off in flight – a tundra swan. I circle the sculpture and read the inscription. On one outstretched wing: FOR ROSIE. And on the other: FOR WHEN YOU RETURN . . .

A wind blows off the bay, and with it, a frenzy of tundra swans arrive, darkening the golden morning sky. The swans pat across the mudflats. The melancholic change between autumn and winter is in the air – they must feel it, too, the restless call, an ancient inscription written in their wings.

Dad unwraps a thermos from his towel, unscrews the cap. The liquid steams as he pours it into the lid and screws the cap back in place. He offers it to me. I take a sip and hand it back. Our breath is cold and steamy on the air.

'Listen,' he says. 'Ever hear anything like it?'

And, I have to admit, I have not.

The cacophony strikes a chord as ancient as the first hands that bent to shape the sapling, marking a way home: a memory, wired on avian wings, sounding anew from avian throats. It will continue long after the misshapen tree has fallen, long after the memory of us fades from these woods.

Dad makes a sound and swallows hard. 'That sound,' he says, 'it's awfully full of lonesome.'

His words ache in my throat, burn in my chest. A fat tear rolls down his cheek. Then another. He wipes them with the back of his hand.

The sun rises, shattering the water into platinum shards. The first swan sounds the ancient call; a desolate cry fills the marsh. A wedge of tundra swans answer in response, their sun-touched wings beating the air. They rise, turning and disappearing east toward the morning star, ascending once again in terrible flight.

30

I FIND IT ON a weekend before Thanksgiving, on the day of my seventeenth birthday.

Aunt Rita is coming to collect us to visit Mom in the apartment above the Treasure Chest. She will let me drive the bus. The weather is unseasonably mild for this time of year and she says I must get all my practice in now while the roads are still clear of snow. I will grip the steering wheel with white knuckles, and she will grit her teeth the entire way into the city.

I rummage through the coffee tins in Mom's workshop, finding a collection of wooden knobs that I think she might like to have. She has begun painting intricately delicate scenes onto their tiny surfaces, scenes of wildlife at Mulberry Point: cattails, fox, waterfowl, deer, all against a backdrop of the seasons. I gather sandpaper and paint, and search for turpentine and her stash of paintbrushes. On a cement hip in the foundation, in the underbelly of the floorboards, I shift an antique chair, a child's potty seat, pushing it to one side. The chair is heavier than expected. I pull it down and lift the lid.

Inside the chamber pot there is an urn. It is about the size of the Infant of Prague.

It isn't difficult to figure that these are the missing ashes of the Irish ancestor, the ones my grandmother still believes she clutches.

The lake at this time of year holds onto the last of its heat, as though it knows the toll of the brutal winter ahead. I wrap the urn in a towel. The branches are bare against a cobalt sky. The view of the cabin shows through the empty limbs once again.

I pull the urn out of the bag; the marble is cold in my hands. I run my finger along the curved, patinated stone and imagine Mom holding this on her wedding day. Had her hopes already been crushed? Had her dreams dimmed so low to make her pull this from the reception and stash it away? Is this all she could do when she awoke to find that becoming a bride had not lifted her from this cage of herself, that all her traumas had not gone away, that she could not leave them behind? How devastating to arrive in Danny Kennedy's life, unwelcomed and uncherished, still the outlier, no chance of refurbishing the family's hearts, burnishing their prejudices, no hope of coaxing them into fulfilling her longings, her dreams. And Aunt Rita, who had found the stamina, the self-preservation, the self-love – call it what you will – had to witness her sister slowly taking this path in which there was no redemption.

I pitch the urn far out into the middle of the kettle lake; the water receives it, sinks the vessel in its hold. How quickly the waters close in on themselves: no sign to mark the watery grave, only the dead birch to break the surface.

I feel the pull of the water now. I take off my clothes and step into the lake. The water meets my toes, my ankles, my knees. They disappear once again, merging with the cold. I no longer brace myself against the shock. I feel it, absorb it, let the sting separate all the parts of me from myself until I can no longer feel my limbs, my chest, my neck. Then I swim out.

I swim to the middle of the lake. I let go and sink like a stone, staying as long as the waters will hold. My buoyancy pushes me, returns me to the surface, and I lie here and float, thinking about Cathy, thinking of what I would have said if I had managed to speak to her parents on the beach that day.

There are the truths we have always known. I knew I watched a girl floating, not drowning. I should never have doubted that. But I wanted to tell her parents something else – I wanted to tell them what else I knew: before the terrible drowning came to pass, how I had witnessed their daughter's final moments.

Water carries people away, but it also brings us back: back to the moment of which no memory exists, back to the moment life seized us in its catch, sparked through the chambers, caught fire in our heart.

I saw Cathy swimming in the same way I swim.

Spreading open my palms, I tilt my chin to the sky; the sun, the water, the clouds sheer across the sky like the bright, white bones of fish. I am absolved, dissolved, and for a moment, the water holds my weight.

And there it is again. Swimming brings me back to the source of that first pulse. Before thoughts, before breath, before bone – before Kettle Lake.

This is it. This is all there is.

Acknowledgements

THANK YOU TO Deirdre Nolan for finding, loving and knowing exactly what to do with this book. Also to Clare Kelly, Francesca Eades, Ella Holden, Katie Lumsden, Djinn von Noorden, Emma Rogers, and all at Eriu and Bonnier Books UK. To Brian Langan for his faith, insights and early edits. To Lisa Gilmour for her support and encouragement. Love and thanks beyond words to The Misfit Pop-Up Gin Club. My gratitude to the Irish writing community for their generosity, especially Olivia and Michelle for their unwavering belief. To UCD Creative Writing staff past and present. To the Arts Council and dlr Creative Ireland for your support. I am indebted to Lia Mills, Maria McManus, Patsy Horton, and also Valerie Bistany, Betty Stenson, and the Irish Writers Centre for the opportunities you have offered. To the 2019 Cill Rialaig Seven, for the ten mad, lovely days on the cliff. The warmest thank you to everyone at Annaghmakerrig for making a residency feel like a homecoming. A special thank you to Diana Souhami, for her wisdom and kindness. A mention for Mario Vittone, whose articles on drowning sparked a parallel with mental illness. For the early readers, especially Theresa (for lessons in grammar), Shelley Puhak,

Julie, Riley, Sandy, Mary, Martha, Fiona, and Lisa. Ah, Lisa, I will miss you. Also Anne Margaret for her expertise in lakes and emergencies, and in memory of Colin. For Sarah, who was too busy looking after everyone. To Kathleen, Larry and April for their encouragement. My Irish sisters Sinéad, Karen, Jen and Barbara – you have kept me afloat. Conor's family, especially Mary and Benny. Love to Laura. In memory of my cousin David, who lived courageously, true to himself, for too short a time. In fond memory of Florence 'Crosspatch' Preuss, Pinckney town librarian, and patient soul. For Sue, my best friend and the best person I know, thank you for a lifetime of friendship and mischief. In memory of Mom and Dad, who loved us and did so much with so little. Love and thanks to my 'freakishly large family': my one and only brother, seven sisters, partners, nieces, nephews, my amazing aunts, and the extended Gorman/Hurtubise family. I miss you every day.

With immeasurable love and gratitude to Conor, Dearbhaile, Donnchadh and Ruaidhrí. So many years, so many words, so many cups of tea later – finally, here is your book. I dedicate this to you.